The Way an Apple Falls

By Merenptah Asante-Douglas

The Way an Apple Falls

By Merenptah Asante-Douglas

First published 2012 By Merenptah Asante-Douglas, Copyright ©.
TamaRe House Publishers
www.tamarehouse.co.uk
info@tamarehouse.com
0044 (0)844 357 2592

This publication employs acid free paper and meets all ANSI standards for archival quality paper as well as meets all FSC standards for certification.

A CIP record of this publication is available from the British Library.

The right of Merenptah Asante-Douglas to be identified as the Author of this work has been asserted by him in accordance with the Copyright, Designs and Patents Act 1998.

ISBN: 978-1-908552-01-3

All rights are reserved. No parts of this book are to be reprinted, copied or stored in retrieval systems of any type, except by written permission from the Author. Parts of this book may however be used only in reference to support related documents or subjects.

Dedication

I dedicate this novel to Ras Tafari, HIM Haile Sellassie 1, of Ethiopia, and to the memory of Claude McKay born, Jamaica 15 September 1890, died Chicago May 22, 1948. Selah.

Acknowledgements

Paul Simons: Publisher
Gail Hill: Editor and typeset designer
Michelle Grant: Marketing Consultant
Bola Roberts: PR Campaign Advisor
Aundrieux Sankofa: Graphic designer
Charles Norman: Cover illustrator
Rudy Attwell: Photographer
Amenemhet Asante-Douglas: Cover concept designer
Ankhesenenpaaten and Amenophis Asante-Douglas: Cultural critique

A Dream Deferred

Langston Hughes. 1 February 1902 - 22 May 1967

What happens to a dream deferred?
Does it dry up
Like a raisin in the sun?
Or fester like a sore--
And then run?
Does it stink like rotten meat?
Or crust and sugar over--
like a syrupy sweet?
Maybe it just sags
like a heavy load.
Or does it explode?

Chapter One

Sadie McDuncanning made her way along Dalston Lane; she walked slowly, measuring her steps, seemingly oblivious to the persons in cars who blew their horns to attract her attention. The neighbourhood had become a hunting ground for women when they walked alone or with their children. So, mindful of this she concentrated on her journey; her locks piled high on her head, one lock falling over her forehead.

Sadie wore a short white blouse that accentuated her bee - like waist – line, her favourite black skirt that was long and flowing hugged her shape and gave her wide hips an even more sensual sway as she strolled. Her deportment was graceful and cat - like; she pitched as she strolled, the breeze blowing her skirt and slip about her ankles.

She was small boned, slightly built, rounded and about five feet ten inches in height. She walked from the base of her spine as if her mother or grandmother had turned her upside down and stretched her limbs after every bath as an infant, as they often do in the Caribbean to shape the muscles of their children.

Her limbs were long and her frame round. Her face was heart shaped and her cheekbones high. She was by any standard an attractive person.

As Sadie turned off the lane into Falcon Terrace, she was in two minds whether to see Ralph or not; so she went for her favourite spot in Falcon Square instead, and sat down under a large field maple tree. Across the lawn there was an apple orchard where coxes were in full bloom, and she watched awe struck as one by one, a branch of apples fell from the trees, and suddenly she began to reminisce. Last summer she had been stricken with Raul, and despite she had given him her all he had abandoned her. That year she failed her degree, had an abortion and lost her man.

She sat reflecting on her past experiences: her girlhood, her relationship with Lottie, the first child, the second, the third and the fourth child with Ivan, and grew sad. It seemed to her that she had surrendered herself too willingly to the will of others. These individuals had interfered with her life, her love of books and her studies, things that really mattered to her. All the dreams she had had of marriage as a young girl had now faded, and as to her studies, her dream of eventually going to university had once again begun to pale into insignificance, and to her it seemed inevitable, the way those clusters of apples were now continually falling from the trees, in the orchard across the lawn.

Unsure of what to do, Sadie looked around at the hydrangeas and daisies in the small square, the sprinkling of irises and roses and smiled. At least, she could find solace here. There was the sing - song of birds as they flit from the limes and oak trees, and now and then, a sparrow or blackbird would fly to the statue of St Fiacre. There to quench its thirst in the trough filled with water beneath his feet. She sat reminiscing until the afternoon bell began to ring out the hour of three and got up, suddenly, remembering that she had made a promise to Ralph to visit him at his flat at Falcon Terrace. So she set out, turned right into Falcon Square, then right at the corner; she crossed Greenwood Road, and eventually arrived at Falcon Terrace. She mounted the steps to a large Victorian house and rang the top bell. Ralph was looking out of the window and ran downstairs.

"Hello!" he said as she entered the door, "Where have you been all my life?"

Sadie laughed and followed him up the stairs.

It was her first visit and she knew the moment she entered that Ralph was just the person she had wanted to meet. She needed someone to help with her studies, and whatever else came of it would be a bonus. The place was simply furnished, but with an air of not having been lived in continuously over the years. There were books on different subjects such as art, philosophy, literature, and even science and mathematics. There were a few paintings, photographs on the wall, one large sofa, armchairs, and four beautifully carved yellow cane dining chairs, which attracted her attention; she felt curious about them as they had the initials NF cut into their armatures, but she said nothing. Ralph had bought the chairs in Shoreditch Market, years ago when he was an innocent in London. He weren't to know that the newspaper he had bought criticising kosher and halal butchers, or that the two gentlemen who had sold him the chairs were representatives of what was to become the

British National Party. Despite their origins, he loved the chairs. He saw her looking at them and smiled.

Sadie continued to look around the flat. There was a large sofa and various plants; a music centre, but no television. They sat on the sofa. "It seems to me you are hardly ever here," she said, taking a deep breath.

"You are partly right," he replied, "I've only just moved back in after a couple of months, I've been staying with relatives in South London." What he really meant was that he had been staying at his parents' house in Guidea Park, in Essex.

"So you raced back here to see me!" She did not know why she was saying this, but she said it any way. Subconsciously, she was establishing how often he would be available. Ralph smiled, "You're pretty forthright, but no, I didn't race back here to see you."

Sadie smiled, "That's what you say," and she added incredulously, "That's what you want me to believe."

Ralph laughed, "I told you I have been back in Hackney a couple of weeks the last time I saw you."

"Seeing some woman I bet," she teased.

Ralph laughed loudly, "My we have a suspicious one here."

"Of course, you men can get up to all sorts; it's us woman who have to look after the children." Sadie's matter of fact manner was pleasant, but Ralph felt that she was trying to let him know more about her situation.

"So what about your children?" he asked after a pause.

"I have no one to help me look after them," she lied, but continued. "Sometimes I have to go to college and leave them, and I have exams soon. Yesterday, Ali threatened Anum with a knife. I don't know what's wrong with the children."

Ralph was concerned. "That's not just the problem. It's you; you just can't cope. You look absolutely stressed out." He put his arm around her. "You need to go for a bit of a run in the park. Let's go to your place, since the children are alone."

They took the route through the High Street, along the pedestrian walkway, and were at Gladstone Heights, where she occupied a two bedroom flat in a maisonette. They ascended the stair well. There was the customary long corridor off each unit, which overlooked the whole complex as there were also units on the lower level. They arrived at the door, where three children were standing around. "Where's Anum?" she asked as they approached. The little girl about seven years old ran to Sadie; the boy about eleven and the other girl about twelve years old were laughing. "This is Aisha, and Haley, and Ali," Sadie said to Ralph pointing to each child, respectively. Then suddenly, her accent changed, "Haley is mi gad pickny!" Ralph was slightly taken aback, by the sudden change to Creole, but adapted quickly. He knew that changing one's accent in an area such as this gave some street credibility and the ability to do so was evident that Sadie was the kind of woman that he had been looking for.

"Mummy," Ali said, "Anum pulled a knife on me!"

"He did what?" said Sadie, alarmed.

"He said he was going to kill me!"

Suddenly a boy about nine years old perched his head out of the flat next door. "Anum, come here!" Sadie shouted, "Come here now!" Anum came to her reluctantly. "He is always fighting me, mummy – always bullying me, mummy!"

"That's no excuse," Sadie said reprimanding the child, "That's violence; you mustn't pull knives on your brother or anyone else!" There was a few seconds pause, after which Ralph said, "Let's all go to the park."

Chapter Two

Aisha was gleeful; as they entered the park she jumped and skipped on the pathway and on the grass, and jiggled about joyfully. When they finally reached the swings she jumped in. "Push me," she insisted to Ralph, with a child's innocence.

Ralph pushed the swing slowly. "That's too slow," she said, "too slowly!"

"OK then," he laughed and pushed the swing forward, when it came back, he pushed it out again, and as it gathered momentum she swung herself, and as it went out and came back, he watched it gather momentum and pushed it out again. Aisha screamed with glee, and finally learned to control the swing. Satisfied that she could manage, Ralph walked towards Sadie, who was standing against the railings of the play area, "Let's go for a run," he said. She was reluctant at first, but then agreed. "Anum look after your sister," she said and joined Ralph who had already started jogging away from the play area.

"Let's run around the other way," he said as they set off together.

They ran the perimeter of the park; stopped intermittently to check on the children and then set off again. Sadie could feel her heart beating as they raced, the way it had not beaten for years. She had that excitement back and was elated, for it was as if she had forgotten the sheer joy of feeling her heart beat fast and then faster inside her chest, and her blood pumping fast and faster, through her heart and her veins. For the first time in years she could breathe deeply and now relished the exhilaration and the fresh air. They were racing around the park when Sadie stopped suddenly and pointed at the sky. "Look!" she said, "It's going to rain!"

It was sudden; the rain came swiftly over the trees and they ran back to the children, who had taken shelter under the roof of the park house. From there they watched as the rain washed over the roofs of the nearby houses, and shouted as the wind took the wash of water and wafted it across the streets and over the trees. The rain fell in buckets and, occasionally, they had to move away from the draft as the wind intermittently drew streams of the rain and blew it against the roof, which dripped down the rafters threatening to douse them. The children were singing, rain, rain, go away. Come back another day, which was amusing and Ralph and Sadie joined in. This continued with laughter and teasing by the children, until minutes after their voices had begun to get hoarse and tired." Ralph put his hand out to test the rain which had become spitting, then it stopped as suddenly as it had begun.

"Look!" he said, "the rain has stopped."

They made their way out of the park and the children followed, chattering and playing. Aisha jumped and skipped as they walked along the path and out onto the pavement. They made their way back to Gladstone Heights, and there Ralph left them.

"Goodbye," he said as he left.

The children waved goodbye as he walked away. He made his way home as if walking on air.

Chapter Three

Three whole days had passed since Ralph walked with Sadie and the children in the park; she had not telephoned him. He had thoughts of going to her home, but was sure that Ivan would be there, so he decided to give her time.

On the fourth day while he was taking his midday nap the door bell rang. He had been helping Owen Izak to move furniture the day before and had taken time off to rest as he was tired. They had done most of the removal and Izak was off to St Kitts Nevis, the following week. He had no intention of returning to England if prospects were good for him in the Caribbean. For him, that was the true meaning of Exodus and he had already informed Ralph that if he wanted to dangle in England, or anywhere else, for that matter, then it was his choice and that he would leave him behind to dangle, and he had ended his sentence with the customary tail ender "whenever."

So when the door bell rang he thought it was Owen Izak who had come to finish off the rest of the removal, but when he leaned his head out of the window, he saw Sadie's slim figure, standing on the steps and raced downstairs to open the door.

The moment she entered, they kissed and embraced as if time their great enemy had wilfully kept them apart. Minutes later, Ralph washed his hands, made tea, took the biscuits from the cupboard and they sat down. Sadie was first to speak. "What we did the other day seems a bit unfinished." Ralph got up, went to the bathroom, washed his hands and mouth and came back, grabbed Sadie around the waist, and they walked towards the bedroom.

***

Ivan Isaac drove at break neck speed as he raced home from Luton; it had rained earlier in the afternoon and now at dusk the road glistened with the wetness of the downpour on the tarmac surface which gave each stretch of road an eerie light, like bubbles floating and suddenly disintegrating. It had been a good week for business and he had money in his pocket and, more importantly, petrol in the car. The old Sierra was like his woman, always giving him problems, but he knew her well. Picking up the M1 at Bury Park, he passed Hendon, took the exit there and then onto Golders Green; Highgate Village, down Holloway Road, towards Finsbury Park, through to Stamford Hill and reached Hackney at seven thirty. This had become a regular route for him, so he drove without really having to think where he was going or what direction to take. He was in automatic in his eagerness to get there, like a racing pigeon homing after a long race in a storm.

He was reasonably happy there was shopping in the boot of the car and two thousand pounds in his pocket. Sadie would be pleased to have some money, he thought as he remembered the look on her face on the last occasion that he took this amount of money home. The carpenters, Shaba and Shabaaz had been paid; he owed them from the last job, but he would be able to pay them off after he had worked

The Way an Apple Falls | 17

on Sunday morning. He had promised Kahn that he would be in by ten o'clock and that he would work up until six thirty to finish off the work, so that the shop could be ready to be opened without any risks to his customers on Monday morning.

He arrived at Gladstone Estate at eight o'clock and parked on the road off the estate. The youths in the neighbourhood were lately apprenticed in car stripping and while he was well known in the area, he was in two minds about parking in the estate. This after all was his livelihood and without a car, he would have to disappoint Kahn on Sunday and this would delay the work on the shop in Luton for another week. Although he still signed on, this trifling money could not keep his family in food or clothing and so he had had to cheat. After all, he had given up on seeking mainstream employment because despite his skills no one it seemed wanted to employ him. Therefore, money had to be regularly made. He wanted to see Glendina though, just for a few minutes, and he reasoned that this would be no problem once he had parked safely.

Glendina Chin, a dark brown woman of about thirty years old was standing by her window looking out onto the street when she spied the blue Sierra pull up and Ivan's long legs emerged from the front seat of the car. She had been willing him there since mid afternoon after she had picked up Jamal from school and Natasha from nursery.

Canaan at play centre would join the other children at her mother's house. So when he made his way up the stairs to her maisonette, he did not have to knock. She had already opened the door and left it ajar.

"Hey!" she said quietly as he entered.

"Hey!" he replied and they both laughed out loud.

"I didn't want you disturbing my neighbours by blowing your horn and annoying everybody," she said.

"I know!" he retorted, and added, "Just in case you had somebody in, cheating on me again."

"He is already gone," she joked.

"Where are the children?" he asked, looking around the flat. "What have you done with my children?"

"Oh! Massa kum by, ana gi dem tu massa!"

Ivan was highly amused and laughed, chuckling at the end; and grabbed her around the waist, "You 're always making me laugh, you are so much like the old people, as if you were not born here."

"Dat whye ya luv mi!" Then she spoke in English.

"Don't worry I only sent them to spend the afternoon with mummy, she said she was missing them." She disentangled herself from his embrace. "You need a bath;" and walked towards the bathroom.

Ivan stretched languishingly on the settee and yawned. He was tired, but feeling Glendina's soft body had aroused him. After a few minutes she returned and started undressing him: she pulled at his zip, unloosened the button of his jeans and his shirt and pulled him towards the bathroom. He allowed her to lead him into the bathroom where to his surprise the water had already been run with a fresh towel and new clothes that had been put out for him.

"See, there you have coconut oil with rosemary, so you won't forget me."

"And what after that?" he asked.

"If you are a good boy, you can have some pussy," she laughed and ran out of the bathroom.

Ivan washed himself without a single thought of Sadie; he had two sets of families and as a man of the faith, he was doing what was only natural, or what came naturally or should come naturally to any man. It was his prerogative and it didn't matter because both the women and the children knew of each other. It was no longer the great secret that it was a year or so ago when Canaan had come home from school complaining that his friends were saying that Anum looked like his twin and were they friends or brothers, or both. Ivan remembered how Glendina had taken him aside and after getting the confession out of him had cried all night and could not be consoled. She had somehow got over the shock and now lived with the reality that he would be shared among his various women.

Sadie was not her only rival that is if she could be classed as one. But now he was with her and as the children were at her parents' home they had the house to themselves for a short while. So after soaking away the stress and strains of the day, Ivan stepped out of the bath and began to dry his skin.

Glendina was different to Sadie in her ways, although they could almost pass as sisters. It was as if he had chosen them deliberately, they looked uncannily similar. They both had part coolie grandparents that showed in their delicate features. This was his rebellion as if he had deliberately chosen women who looked remarkably like his paternal great - great- grandmother Georgia Ram, whose father came out of India, but who had married her cousin Jamie McFarlane. The similarities showed in their locks, their slightly flared, upturned nostrils, and high cheekbones with delicate clear cut features. They were slightly built, but while Sadie had a bee – like waist, Glendina's was even smaller; her whole frame was slight and delicate.

He felt refreshed as if the whole week's stress had drained away. The fresh clothes felt like a second skin on his body and from where he sat in the living room, he could see Glendina placing the food on the trays as she prepared to bring them to the dining table. At least, here he could sit and eat in comfort without Sadie's relatives knocking on the door or suddenly turning up at the last minute before dinner, begging favours. He missed the children for unlike the children he had with Sadie, Glendina's children saw her parents often. Sadie's mother on the other hand, never adapted to grandparenthood. For after so many years, she still insisted that her grandchildren should call her Audrene, feeling that she was still too young to be a grandmother. Anyway, the confusion of his other household seemed very far away now as he settled down to his meal of rice and peas, with oxtail and butter bean stew.

It was always the ritual with Glendina: the unexpected arrival, the running of the bath, the meal, and then they would make love, sometimes on the living room floor, or in the bedroom. Today, however, she cleaned away the plates, and hinted where they would go.

And after they had washed their hands and mouths free of the scent of the food with lime, she kissed him hard on the mouth and sat on his lap. As always she was passionate. But today there was urgency to her, as if she needed reassurance, somehow. Ivan responded to her passionate kisses until both their needs became too unbearable to hold back any longer and they rushed to the bedroom, closing the door, as if afraid that Anna would return with the children unexpectedly, and bursting in on them, find them on the floor, naked as they were born.

In the bedroom, Ivan sat on the chair; Glendina sat on him, her right leg over his and her left leg between his thighs, pointing forward as he grabbed her around the thighs from behind; she began to move hesitantly, as if uncertain whether it was safe, but as he sat so pointedly with her on his lap she balanced herself and gradually developed the confidence to move and maintain the momentum, and they kept the position with her back turned towards him for an hour. He then began to massage the back of her hands, tracing little circles around the stress points and kissing between her fingers. Then he began kissing her nape and nibbling her ears. All their energies were focused and channelled into one flow of ecstasy as Glendina swung herself as if on a swing.

After Ivan had eased her off him slowly, they faced each other on the floor. Glendina placed her legs between Ivan's and while he sat with his arms forward; her legs locked his chest and rested underneath his arms, placing her arms behind her on the floor, she threw her head back as Ivan forced his way into her body. They moved in unison, up, right, to the left and at times, almost uncontrollably, as their respiration changed and their hearts began to beat faster and faster, until their pulses raced and their chests began to pound and they could not stop, they moved instinctively like two horses galloping, until they both realised that they might hurt each other.

Then they resumed the position with which they had begun for the sake of symmetry. Ivan sat on the chair and placed his right leg on the bed while Glendina leant forward and rested her head on the chest of drawers, and they continued to move, hard soft, soft and hard; slow fast, slow, until Glendina began to count, until she climaxed; her voice trailing off into an exhaustive whisper and she felt revitalised. She breathed in deeply and exhaled as Ivan suddenly stood up and filled her with the force of all the vitality that he could channel from the core of his very being.

That one movement had changed the position and she gasped, exhaling swiftly, for the quickness of the movement had stopped her breath. Glendina extended her arms and grabbed the edge of the drawer as he held the small of her back, pulling her feet around the back of his thighs, and she screamed his name.

Then when at last they manoeuvred their way onto the bed and he lay back, she took him in her mouth and began to blow kisses that fell like gentle breezes on the tip of it. She squeezed it between her fist and felt him as he grew bigger in her mouth, then when he was hard and extended, she began licking and squeezing the tip of his penis, until he stiffened as the sensation spread from there to his spine, and the vibration throbbed in his head and he ushered forth; and as he tried to pull away, Glendina held him firmly but gentle enough to make it pleasurable and as the throbbing relented, she drained him into her and ate him, delicately. "I got you!" she said.

Chapter Four

The sensation began somewhere in her head, a spot behind her left ear throbbed. It moved down her body and stopped as suddenly as it began. The pleasure began to stir inside her and her feelings began to explode; Sadie felt somewhere between longing for and finding ecstasy. Ralph dropped his hands under her behind and raised her against the wall; he stood up and her voice trailed off into a swoon. Then he let her down, onto the floor and moved towards the bed, lying down. She joined him, turning over on her belly, and he lay on top of her back.

Looking back, Sadie smiled, "I've got you!" she said, laughing out loud.

"Oh you have!" he replied; and they both laughed.

Those years ago when I saw you at the Roots Pool Centre, I used to think, "Why can't I get a Rastaman like that, but I thought you wouldn't be interested in me."

"Oh, no!" said Ralph.

Sadie gritted her teeth and breathed, exhaling and inhaling, "Do you mean no, not interested in me, or no, you didn't see me?"

"I couldn't do that then, I had Barbara and the children and you had Ivan. I wouldn't interfere."

"That day when you were at the centre and you went upstairs, I followed you and spoke, but you didn't hear me."

"Oh I was looking at the building – the architecture, the way it was being used. The upstairs had a fine sweep. I liked the seats and the ceiling with the big glass dome. It was a good place."

"But they spoilt it; all those men masquerading as youths. I used to go there with Ivan."

"Yes, I saw you there another time. You were downstairs dancing and I thought why all the beautiful princesses prefer the wild ones?"

"Let's come together," she groaned and turned over on her back as he released her.

Sadie held her legs up, her toes pointed to the ceiling, and then she brought her feet down and placed her legs over his shoulders. Ralph looked her in the eyes and placed his finger on the perineum, kissing her breasts. She lowered her eyes and moved towards him, she kissed him hard on the mouth and bit his earlobes. His ears tingled and he inhaled deeply and exhaled, and blew air through his mouth.

"I've got you!" she said as she moved from left to right.

Ralph's legs began to tremble as she carried him to the point of ecstasy that he had always dreamt of, but could never go, until that moment, for she maintained eye contact with him and suddenly closed her eyes as if they were dancers blindfolded, in search of their own ecstatic relief, but using each other's body as vehicles to attain that indomitable state of bliss. Suddenly she linked both arms around his shoulders and began scratching the back of his shoulder blades and biting his cheeks playfully. Then stretching her body, she felt an intensity of pleasure that gave her an immense feeling of happiness, and lifting her left leg she pulled him closer to her, and moved from left to right, then stretching her body again, she closed her eyes tightly and raised her breasts to his face. Ralph kissed them gently and began to blow bubbles of air on the nipples. Suddenly her limbs relaxed and she cried in great release, and held him tightly to her as if she would have them merge into one being, and that she would never let him go.

Now she felt healed, but Ralph did not release and continued to move with deep and shallow strokes; and pulling back he looked down on her face. Her eyes were closed tightly again as she continued to murmur and still he did not stop his movements, but continued to alternate both his breathing and his strokes. Sadie found herself crying softly, streams of tears ran down her face and she was wet and slippery underneath, and still he relented slightly, only to resume again, with a subtlety and gentleness that astonished and pleased her. Never before had she been so completely and utterly overwhelmed. For the first time in her life, as a woman, she felt consumed and feminine, utterly feminine. Then he stopped.

Chapter Five

Later as he walked her home, Sadie talked about Ivan; she recounted the many times that Ivan would go off to Birmingham, or Luton, and even as far north as Manchester following his favourite sound system, when she would be left alone with the children. Every woman came with her own story and hers was the stuff that you either believed or found incredible, at least, that was the case for a man coming from Ralph's background. Then she told him how she hated the estate and that she had been trying to get a transfer for over ten years. Of course, Ralph felt sympathetic, for she had good ambition and was taking an access course at the local college, which if she passed would see her at university the coming September. He agreed that Hackney was not a good place to bring up a family, but they were all trying as best as they could because life was short.

They reached Mare Street Parade, passed McDonald's, and turned left into the estate. Sadie found a secluded spot and led him down the basement. Ralph was intrigued for he realised how little he knew the area. Sadie lived at the top of the stairs, and even though he had walked her home before, he was surprised that the estate had such secret places. They embraced and kissed for some minutes before she pulled away and ran up the steps laughing.

"Come here tomorrow," she said and disappeared.

Ralph made his way out of the basement and took the exit for the street. He wanted more cannabis and he knew that Barton would have opened shop by now.

Chapter Six

Sadie went to the kitchen and opened the cupboard under the sink; she felt under the shelf behind the piping and pulled out a polythene bag folded up with papers, which she opened. It was half past three and the children were at their godmother's house, so she felt comfortable that she would not be disturbed. These were Raul's letters, and selecting one she began to read it. But her mind could not concentrate on the words, as if there was something stopping her from reading the letter, so she ran herself a bath and changed her clothes. She spent the afternoon and the evening reading, until the children returned at eight, when she made them tea, played with them and turned on the cinema for them to watch cartoons.

At Gladstone Estate, Ivan turned in his sleep, half-awake. He was sure that he had left Glendina and that the woman beside him was Sadie. He rolled over, feeling her warmth, the smell of her and embracing her slim waist. Glendina could feel him hard against her and pushed back. He moaned and whispered some incoherent name. Glendina smiled and slid from his grasp silently, and stood at the side of the bed. Ivan stretched his long legs which were longer than the bed and turned on his belly.

"Sadie man!" he gasped. "What's wrong with you man, where you gone, where you goin' now?"

Glendina slapped her thigh, walked over to his side of the bed and poked him in the side.

"Wake up you bitch!" she said.

Ivan stretched his arms over his head and opened his eyes. He was confused, he thought that he had left and was at home with Sadie. Then came the accusation, was she right, he thought.

"What the hell you playin' at?" she asked angrily, "Calling her name in my bed!"

"What?" he asked sleepily. "What time is it?" he yawned, rubbing his eyes and getting to his feet.

"It's ten past ten."

Ivan reached for his trousers and dressed himself. "I'll be late for shopping. But I got lots of food in the car already." This was it Glendina thought and panicked; now he was going without giving her keep.

"I don't mind sharing you, you know you is the only man I had since school days and I don't want anyone else. You know I'll stay without a man if only for the sake of the children."

Ivan took a wad of notes from his pocket and pressed them into her hand. "I coming back later to see the children. Make sure they're here." Glendina held on to him tightly, but he kissed her forehead and held her away from him. "Make sure the children are here."

"Yes!" she said, as he walked towards the door.

The drive from Gladstone Estates to Gladstone Heights took Ivan fifteen minutes. He looked at his watch as he took the last corner which led into the drive way. It was ten forty five when he pulled up in the alley way off the estate entrance. On arriving in the drive way he parked quietly in his usual spot, placed the lock on the steering wheel and took the tapes that Kahn had given him from the glove compartment. He took the keys and stepped out of the car; looked up at the bedroom window directly above the drive way. The lights were on and he knew that Sadie was at home waiting. Assured he opened the boot of the car and took out four carrier bags of shopping, and slowly made his way up the stairs.

The door opened and Sadie stood dressed in black as she often did at weekends. "What time do you call this Ivan?" She helped him with the bags of shopping; he followed her into the kitchen. "The children have been waiting all evening for you?"

"I had a puncture on the way home," he said defensively.

"Oh, really?"

"Yes!"

"You seem to be having puncture after puncture after puncture these days."

"See!"

"See what?"

"You're always using your brains on me."

"That's because you are always lying."

"What makes you think that I'm always lying?"

He took off his boots, placed them in the passage, by the front door and returned to sit at the table. Taking a wad of notes from his pocket, he counted one hundred pounds and handed her the money. She took the money and smiled.

"See how you love money, eh," he said.

"That don't mean zero," she said. "You always come home late when you get paid, when you have money, as if you have another family somewhere that you have to look after."

"That's not the point, the thing is I can't get zero from you. Yet you are my woman and its months now and people see us as a family, but I can't get nothing from you."

"That's it you think screwing is everything." She stepped out of the kitchen.

"We don't have to screw to be a family again. You're too damn lie – as if you would tell me the truth."

"Truth, truth, you wouldn't know what the truth is. "If you saw the truth you wouldn't know it. If it hit you a hundred miles per second in your face, you wouldn't see it." The past loomed in Ivan's mind as he spoke; she had betrayed him before and he was guilty of the same betrayal as well, as if he had pushed her there, pushed her to do it.

"My, my," Sadie retorted. "You are really steaming tonight. You see your other woman again, that's why you come home brazen with lies and confrontation?"

"Your behaviour last year with that college boy is still preying on your conscience."

That was it, they were both on familiar ground, with no holds barred, and they would fling back dirt for dirt.

"You have been screwing with me all along; don't think I don't know – people talk. You want me here to screw while you're screwing somebody else, and I don't get love, but look after you, look after the house and the children, like am some idiot or domestic for you and them!"

"Yes people talk and they still talk and will talk – you and people. Which people talk about what, me or you?"

He stood up and took off his belt. "I feel to beat you."

"Beat who, you think I am a child. This is England the air is free and you didn't pay me passage here. My people did."

Ivan wound the belt around his right wrist, twirled it in a little and threw it onto the table. "You might even enjoy it."

"I aint arguing with you," Sadie replied softly and began putting away the shopping.

Ivan felt good after Glendina and Sadie's hotness inflamed him. He wanted her but knew that she would not allow this to happen. Resigned he took a wad of notes from his pocket, counted out a hundred and handed it to her.

Sadie took the money putting it on top the fridge. "Thank you," she said.

Ivan remained seated at the table, while Sadie finished off her work in the kitchen. He watched her as she put way the last items of shopping into the fridge and got up going towards her. Sadie turned around to hold him, she wanted him to touch her; to hold and reassure her that what she was saying were all allegations and not the truth. Ivan made to move towards her, until he remembered the smell of Glendina's s body, and turned, holding her at the side.

"Oh that's not a hold, that's a side hold," she said.

"I thought you said you didn't like it when I come in sweaty and want to hold you."

Suddenly the telephone rang. Sadie pushed him away gently and went towards the phone on the small table in the hall. "Hello, who is it?" But all that she heard was a click as the person at the other end hung up.

Ivan was silent as she busied herself in the kitchen, then turned to the dining table with a plate of rice and steamed fish on a tray. Putting his dinner down before him, she returned to the kitchen and brought him a drink of punch. Having served the food, a mood of pleasantness seemed to come over her.

"Well, how was your day?" she inquired softly. "I suppose you were late this morning for your breakfast at the café because Shaba phoned asking for you at seven thirty; just a few minutes after you left." Suddenly, she paused and stood at the entrance to the kitchen and returned swiftly.

"Want me to run you a bath?"

"Yeah!" Ivan said, looking up from his meal. "Thanks!" he added.

Sadie looked at him as if to bring into mind some question which has been puzzling her for quite some time, while Ivan continued eating. "Ivan!" she began softly. "I know that you think am holding out on you, but it's not me, you know; it was you who said you can do what you want; anything you want at all because you are a man, and that you don't have to give me sex too often. Ivan, you know I like doing it with you and no one else. I started burning up

34 | Merenptah Asante-Douglas

when you wouldn't come home, and seeing Glendina in your car, not out of the area but in the neighbourhood. Ivan you don't care how I feel."

"Feel as you will," he retorted, shrugging his shoulders.

"Ivan! I'm appealing to you, I know I did all those silly things before but you been fooling round for years. Ever since the first time I let you into my heart, you been fooling with me and you won't stop."

"Look Sadie," Ivan replied lowering his tone of voice, "I had a hard drive home; it's late, I'm hungry and tired and leave me alone, no man!"

"Listen Ivan, I aint no man."

Ivan looked up from his plate and took a sip of his drink. It tasted fresh and complimented the rice and peas and fish well. He took a serviette and wiped his mouth. He loved Sadie's cooking, her food, her wifely endearments, but there was always some restlessness around her; not like Glendina, who was different; simple, not complicated.

He smiled, feeling guilty, he commented, "This is good!"

"Is it?" she inquired incredulously. "That's all am good for isn't it, to have your children – to clean wash and have your children!"

"Since you started college, you feel you're better than me. Remember the last college you went to, you and that student that you took up with?"

"That was last time," she said, "I'm older now and I know what I want, and that had nothing to do with books. Since you know me I have been into books."

"Yes, you're always reading – in some damn dream with your head in some damn book."

Sadie looked at him, raising her eyebrows as if more to register her shock at his outburst.

"You and your family believe in going for what they want; what's wrong with other people doing the same; with me going for a degree?"

"You will find some jackass intellectual like the one you used to get so excited about years ago at the centre. I don't forget him – you know he's a bald head now, so much for conviction."

"Is that so?"

Sadie suddenly became silent as if she considered the matter closed.

"Is that so what?" he exclaimed. But she looked at him blankly, but said nothing.

"See you always using your brains on me."

"Because you too lie."

Ivan got up and walked towards the kitchen. Sadie looked at him and disappeared up the stairs. Minutes later he heard the bath running and Sadie singing as she prepared it.

Then the phone rang as Ivan returned to his dinner on the table. He walked to the small table and picked up the phone. "Hello," he said.

"It's me Glendina!" the voice boomed in his ears.

"Can't talk now," he whispered.

There was a click as he put the phone down.

Some minutes later, Sadie raced downstairs. Ivan could hear her footsteps resounding from the bath room, then the passage way upstairs and down the stairs as she approached. He was irritated by Glendina's call and suspected that Sadie may have listened in on the extension upstairs and braced himself for more argument.

"Your bath is ready!" She smiled, and added, "Going out later?"

"Yes," he said.

Chapter Seven

It was evening. Sadie peeled each layer of clothing from her body, placing them neatly on the bed. Ralph handed her the two large white towels. Sadie looked at the large kente cloth that covered the bed and smiled. Ralph walked out of the bedroom and returned with a small bag. "Here you are," he said.

Sadie took the bag and retrieved two pairs of French knickers: one black, one white. These she placed on the bed. She felt sexy; they smelt fresh as if they had been sprayed with perfume. "Will this be a wedding of the soul?" she asked.

Ralph smiled; she could feel her blood rising, coursing through her veins; she was excited, her mouth was becoming dry and she found it difficult to swallow, as they moved to the bathroom. The water was warm and she felt overwhelmed, like a great wave had washed over her; she felt butterflies. Together they began to rock to and fro.

"You are so sweet," she said emotively, for she loved words and endearments, as all sensitive women do, and for her, love was this, if nothing else; gentleness and sweetness – sweet talk. "We should write a book to celebrate our union," she sighed.

"Do you like it?" Ralph asked.

"No!" she replied teasingly.

Ralph laughed.

"We are Gods!" she sighed.

Then she turned, facing Ralph. "How many marriages are there?"

"Many."

"Today, let's do a ceremony; we will do the ceremony together – we will marry our souls together."

Ralph took the bucket, filled it with water and poured it over Sadie's head. Then he took the soap and lathered her body; refilled the bucket and washed her. Then it was her turn to wash him. Finally they stepped out of the bath together and began drying and creaming themselves.

Ralph pulled her towards him and bit her ear lobe, then whispered in her ear. Sadie punched him playfully, pushing him away. Ralph doubled up, feigning pain and laughing.

"Sadie, don't hit me so hard man; it's just that you made it sound so extraordinary."

Volume Two

Chapter Eight

Two years had passed since that afternoon in the park when Sadie and Ralph walked with the children along the path. Aisha was now nine years old, Anum, like his own son Alexander was now eleven; his daughter Aisha Nana had developed a close bond with her namesake, not because they were both girls, but they also shared the same name. Ali was now thirteen and Joachim, her eldest son, sixteen. Alexis was born in October and was now six months old.

Sadie was looking over the balcony of the flat when Roland approached with Maxmillian. The latter was short and, compactly built and of a smouldering personality. Roland on the other hand was calmer, more self assured; Sadie noticed that he carried himself a little like Ralph, but apart from that, his general demeanour was rough-diamond, which to her made him likable. They had come to look at the computer. Ralph was at work and Sadie was at home as it was reading week at university. There was a knock at the door downstairs and Sadie hesitated a moment, but then decided to let them in. There was another knock as she made her way downstairs.

"Hello, girl!" said Roland. "We've come to fix your computer!"

"We've come to fix your computer!" Maxmillian repeated.

Roland smiled and stepped into the flat; Maxmillian followed as Sadie moved aside to let them in.

"So, where's he then?" Roland asked.

"Where's who?" she replied defensively.

"Why don't you leave the woman alone, Roland (he pronounced the name Roll-on), "er man is at work," said Maxmillian.

"He got you like a queen bee, someone should tell him, he's a big head," said Roland.

"Ralph is a dreamer," exclaimed Maxmillian.

"Not practical," retorted Roland.

"Ralph is helping me with a transfer off the estate," Sadie said proudly.

"That won't happen, I know these clever types. They pretend they know everything!" said Roland.

"Oh. That's true!" Maxmillian intoned.

"He's helping me with my work; it's my final year."

"That won't happen!" Roland said.

"Why not?" she asked.

"Not if he knows am fucking you!"

"But you're not." Sadie said indignantly.

"I soon will be; just as you get bored with that coconut who thinks you're the Virgin Mary!"

Sadie moved from the passage into the dining area. She was annoyed at this self assured stranger and yet, she had no wish to let him see the other side of her which could be, to say the least. She took a deep breath before she spoke again.

"Maxmillian, the computer is upstairs; bring it down, please, so you and your friend could fix it. Here's twenty pounds."

"What about breakfast?"

"Ralph said, no breakfast; business is business," she said teasingly.

"See," said Roland. "You and this Ralph; everything is you and this Ralph, like this Ralph is everything to you!"

"You're obsessed with Ralph, everything is Ralph and you," said Maxmillian.

"Yeah, what the hell he got?" said Roland.

"You come to fix the computer or not?" Sadie said firmly.

"We'll have to take it away," said Roland.

"All my work is on it and so is Ralph's, I thought you would update it here."

"What the hell has he got, I thought he was just a workaholic," Roland said firmly, sucking his teeth in disgust.

"He writes!" said Sadie.

"Writes, writes what?" said Maxmillian.

"He's got you fooled eh!" said Roland.

"Look!" Sadie said. "The computer is upstairs, take it; but Maxmillian, I hold you responsible for the work on it. You have my money and you owe me forty pounds already."

The Way an Apple Falls | 45

Maxmillian made his way upstairs, followed by Roland, with Sadie behind them. As they reached the top of the stairs, Roland turned to Sadie, immediately behind him, and put his arms around her. "You look like you falling over," he said, letting his hands fall to her waist. "Ehem, you look small, but you firm and round, just how I like them," he said.

Sadie pushed his hands away. "Like them, who are them?"

"Black bitches," he said curtly.

"Maxmillian, where you find your friend?" she asked as she pushed past them. "The computer is in the bedroom," she added – "Oh no! I lie; it's in the living room. Ralph put it there; he doesn't like people other than the children coming to the bedroom."

"He's kinky as well, eh," said Roland, winking at Maxmillian.

"I never used to go into my parents bedroom," said Maxmillian. He stopped abruptly, "that is my mother and her man's bedroom."

"He must be funny – weird," said Roland.

"I think he was brought up different to us, you could see that in Ralph. The first time I saw Ralph, I couldn't stand him. I still can't stand him, but he thinks I like him; he thinks am his friend," said Maxmillian.

"But Ralph respects you Maxmillian," said Sadie.

"That doesn't mean he wouldn't have you," said Roland.

Maxmillian smiled. "Well you have a nice shape Sadie; I don't know how Ralph saw you first," he laughed.

"Look Maxmillian!" Sadie said sharply. "Don't play with my generosity – I thought you were running a business."

"This is it," Roland exclaimed.

"OK, you lift while I disconnect."

"OK," mocked Roland.

It took them very little time to disconnect the scanner and printer from the processor, and pack all the bits and pieces into the large card board box which they had brought.

Now they were ready to go, or so Sadie thought, until Maxmillian held out his hand.

"I need a tenner off you."

"That's just for the accessories," said Roland. "You get me for the call out service."

"Look here," Sadie began but stopped abruptly. "What's your name again?"

Maxmillian laughed and couldn't contain himself. He slapped his thighs and shrugged his shoulders, groaning with mirth. "His name is Roll-on."

"Roland?" she exclaimed incredulously. "Roland!" she repeated, trying not to laugh.

"See you got the pronunciation right," Roland said, "I'm very proud of my name!"

Maxmillian laughed loudly. This time Sadie could see the humour in the name being pronounced Roll-on, and she started laughing, at first reluctantly, until she could not hold

The Way an Apple Falls | 47

back the laughter anymore; she laughed, almost breaking into tears.

Roland held out his hand with mocked courtesy. "My name is Rollon Austin, nice to meet you. Bet coconut hasn't made you laugh like that for a long time."

Sadie disregarded the comment and mockingly took his hand; as she took his hand he pulled her towards him, and kissed her on the cheek. Sadie felt her body stiffen; shocked and stunned, she felt herself looking at Roland, before she backed away confused. Then suddenly coming to her senses, she turned and laughed, embarrassed.

"You got no manners," she said faintly.

"I'm a dog!" said Roland, laughing out loud.

Chapter Nine

The year before Aisha and Aisha had their birthday party together. Now the time had come around again. And this time Sadie had invited her school friend to stay over as she had written earlier asking if she could put her up while she was in England. At least, she would have a hand in baking the cakes that the children were so fond of at birthday parties. This was the situation that Juanita saw that Friday afternoon when she arrived at Sadie's place. But for Juanita there was something different about Sadie – even odd, she thought as she sat in the kitchen - even the children were better behaved and as for Sadie, she had remained slim, and still very shapely. She had just finished helping Sadie put the icing on the three cakes, when Ralph arrived.

Ralph entered the flat putting down his brief case in the passage near the kitchen. "Good afternoon," he said.

"Hello," Sadie said. "This is Juanita," she laughed, "we used to get up to all sorts at home; she's a good friend of mine. This is Ralph."

"Hi!" said Ralph, holding out his hand. "Nice to meet you, I've heard good things about you. Hello," he added amicably.

Juanita shook his hand and smiled. "Me as well," she said, "Coming from work?"

"Yes" said Ralph. Turning to Sadie, he kissed her on the cheek. She returned the kiss and held his hand, smiling. "How was work?"

"It was tiring!" Ralph said. He looked at her lovingly and added, "It's good to be home though, and to be home early tonight."

"Well, it's better than nine thirty."

"Exactly, I told them it's not on any more." He turned, making his way up the stairs.

"Excuse me," said Sadie to Juanita, as she followed Ralph up the stairs to the bedroom.

They were alone now, except for little Alexis asleep on the bed; she placed her body against the door and drew him to her. Ralph turned his head and looked at Alexis, asleep.

"Don't worry about baby; he only went to sleep a few minutes before you came. That's why Juanita is here helping with the cakes. You know their birthday is on Saturday."

She pulled him closer, kissing him on the lips. Ralph returned her kiss and began to unbutton his shirt. Then he pulled the tie from around his neck and began to undress. He sat on the bed pulling off his socks. "Where are the children?"

"At club," she replied, and pulled him against the door.

"How do you want it?" he asked.

"Quick!"

Ralph kissed the top of her upper lip and linked his arms around her waist; he began to nibble and suck her upper lip and ears. Sadie sighed as she felt a surge of intense emotions and closed her eyes tightly breathing in gulps of air; she felt butterflies, as if her breath had stopped. She pushed him away gently and lay on the floor; raised her legs under her thighs and pulled him towards her. Ralph bore down on her, filled her and retreated, pausing. Sadie sighed, pushing her hips from right to left, moving up and down, while Ralph continued pushing in, pulling out and pausing. She pulled her legs further apart by placing her hands under her ankles. Ralph stroked deep inside her, then shallow, and paused, holding her eyes within his stare, he looked intensely into her soul. Filled with emotion, Sadie moved slowly pushing forward, then moving swiftly, then very slowly; she pushed her hips upwards while Ralph pushed down with intense force deep inside her: six deep to two shallow strokes. Sadie started counting, until suddenly her voice trailed off and she closed her eyes tightly, screaming under her breath, as she attempted to pull her knees together, and then paused. After a pause they ran to the bathroom and took a quick shower.

Sadie returned downstairs while Ralph reclined on the bed, freeing his mind of all the worries he had encountered during the course of the day. There is a pain in my head he told himself in quiet thought. Where in my head? In the front of my head; it has the colour red; it is hot. I want to make it blue, he told himself quietly, I want it warm and blue, warm and blue, as he willed himself into a trance like state. As he drifted into what seemed a light sleep, he could hear Sadie and Juanita talking and joking downstairs.

He knew he was dreaming as he stirred in his sleep. He pulled himself towards the head of the bed beside Alexis. He could feel Alexis's little body beside him. He fell deeper into sleep and the dream began again under a sky filled with rain and he was standing outside the house of Barclay – something had drawn him there.

"Let me see your hand," Abba said, as he came down the stairs to the kitchen, where Barclay was cooking. Abba carried himself with such dignity that Ralph did not mind the request. He was curious.

"This is Ralph," Barclay said by way of introduction.

"Hi!" said Abba, smiling. "I just woke up; I saw you coming here."

"Hello!" said Ralph holding out his hand.

Abba's grip was firm; he shook Ralph's hand for a long time. "You been through a lot, but you look alright."

"Thank you," Ralph replied.

"Look," said Barclay, "read his palm for him."

Ralph looked troubled; he was broke.

"It's free," said Abba and laughed.

"Oh, never mind him," Barclay said, making fun of Ralph's embarrassment. "He thinks the class is full of queens – and in a way, he's right!"

"Oh, never mind your friend Ralphie," Abba said. "He's just showing that he's been cured of love; you should visit me in Trinidad." They all laughed, and there was a pause.

"Now, as I was saying," Abba continued, "I saw you coming here; your mother was a healer!"

"Yes" said Ralph.

Abba cleared his throat, "I aint asking you; am telling you!" He snapped his fingers and made a hissing noise. "You need protection! "Ooh!" He turned away abruptly.

"What's your favourite animal – shut up, shut up," he said softly, "I see a cat!"

"Give the man a reading, then," Barclay insisted, stirring the food on the cooker.

"Oh never mind him Ralphie, he does go on like a woman," Abba laughed.

Barclay enjoyed the joke and laughed himself. Ralph found their mutual respect amusing.

"But maybe he has a point," Abba said. He looked at Ralph.

"See you later, enjoy your meal," as he left the kitchen and made his way up the stairs.

"Don't worry Ralphie!" Barclay said. He pointed to a bottle of red wine on the table. "Open that Ralphie," he said and laughed. "Don't worry, he added, "He is not a queen!"

Suddenly there was a little hand across Ralph's face and a soft thud in his side. Alexis had awakened and was playing. Ralph opened his eyes, "Hello baby," he said, kissing the child.

"So you fell asleep again," Sadie said as she entered the bedroom.

But Ralph had no chance to answer. Suddenly there was an urgent call downstairs.

"Sadie, Sadie!" Juanita's voice trailed up the stairs with an alarming urgency. Sadie and Ralph looked at each other;

Alexis was startled. Ralph took Alexis and Sadie made her way downstairs.

"Ehem," Juanita said ominously; she patted her hair, flashing her gold ring. "Ehem."

"What?" Sadie said, incoherently.

"You a walk a look husband!"

"What?" Sadie said.

"This man has so much power over you." She paused, looking at her intensely, patted her hair with her left hand, turning her finger so that the gold engagement ring glistened. "And this child, I never see you so fixated on an idea before. You well domesticated, like a kitten, meow!"

"What's that? Come again!"

"You aint got no life. You think you is a wife, but you acting like a little girl – like you find a father."

"So I aint suppose to have nothing then?"

"Look at it, you and he is like chalk and cheese and I hear he has a wife."

"You just come and you know everything. Where you get all that information from?"

"Somebody tell me," Juanita said curtly, a malicious tone to her voice.

"Who said that?"

"His friend," Juanita said. There was a pause as both women looked at each other.

"I bet if you ask him to look after the children while we go out I bet he wouldn't. You remember the last time I was up we went to this place called Peaceful Valley. Why don't we go there on a Saturday?" This was the temptation which Juanita proposed; threw down like a gauntlet. And she knew either way she couldn't lose. Even if Ralph looked after the children, it would aid his down fall and prove his weakness.

"What you doing with this man?" Juanita said sourly. "Where's he from?"

"St Kitts," Sadie replied.

"Oh that's not far from Montserrat," Juanita said, smoothing down the hem of her skirt, "They is funny people, very changeable, I hear. I never been there but I hear they bad – not like people from Antigua, or our island. They more like Jamaicans. They so near to us but different – very different; especially now they thing they big," she added.

"But Ralphie was brought up over here in England; he doesn't even identify with them much. More than a third of his life is spent over here, he has very British ideas – and his education is from here."

"I met his kind back home; he's from that dangerous class. He can't see why Montserrat is still a colony; why Anguilla is still a colony; why the Virgin Islands and the Dutch ones can't see themselves as West Indians, first. He is troublesome."

"He thinks African," Sadie said flatly, attempting to diffuse Juanita's prejudices.

Juanita laughed out loudly, slapping her thighs.

"Whey de arse he gets that from. Doesn't he know they call us slave babies; that they hate us even more than the Indians?"

And she laughed even more loudly, adding, "What damn nonsense. Ralph is of the troublesome type; he thinks too much of himself."

"He's very pan African," Sadie retorted sharply.

"Well, he's still a Kittitian – one a them – push him and you will see it come out," Juanita added, ominously.

"It's not one a them who will come out; it's the way of life here. He's really from here, since he moved here years ago – he's well known in the area," Sadie eulogised, as if giving vital information to Juanita to correct the distorted picture she had of Ralph.

"He sounds like an Englishman, who the hell does he think he is talking like that?"

"Ralph tries to speak like us sometimes and sounds stupid, I guess. But you must realise it's the kind of work he does, Sadie replied.

"What he got qualifications?"

"Yes!" Sadie replied proudly. "He's really a hard working man. I'm well kept."

"Like a Queen Bee, Juanita retorted.

"What do you mean?" Sadie asked concernedly.

"Oh so you don't know?" Juanita remarked ominously. She paused briefly, made as if she had some urgent information to add, and then shrugged her shoulders. After a pause she began slowly.

"What special about this child and this man. You find a daddy?"

Sadie got up and walked towards the balcony, looking out. From the flat she could see Grantham Heights, where it joined Gladstone Heights. She lived at Hackney Central and Juanita had come all the way from Stonebridge to see her. But she was in two minds now. She didn't like Ralph and she had made it plain to her. That her loyalty could be so divided hurt Sadie and threatened her confidence, because she wanted Juanita to congratulate her, to give her the credit for having turned her life around. It was clear to Sadie that Juanita would continue to undermine her relationship with Ralph. He was unlike anyone she had ever met. Sadie for her part was beginning to question her reasons for being with Ralph, because he was different to Maxmillian, Roland, and all the other men she knew in the neighbourhood. He was different to her brothers Allen and Tremolo, different even to Lottie, Ivan, Raul, and Edison. And she found herself questioning his personality even more than she had ever done before Juanita had arrived.

Juanita wanted to break up the relationship and had certainly undermined it, and therefore, went about it systematically. She knew Sadie's likes and dislikes: whereas stability was yearned for, excitation was equally important. And Sadie yearned for all of these things; this Juanita knew. But most importantly, they had made pact years ago, and Ralph was not one of them and could never assume a place within their community; he was an outsider and this relationship would be short lived.

Ralph was generous; over the years he had unwittingly buried his individualism and had, because of continuous episodes of identity crises become, first, an academic failure and then a fop. As if he could not reconcile his needs and interests within the bounds of the people around him; he had become afraid of his own individualism.

Hence he had failed to achieve his potential. He felt he needed a change, but was too afraid to initiate that change. But meanwhile Sadie, in deep contemplation with her childhood friend would become that agent of change. But for the time being, any way, the mirage of domestic bliss seemed not to be imperilled. Yet powerful forces were against their protracted relationship.

Chapter Ten

The next day Juanita arrived without her children, although Sadie had invited them to the party. Maxmillian had brought his daughter Sarafina and his sister Plum. The flat was a hive of activity, with music playing, children dancing, and the adults, some dancing while others were in conversation. Several of the neighbours came as well and the food which Juanita and Sadie had prepared was well appreciated by the guests.

At about seven thirty the music was turned down and the table opened; the cakes were brought in with candles for the two Aishas and placed on the table. Sadie and Ralph opened the table, toasts were offered, with libations poured; there was much laughter as many of the guests found the pouring of libation ludicrous.

The table was opened; Candida, a relative of Sadie's whom Ralph had not met before, strode up to the table and confiscated the cakes, saying they would be held for the next year and placed a price of ten pounds for anyone who wanted them cut then and eaten. She just mentioned the sum and produced no money. The two children were very distraught at this. And rightly so, for the children had always seen Sadie and Ralph as the adults in charge; now this complete stranger had become the owner of the cakes and the party guests stood bemused, while Ralph tried to reason that this was unnecessary. He had given all the money he had to make sure that the party went ahead. He had bought the ingredients for the cakes, but now this stranger, taking advantage of her relations with Sadie had suddenly changed the rules.

Candida took the cakes into the kitchen; the disc jockey started the music again and dancing resumed. Later as they danced, Ralph took the children down stairs and shared out the cakes. Candida was by then too far gone in her infatuation with Maxmillian to care about anything than dancing closely with him in the corner. The party continued well into Sunday morning with the last guests leaving at around seven o'clock; Ralph and Sadie immediately set about clearing up and retired to bed around nine o'clock.

Chapter Eleven

The two Aisha's and Alexis the baby slept in the bedroom and at about twelve o'clock they could be heard playing with the child. There was no need to make breakfast, lunch or dinner as enough food had been left over from the party. The boys were in their rooms playing their play stations.

At three o'clock, the children got up and bathed and were impatient to go to the park; so after taking a bath together, Sadie and Ralph set out for the park. At the park Sadie and Ralph followed both Aishas into the play area; the younger girl made for the sand pit. She pulled off her shoes and jumped in. Sadie put the brakes on the push chair and took Alexis out, placing him in the sand pit with his younger sister. Sadie and Ralph took off their shoes and joined the girls. The boys, however, had wandered off to the football pitch and were running around with other boys whom they had met some Sunday before.

There were other parents in the sand pit and the couples nodded amicably, acknowledging each other. This was a day for families and Ralph and Sadie teamed up with the Wades, who were there with their three children, who normally came to the park on a Sunday.

Today however, Ralph's cousin, Pervase had turned up unexpectedly. Pervase who was always more talkative than his wife Abby sauntered over to Ralph and greeted him, engaging in polite conversation. As they spoke Abby wandered off, instructing Alfa and Rashan, the twins who were on the swings.

"It's good to see you guys," Pervase said in a Trinidadian drawl. "I like it, any where I go on a Sunday my family goes."

Then he grinned, mimicking the old Uncle Tom characters in old Hollywood movies. He began to roll his eyes. Pervase had always had a knack in mimicking all the different West Indian accents; his Bajan drawl was the most hilarious, but the Trini accent would also have everyone laughing hilariously.

"Yessuh massa, any wheyre I goes, they goes!" They laughed, as did the other couples.

Pervase was two years younger than Ralph and had lived a Casanova life style during his university years; he liked sports – anything physical. It was basketball that had placed him in constant interaction with many of his conquests. After university he had applied to go to Africa, immediately after graduation. The entire family apart from Ralph was set against this decision, but Pervase went any way. After eight years in Africa he had returned with a woman whom all the family immediately nicknamed Mugabe. They did not work hard at breaking up the relationship, but feared more for her safety than his own, for they all knew that women were Pervase's weakness.

Elizabeth Kalinda was a beautiful, full bodied woman, who adored Pervase. However, true to form, Pervase could not change his independent ways and many of his women friends, realising that he was back in the country would look him up, some out of curiosity, others to find out about his experience in Africa. When finally she left Pervase, no one was surprised for she needed her stay; he had by then married her. That she had found a white man in Bath did not worry Pervase; he promptly gave her a divorce.

It was the first time a woman had left Pervase, but at the first break up, she had made off with a woman friend of his who played basketball; one of his favourite girls at that. Far from being bitter or devastated, Pervase was delighted that she had chosen Margaret Ford, whose parents came from Jamaica. Rumour had it that they stole away one weekend in Brighton where they had bought a house. True to his style, Pervase had visited them not to protest, but to congratulate them and give his blessing, and had slept with them both in the same bed that visiting weekend. Years after the girls had parted by mutual agreement and Kalinda had married Robert Ferguson. And, of course, Pervase had given the couple his blessing, apparently in more ways than one, and unbeknown to Robert.

Pervase lived in Wimbledon, but occasionally brought his family into Hackney to give them what he called orientation and direction. They both shared similar attitudes, and were more unlike other members of the family. Years ago when Ralph had moved from south London to live in Hackney, all the family were horrified; for coming from Leeds and Birmingham, they considered London as most northerners did, a foreign country; not quite England. And any where you could not get scallops with your chips, could only be too foreign to live. That he had moved from south to north was a surprise; that he had moved further from north to east was a catastrophe and they said no good would come of it. Today Pervase had come to the park, in pretence that he was bringing his family for recreation, but he really had been looking for Ralph, whom they had not seen for three years.

Within that time Ralph had lived alone at his house in Bury Park, Luton, and reverted to Islam where he attended Friday prayers every other weekend when he was not collecting Aisha and Alexander to spend the weekend with him. He had taken the name Idris Suleiman, and had proudly informed his Seventh Day Adventist clan, who took no notice of the change of name and continued to call him Ralph. Occasionally, they would add insult to injury by addressing him as Ralph Regan Jamieson McFarlane, which included his hated middle names, the first one being unisex.

Frank would sometimes tease: 'Ralph Lear's daughter's son, grandson of the third Jamie McFarlane.' Since the early days he had become a secret Muslim and went about his daily life unhinged by the rigours of faith or community. In the last year he had rented out the house and bought a studio flat in Hackney, where he lived until he met Sadie and decided to move in with her, often leaving his flat unoccupied, much to the consternation of his close friends who occasionally rented it.

Sadie leaned towards Abby and smiled; the two women felt an affinity and moved closer to each other. Ralph and Pervase sensing this took the opportunity for a stroll around the park.

"As you know," Pervase began, "I've only just decided to give Caribbean women another try; if Abby and me finishes, that's it. As you know, I am very fixated on women from Africa."

"I know," Ralph replied.

"I have a weakness; they always have better arses." He smiled, taking a deep breath. "That's like you and Indians."

Ralph laughed. "What makes you say that?"

"Don't you remember the day you went to Sofia's house and sent her little brother to call her out, and all the brothers and uncles came out and you took off, and you never saw her again?"

"And you remember that?"

"I bet you they sent the poor girl back to Pakistan or India or where ever they came from, they probably killed her. Don't pretend that you have forgotten her Ralphie."

But Ralph remained silent.

Ralph and Pervase held specific ideas about India and Africa. At university they had mixed freely with all types of nationalities, but it was the Indian subcontinent and Africa which held their interests. Ralph recalled that one of Pervase's encounters had openly referred to him as a slave baby, after Pervase had used his flat to entertain her for six months, only to move on; a situation which she would not accept and would visit the flat looking for Pervase. It happened one Saturday that she had turned up in a beautiful dress that was made to fit her and show off the tantalising curves of her body, and when told that Pervase was not there, barged in and refused to leave. He could not persuade her to go, and at one point she offered him sex, which Ralph had refused. In the end he pretended to take her to see Pervase at some place and had run off, leaving her. It was the only way that he could get rid of her. Looking back now, Ralph concluded that he should have taken her up on the offer.

"That was the best pierce of arse I've ever had."

"Really?" said Ralph.

"Of course, I think Asian and African women were born to please a man. I mean they train them in the arts and science of love. When our women have that sort of thing it's when they listen to the older members of the family. They must tell them what to do. Amar was exceptionally skilled."

"If you say so," chimed Ralph. "I mean, I have only your word for it, and, of course, I never tried her."

"Exceptional," Pervase repeated. "I should have married her, but she became too jealous and obsessive. I had to take out a summons against her as she kept stalking me."

"What made her do that?"

"What do you think, don't you know once they eat you, you become a part of them; once they swallow you and you taste good, they can't resist?"

"Ralph laughed, so you've been up to that with her, poor girl."

"She would have done the same to you. Didn't you see the way she used to look at you?"

"But I wouldn't want to go where you go."

Ralph remembered years ago when they were teenagers and went to discos, they would toss a coin to decide which of the two girls they would go for. As teenagers growing up together this had always been a rule among them, which had only been broken twice. Once when on vacation in Leeds, Pervase had moved in on Lydia, a girl whom Ralph had begun to chat up at one of their parties. The other when

Janis who had slept with Frank, Pervase's brother had virtually kidnapped Ralph at a dance, taken him home to her apartment and screwed him legless; only for Ralph to discover that she had done the same to Frank some months before. This became a family joke; and there was the near miss when Frank had visited Ralph at his bed-sit in Stoke Newington; he had met Ralph's neighbour Alba, and spent the night, after she had been chasing Ralph for months, and couldn't persuade him to have sex with her. Frank had later complained to Ralph that he was losing his touch and letting the family down because Alba had confided in him how much she fancied Ralph, and despite all her entreaties Ralph did not find her attractive.

"You are acting crazy!" Frank had told him.

"You haven't started eating pork, have you?" Pervase asked.

"No, no Ralph stammered," wondering what had prompted the question.

"See, after you start eating pig, the chemistry of your sperm changes and we are supposed to be sweet; that's why as long as we remain true to our genes we can't lose; we are expected to impregnate them all. You know that song that was the road march in St Kitts Nevis Carnival, "Put Fire in dey pumpum," Pervase let out a shrill.

Ralph laughed. "I heard Cousin Clarence playing it the other day."

"Some singer calls himself Lord La Place," Pervase added.

"These Caribbeans; they're all pumpum mad," Ralph said.

"This is a white one," said Pervase.

"Still crazy!" said Ralph.

Chapter Twelve

They were walking up the hill back to the play area when Pervase stopped; for they could see Abby, Sadie and the girls with little Alexis toddling among the daffodils in the enclosure, which was separated from the road by a wooden fence. Ralph watched the women and the girls as they were joined by the boys. They were running and skipping along the edge of the garden; stopping now and then, picking up feathers and flowers. The crowns of the yellow daffodils blazed against the green grass of the midsummer and Ralph had a premonition. He wondered what tumult in the world was happening to interrupt this episodic tranquillity, what eruption would tear him from such a stabilising environment. There was no doubt in his mind that he loved Sadie, and that he would not do anything to disrupt the sense of balance that they had tried so hard to achieve.

Pervase quickened his steps as they reached the lime trees, where in autumn horse chestnuts would let fall their yellow and golden leaves to let the wind weave a carpet of banked leaves to meet the red orange of the October skies. What did Pervase see? He pondered.

Minutes before, a van had passed along the road and pulled up about twenty yards from the fence of the enclosure; Sadie had stopped what she was doing abruptly, and walked towards the van through a gap in the fence, as if mesmerised by the sound of the horn. Roland got out and they stood talking, as Pervase and Ralph neared the group, then Roland got back into the van and drove off. Ralph could see it happening, but blinked a few times to make sure that what he was seeing was taking place. He had no idea Roland and Sadie had become friends. Pervase looked at him, "Looks like you have to bite the bullet, coz."

Pervase had seen it with Barbara years ago; Ralph had that uncanny way of letting people take advantage of him, he had become so unlike himself since university. Had he not been warned years ago, before he took it upon himself to move out of the family circle; and Frank had warned him how middle class he was; yet he continued to under sell himself; refusing to admit that the majority of the people around him were acquaintances and not friends, and what's more, they couldn't measure up.

Not only had he squandered his money in building an organisation from which he was now banned; the people whom he had helped and brought into it had sold it while Ralph was still struggling to find his former self. Now another of his delusions had landed him a fish. Pervase recalled how Frank had reacted when Ralph had turned up at his daughter's christening with Donald Thumb, the one who was a ganja seller, and as the godfather Ralph had argued his case by alluding to what he called commitment to community. Now, he would learn that community meant nothing; family and bloodlines meant everything. Surely now Ralph must realise that it was over after that, the end had begun. His duty was to tell him this with as much subtlety as he could. Make a credible excuse to Sadie and be off. Taking

Ralph aside, Pervase said, "He's been there already Ralphie; let her go!"

Chapter Thirteen

That night Abba and Barclay came back to him in a dream. Ralph had gone to bed after dinner and Sadie and the children were preparing for the Sunday Play in the living room. The children often did such things. They would write the script on the computer, print out so many copies and arrange the props and curtain calls. At other times they would hold dancing competitions or just dance dramas. He felt tired after the park and went to bed. He knew it was a continuation of the same dream, for Abba and Barclay were there, and he was in the same house; and he sat opposite Abba, who was reading his palms.

"About the same time," Abba hissed. "You will have something wrong with you down below – an operation. You can take precaution. There's nothing wrong with celibacy; you can try it."

Ralph looked at him bemused, but still not wishing to offend, he smiled. He felt hot under his clothes and shifted his behind on the chair, to be more at ease. "They will take your child," he said, and he hissed, closed his eyes and made a snapping sound. "But you will get him back; I see two women: one in black and one in purple. They are reaching out to you and I see two men following behind them. These two men, you are very much like them. All of these people love you from the grave."

Ralph was quick enough to retrieve his handkerchief from his back pocket with his free hand and coughed into it. "Sorry," he said. He could feel the hair at the back of his neck stand on end; a shiver shook his body and his pulse began to race. He wanted to flee, but perhaps, there was some truth in all this; he would feel like a coward any way; so he braced himself and waited.

Abba began to rock from side to side, and made a ululating sound. "But I see a woman, so black that even her black dress makes her looks blue. Ohh, she is even more powerful than the rest – she's restless; she's angry with you." Then he moved to the right hand. "Ohh," he sighed, "They are still there - all of them - still there," and he blinked and made a hissing sound, clearing his throat. "I see a fair woman now; she loves you more than from the grave, and Oh Lord, two angels, a boy and a girl walking beside you; you in the middle. You go to a house and there's another girl, a living one, very similar with the dead woman, Ohh, I see it now," he said joyfully, "I see it now!"

Ralph was losing his concentration; he knew that it was a dream; that he was dreaming but could not wake up. It was as if his soul had left his body and only the shell was there. This was the same vision, the same story of his life, recurring over again.

"I see a man in a car and a woman; they will take your woman, but you will find one more beautiful and younger than all the others, you have ever known, like this fair woman, who is angry with you, because you have disowned her."

"Ouch, he breathed loudly," But that fair woman and her daughter, that black one they will pursue you for not loving them enough, and the Indian looking one, Ohh, you disowned her as well. You must make peace with your soul. These children you have are guarded by all these, just like yourself; but you must do right; some bad men robbed you years ago, you could be rich beyond your wildest dreams." Abba shook himself as if waking from a trance and opened his eyes. Ralph's eyes were closed tightly, but when he opened them they were filled with tears. Suddenly there was a knock at the door and he woke up; it was Aisha, "Daddy, we are ready to begin the play," she said.

Chapter Fourteen

The dream did nothing to disturb Ralph's resolve nor did Sadie's recent arrangement of sex once a month diminish his love or trust in her. But he was living in a fool's paradise for circumstances had changed in a way which could never be recovered. The relationship was over. It was irreconcilable between them. Yet Ralph could not let go.

For Sadie, her relationship with Ralph was over because she had found excitement in Roland. From the very beginning of his advances he had both scared and excited her, and Ralph had continued to act the husband, much to her annoyance; he had become weak and pathetic; instead of the strong, robust and sexy person whom she had yearned and longed for so many years ago. So while Ralph made the shopping she would be visit Maxmillian and Roland, with Juanita, at Roland's home in Leyton. That pact between the girls when they would abscond from school to play among the rocks and to visit exciting places back home was revived, and the excitation had grown out of all proportions. They were both having illicit affairs.

As Juanita had embarked on an affair with Maxmillian, almost immediately, it was inevitable that Sadie and Roland would become lovers. So they began to meet at regular intervals, having foursomes and close dances and lunches together. Much of this took place in the day time while

Ralph was at work. Juanita was surprised and flattered by Maxmillian's attention. Although she didn't like the country she was determined to broaden her experience of life and enjoy her stay, so that when she returned home she would at least be able to say that she enjoyed her captivity in England and that she had a good time with Sadie; and if she experienced a black Englishman, what was wrong with that? Lloyd, the father of her children would understand; for after all, didn't he boast about his exploits in the United States and Canada?

So that afternoon when Maxmillian pulled her to him and pinned her against the wall, she did not resist, for it had been six months since she had been made love to, and during the winter months, she was at the end of her tether as England was cold, so cold. The music was blaring and while Sadie and Roland had retired to the bedroom, they had been left in the living room, talking.

He had begun to dance close and squeezed her against the wall, and she began to make moaning sounds, so that she became embarrassed. But she was excited, even though she knew that he lived with Carole, and had even visited the house with Sadie and met Carole, who seemed a very nice person, she still wanted him. It was not her usual way.

But she needed to feel her body on fire, and she held a secret passion for Maxmillian the very first time they had met. That this was reciprocated meant that placing them in the same room together and leaving them alone, the inevitable was bound to happen. It was only natural because what she called the vibrations were good; after all, they were two fit, attractive, healthy and head strong individuals. For his part Maxmillian could not resist "a piece of

Caribbean arse," as he termed her. Although friends with Ralph all these years he had begun to tire of his protestant morality, his constant ethics, which robbed him of experience which could make his life richer, and more fulfilled. When a few months before he had asked Ralph whether he should give her a try, Ralph had acted so responsible by saying that if he didn't care about her children then he should leave her alone. Ralph was such a fool. He turned Juanita to face the wall and pulled her dress up to her waist.

"Wait there," he told her. Going to the door, he pushed the large settee against it and returned. She did not move, but waited obediently for him to return to fill her; only looking back at him as he returned. She pushed her behind back and arched her back, and shuddered as he pushed into her, pulled out, paused and entered her again. He continued this action nine times. And each time she pushed her behind backwards, arched her back, and waited for the next thrust. She could feel the sensation as it travelled up her spinal column, and she braced herself for whatever Maxmillian had to give, and she denied him nothing, allowing him to grind into her while standing, and eventually, when he had satisfied himself this way, she spread herself on the settee and, laughingly, dared him to come onto her.

Pulling her dress up, he planted himself deep inside her and ripped her dress off her body, including her thong; held his penis in his hand and turned it, whipped and churned it; removed it and plunged with great force into the walls at the back of her vagina. Juanita felt an upsurge of passion as she climaxed. Maxmillian kept up this movement until she screamed. Then he pulled the cushions off the arm chairs of the suite, propped them under her, placed her feet on his shoulders and entered to the right, moving in a rhythmic way. After an hour, he discarded the cushions, forced her to crouch on her hands and knees, and entered her from behind, embracing her waist. Then dismounted her; pulled her up, pushed her to face the wall and entered her as they had begun. When this was over, they went back to the settee, and he entered her without sound or movement.

As they were about to doze off, Sadie knocked on the door, calling out her name. Hurriedly, they arranged their clothes; only to find that Juanita's dress had been ripped off her, and refused to move the settee so that Sadie could enter.

"Sadie," she called out. "Could you bring me a towel please, and one of your dresses."

Some minutes passed and Sadie returned, knocking on the door. They pushed the settee away while she tossed the towel and the dress in. Later they rushed to the bathroom, cleaned themselves up, and got dressed. Sadie and Roland joined them after a few minutes, with Sadie singing teasingly, "My cup is full and running over and I don't know what to do," Juanita kept silent, and refused to comment when Roland asked what she thought of Sadie's singing.

"I can't hear a word!" she said.

Juanita felt no guilt whatsoever in giving her body to Maxmillian, beneath her calm exterior she was a volcano of passion, and this the warm Caribbean Sea and sun, had nurtured. Her sophistication did not mean that she was not a woman; a female of the species with its own wants and desires; with a body with its own bodily functions, neither immortal nor profane, but a living, breathing thing, and she had experienced the rolling of her eyes. That was precisely what she wanted. She had felt passion in an unfamiliar place.

Her blood was thawing, and she felt relaxed; and outside, it was warm enough not to wear underwear, so she felt like suggesting a walk in the park to Maxmillian as the weather seemed good.

"Fancy a walk girl?"

That was sexy, she hadn't been called girl in a long while. She liked the connotation. It reassured her that she was woman, feminine, and that he still held continuing interest. She felt sexy, but in a non - demanding way. After all, they had already done it and it was good. They had both enjoyed themselves, she was sure.

Maxmillian got up and pulled her to her feet; she let him draw her to him, and her body responded with such elasticity that she was shocked by her quick response, obedience and compliance. He had got to her, much the same way as Roland had to Sadie.

"We're going to the park!" Maxmillian said, and winked at Roland. He knew this would be appreciated, for Sadie had been reluctant to allow Roland to have his way, unless he did to her what Ralph had so often refused to do. Ralph used to be such a lucky guy, but now he wandered how he would feel because Sadie would be even more thrilled by Roland, once he had done what she demanded; did what Ralph said he would never do.

Without much else being said, Juanita and Maxmillian walked out the door.

Juanita felt a soft gust of breeze lifting her dress and she held the hem of the dress down and laughed out loud so that Sadie could hear. In their excitement Maxmillian had ripped her thong off, and now she was not wearing any underwear and felt heavenly sensual as the fresh air wafted between her legs.

"What a fresh piece of breeze!" she said. And Maxmillian laughed. Together they made their way down the stair well.

Chapter Fifteen

With them gone, Roland clicked his fingers and Sadie followed him into the bedroom. They had been through this ritual several times before, but nothing ever came of it. That is they never quite got where he thought they would. But today Roland was prepared. He pushed her down onto the bed, took a bandana from his pocket and tied her hands. Sadie crossed her legs, laughing. Roland lay on top of her and tried to force her legs apart, but she would not let him; he tried to kiss her mouth but she kept her mouth shut tightly; for she could not give in to him so easily. With her hands still tied he forced her onto the mattress, raised her behind and lower back; pushed her legs apart so that her knees touched her breasts, using force and controlled firmness as if he was disciplining her, as if he was angry with her. Sadie loved it, loved to be disciplined this way, and her breathing became deep, as her body yielded willingly, and her heart began to beat with excitement and expectation.

Then he looked her straight in the eyes and spoke, but she did not answer; he inserted himself and penetrated her, moved in and out: ten shallow strokes to every nine deep ones. Sadie wanted to embrace him around his neck, his waist; grab at his behind, pull him down by the shoulders but she could not. The deprivation of touch was scintillating and she moaned and inhaled deeply, whooping, then moaned out loud; then she begun to laugh and chatter to him incoherently. Suddenly he stopped, dismounted her; took three large silk bandanas from his pocket, tied them around her ankles and to the foot of the bed stead. He resumed, resting on his knees, begun to caress the upper part of her body, while whispering niceties to her: praising her breasts, her behind, her eyes, ear lobes, voice and, his auditory caresses gave her a plateau of mounting passions. Then he gave her four deep to four shallow strokes, for he knew she loved to be hit there: four beats to the bar; one and two and three and four; one two, one two. Sadie shrieked, and compensated for the tactile deprivation by pushing her behind forward so that she could feel him deep inside her, as if he would enter her uterus. As she became more impassioned he begun to move slowly, and moved two deep strokes for every eight shallow ones, until she climaxed; but as she began her descent Roland stopped; tied the third bandana around her mouth, instructed that she should breathe through it and control her breathing. He made her take four deep breaths, and continued alternating deep with shallow strokes into her as she pushed back and forth. Sadie stopped moving. She felt a new woman as they lay in silence.

Roland rolled off her, untied her hands and feet, took the last bandana from her mouth, rolled her over on her hands and knees; Sadie raised her behind in the air, while he pushed her head down firmly with a little force as if he was still angry with her, knelt behind her and penetrated her deeply. Sadie felt her vagina contract as he penetrated her, she felt its expansion as he made seven shallow to eight deep movements into her, making the thrusts sharp and clean without any hint of uncertainty. Then as she became familiar with his movements and could brace herself for every thrust he stopped, tied her ankles together by joining the bandanas, so that they could reach the end of the bedstead, and began again, until she begged him to stop. But he would not, and this insatiable consumption of her saw her achieve plateau after plateau, again and again, and finally, when she climaxed again, he stopped, for he could feel her wetness around him; he pulled out laughing.

"I've got you!" he said in a deep, soothing and melodious voice.

"I know!" she replied. And she breathed in and out slowly. "I know you got me," she added softly, with almost a hint of regret in her voice.

Chapter Sixteen

It was mid afternoon and Ralph was glad the lesson was over, it was May and the May Day celebrations would be on Monday. He had been working for the same training provider for three years now and felt that he needed a change. Despite this he had continued to take the constant abuse from Libita, a tall lean woman from Albania with questionable English, but his boss any way. John Wayne, the other Caribbean trainer felt equally dubious about her role as boss. Both felt that she had made her career secure by marrying an Englishman of the native soil, for in their own peculiar way they considered themselves English; but skin colour being the vital denominator to be called such, they often referred to themselves as English only when pushed for in depth and detailed information about the Caribbean, by others and more recently by her.

"I'm from Albania" she had told them; "I came here five years ago, when you came from the Caribbean?"

Perhaps it was this astute precision for details that had made her boss, they had both agreed. She had only been here recently in the last decade, while they came to the country as children; had spent all their teen age years here. And only had details of the islands that they had gleaned from attending the embassies and, more recently, for John Wayne, from visits to the islands. But then they would come home; but then being Caribbeans, whose parents were brought here thinking British, who even thought British before they arrived as absolute beginners to the upper end of the culture, which they felt was already theirs by birthright; the shock of the cigarette butt end of the culture to which they had aspired; the fish and chips in newspapers, the loaf of bread in packet left on the door step; the lurid and contradictory aspects of their England that no one had told them about; the wog labelling, racist end of the spectrum that the aristocratic and upper middle class and working class liberals as visitors to the islands had only hinted at – they were still in states of culture shock. Not Libita, however, she had arrived in this country with no expectations and she faced her daily tasks with concise Eastern European and communist precision.

But as Caribbeans she envied their richer spiritual lives; their command of English and despite confusion about their identities, their strong intellects. As trainers they had cut through the volumes of worksheets and found precision to deliver the units and elements of the new Skills for Life curriculum in both numeracy and literacy. But they were not management material; had they been in Eastern Europe, she conceded, they would be heads of such programmes. In the continent with such skills in the language and enthusiasm for learning, they would be in her position. She soon learned that despite their educational achievements Caribbean men were looked upon as not being quite there. That was the stereotype that she had been given as fact; but over the past years her humanist communist training had taught her otherwise. Their country needed them thick, because it was not the women they feared, but the men; and not the athletes, but the thinkers.

And another knowledge she gleaned, for she could not generalise too widely, if these two were a measurement of anything, Caribbean men had a way with women. She had observed John Wayne's style with Zainab, the nineteen year old Asian girl, whom he liked and made no attempt to hide his attraction for her; and as all women would, the girl had been flattered by his attention. But this did not blind him to reason; his was no mundane passion or false attraction, or false love. Within the thirteenth week, he had found Zainab a job and had referred her onto East Ham College to do a part time course in healthcare. He had told Zainab on the first day that he wanted her out of the centre; that he would either marry her – which was a joke, for he commented that he would divorce his present wife for her and become Moslem. Even the men had laughed at his insistence that Zainab had to go. He had a plan for all of them. He wanted them to get on with it, as he had put it in that very cryptic way of his. And Ralph had also agreed with John Wayne and given vocal support that, "Zainab was a dangerous and a wickedly beautiful distraction."

Ralph in contrast had a more reflective humour. Upon arriving he had cleaned out the filing cabinet with all the old portfolios and paper, and dubbed himself the maintenance man. While Sabina, the Moslem teacher had only concentrated her efforts on the Moslems from her region, Ralph treated them all with the same careful attention, at times picking mock arguments with them to give them confidence in conversational English. So that after his last eight weeks on the programme, Mr Patel, whose English was very poor before Ralph arrived, informed Libita that he learnt more in the last eight, than the eighteen weeks that he had attended the programme. Ralph also began to learn how to greet members of his class in their languages, which ranged from Somali to Hindi, Portuguese, French, Lingala, Italian, Bengali, Gujarati, Arabic and Malayalam.

Ralph educated the emotions in a complimentary way to John Wayne's style, and they seemed to be working together without any preconceived plan. As for the humour, Ralph brought in books on the different religions and countries and placed them on the large table where they could be seen; and when a Hindu was found delving into a book on Islam, they would be mockingly reprimanded that they were not Moslem or Hindu – as the case may be – and therefore they should not be reading that book. Yet he had brought the books in for specifically that very purpose; at times he taught by contradictions. In the end the standard replies would be that they all belonged to the same culture and both Ralph and John Wayne would have a discussion, both feigning ignorance of either religions.

The students realising this would begin to laugh, pointing out their contradictions. And they would also insist that the class should swap seats around. One day in passing his room, Libita heard Mrs Das, say, "Look Mr McFarlane we are three different castes of Hindus and we are all sitting together." "And so you should," Ralph had replied. At which John Wayne had rushed in to make a mock complaint against Ralph's liberal seating arrangements. The entire centre experienced uproar of laughter; in the end John Wayne laughed so much at his inability to influence them and her that tears streamed down his cheeks, as she refused his successive pretensions of argument and gave up.

Ralph was in good humour himself. She had by then become accustomed to the underside of Caribbean humour, which was both reflective and reflexive, at the same time.

There was therefore no doubt in Libita's mind that she had a good team. But she could see trouble in the shape of David Dermerec, who although part Irish, part Maltese, had joined Combat Thirteen at the tender age of nineteen and had as an act of a mixture of emotions – bravado, stupidity and belonging – had tattooed on his arm "Death to all Niggers." John Wayne had seen this one morning during a meeting at Head Office, because David had forgotten to roll down his sleeves after washing his hands in the toilet and, quite apart from the protests of other staff members – the company could be sued. David's reaction to this new discovery was heavy handed; he called John Wayne in and had a meeting at which he pledged a greater salary – for they were working for pittance – another disadvantage of the Caribbean male that she had begun to witness - and on top of that, he demanded from John Wayne a commitment of working for the company for the next two years. John Wayne had arrived from that meeting livid, but still retained a touch of his humour. She had heard Ralph and he laughing after the students had all been sent home early on Friday to attend mosque.

Chapter Seventeen

Monday was Ralph's turn for the stand-off, David had decided that the master's approach would work best with these boys – another obstacle that Caribbean men found humiliating - England was not conducive to their machismo, the variant mixtures of genes that had made them men, and would have to emasculate them, make eunuchs of them, and turn them into impish little pussies, before they could accept them, wimps.

The conversation began slowly. David informed Ralph that he had requested a commitment of three years from John Wayne, who would get back to him the following week. He of, course, could not have known that John Wayne had already discussed his imminent resignation with Ralph and had advised the same. During the course of the conversation Ralph kept looking at David's right arm, as if he could not take his eyes off it.

"I don't want to sack you," he said. "I want you to stay with us, but a commitment for two years and more portfolios from you every eight weeks."

Ralph smiled and gave a Marlon Brando shrug, cupped his right hand, put it to his mouth and coughed; retrieved a handkerchief from his pocket, wiped his face, covered his mouth with it and coughed.

"And sometimes if the students can't finish off the writings themselves, you guys can take the work home and finish it off for them – things have changed since I was an assessor." He smiled.

"And I will give you guys a thousand pounds extra, just for the portfolios."

This was insulting; they were both on thirteen thousand pounds a year, with degrees and professional qualifications.

Ralph kept silent. David was becoming agitated by this calmness; he thought that John Wayne was exceptionally indifferent, but never expected tranquillity from both men. After all, he had heard of the explosive personality of the Caribbeans; he at least expected some emotional outburst, some moralising speech about race discrimination and prejudice; he had studied these people and knew them well; just as he had studied the Asian women's respect for men in authority and had the weak ones lining up every Thursday afternoon, so that he could flirt with them to find out which among them were available to be groped and touched up on a regular basis, after which he would have them in his bed. Raj, the other basic skills ethnic had got wind of this and was acting up. He would deal with him later, after he had sorted out these minor problems with these boys.

But Ralph's quietness was dangerous; he was dastardly in attitude; unpredictable and David began to fear for his life as Ralph had fixed him with a stare of utter contempt, with a mixture of indifference as if he was holding himself back from lunging at him, caper over the desks and chairs in the training room and strangle him to death like a thug; these Caribbeans could also become suddenly violent – he had not forgotten poor old Blakelock and the riot years, when the cities of England burned and Combat Eighteen was on the alert to defend the Deutschland. He was beginning to see himself as Ralph was seeing him. He was small, rather skinny from smoking ten packets of cigarettes a day, and had lately been having headaches; he reasoned that if this black man with his animal - like instincts decided to murder him, he could be dead before he could alert the other members of staff, and ambulances tended to arrive only after the police, any way; and he therefore, couldn't be in the same room alone with him a minute longer.

"What I want," Ralph said "is for you to get my papers and hand them to me and I want my payment now."

"OK!" David said and took the opportunity to leave the room.

Ralph sat waiting, but he never came back; instead he went and locked himself in his office, made a cup of tea and sat down to a cigarette. But he never came back out, until fifteen minutes had passed; Ralph was still waiting in the room as he sneaked out and went up the road to the Green Man, where he ordered a pint of ale, lit another cigarette and passed the time at the pool table with his old acquaintances. Carlisle an old friend could see that he was greatly troubled, because since his public renunciation he had not been a visitor to the pub, which was out of bounds to ethnics. Secretly he wanted to hurt Ralph, teach him a lesson; he had dared to even consider taking his life, had disrespected him, and he a combatant of Combat Eighteen. He needed to be taught a lesson, so that he would learn how to treat his betters, with respect.

"I might have a problem that you can help me with," he said. "This black has just threatened me." He lied. If Carlisle could come in on this he was sure the others would follow, for at six foot four and a hundred and ninety pounds, Carlisle was formidable.

"I don't think so," Carlisle said. There was the notion of fair play that David feared he would encounter. "What did he say?" Carlisle continued. But David could not answer and realised that he would have to find the more firebrand type of his old acquaintances if he wanted action on his behalf or even to elicit sympathy.

Ralph sincerely thought that David would return with his papers and his pay; he actually believed what he said he wanted done, but of course, he could not stay a day longer in such a place that wanted him to commit fraud. For this he would be accountable for the rest of his life and long after he was dead.

With that northern fear of nemesis, he was sure such sins would fall on the heads of his children. He wished David every success, if it was possible to call any act that came out of such deceit, success, but he wanted out; wanted nothing to do with it. Neither would he go squealing to the powers that be for he knew when it came to the crunch, they would never believe him.

He waited for the next ten minutes and came out of the room into the passage way where Angela, a pretty girl of about five feet six inches tall, with a wild crown of curls for hair was at reception. She was allegedly of Caribbean origin, but it was becoming so difficult to decide these days, with the Somalis, the Eritreans, the Ethiopians, etc, coming into the country; that made Ralph and the first generation of so called immigrant children, now grown into adults, considered that it was a signal for them to leave. Secretly, they blamed the English Anglo Saxons for this great, unhealthy influx of people.

They were encouraged, aided and abetted to live in their little foreign communities on English soil, when their Caribbean parents had come here shouting yes to integration, if not in bed, at least, over a plate of curry goat and rice, a little beef stew and green bananas with mackerel, a glass of rum, a record or two of, first, calypso, ska, blue beat, rock 'n roll or jazz, and later reggae music and now carnival where all, even the hereditary enemies, the Babylon were encouraged to attend. Now they had gone and fucked things up. Even the Indians, Pakistanis and Bangladeshis were pissed off, with the influx of these coolie Africans, and communist white people from abroad.

Ralph laughed to himself, chuckled madly and left the premises, shaking his head. They had let theses cultural fanatics into the country, including those gangsters from the Caribbean, who went about playing the latest noise which they mistakenly called music, and went about shooting people, or produced children who emulated them.

And to top it all, these bastards had labelled his generation thick for wanting to play football, cricket and rugby, and screw the arse off white girls, once they had consented. As if fucking was suddenly a crime. After all, their ancestors had built their empire fucking other people or fucking up the world. He remembered this all from his school years in Birmingham, and when he and his cousins went to Aunt Rosa's house in Leeds during the summer vacations. Now they were busy gate keeping them out of regular and sustainable employment. Bastards!

Surely, Aunty Rita, Cousin Clarence and Mary his god - aunt and third cousin and her husband John a native English had brought the whole family up with the correct attitude. On holidays in Leeds they would have cheese and macaroni pie with Yorkshire pudding and roast potatoes with their rice and peas and chicken. Then for sweet they would have rhubarb pie and Uncle John would entertain him by filling him up with his elderberry wine when he visited his god aunt and third cousin in Ealing, while supporting the West Indies cricket team all through his life, even when they had begun to lose.

What was wrong with living in two worlds? They had come to England and were only too glad to help to build their Mother Country after the war. They had realised a new age had come and all wanted to rise to its challenges: to be a part of the new age, so they rose to the occasion, instilled in their young the benefits that England had to offer and were grateful for the opportunities to build new lives. As long as the racists did not harm their sons and daughters, that was a different matter; and after the Night of the Machetes at Deptford in nineteen fifty six, and the Notting Hill incident, when they had had to spill English blood, just to show that slavery would never happen again and that it was over, they had respected the good souls of their adopted country. Filled its churches and poured libations in their graveyards and prayed for the souls of the living and the dead. They had risen to the occasion and out of this would come greatness in the end, at some divinely ordained time in the future. But were their efforts recognised? No!

They had accused them of wanting to be white. What was wrong with living in two worlds? Instead they had refused them credit, places to live, and given all fucking assistance to the Asians who only wanted to live among themselves and build enclaves. Bastards! Ralph was insanely angry so he went for a walk in Cranbrook Park, which was only ten minutes away, to calm down.

It was three thirty when he arrived home and found Juanita, Roland, Sadie and Maxmillian in the kitchen at Sadie's home. They were surprised to see him home so early. Sadie had not been expecting him; she had made arrangements for Ivan to pick up the children from school as they would be spending the weekend with him on Friday and Audrene wanted to see them before he took them to see his parents in Bromley as it was Monday, and they were travelling to the United States on Tuesday. Hence the urgency to see their grandchildren straight after school on a Monday evening as the following Monday would be May Day. The arrangement had been made weeks before, also, Ralph's Aisha and Alexander were not expected until May Day Monday, so the two sets of children would not be disappointed in missing each other. Ralph would normally have gone to his flat at Falcon Terrace, changed and visited Sadie. Today, however, fate had decided otherwise. While for Sadie and Juanita, nothing out of the ordinary should have happened that day, if it all went to plan. But, that was not the case. Ralph had caught them.

Chapter Eighteen

They were downstairs in the kitchen laughing and joking when they saw Ralph's shadow as he passed by the window on the communal balcony. Sadie decided to meet him at the front door; she still needed him. After all, he would be inquiring about Alexis, who had been sent off to Juanita's sister Francine, to be looked after. Juanita had made the necessary arrangement so that they could be free to entertain Maxmillian and Roland. That Ralph had just left his job and needed support from someone; not necessarily Sadie did not matter; it was the way of the world, you stood alone in crisis, but if the going was good, and when the going was good, others would benefit from your efforts. Ralph had not realised his predicament and kept holding on to his delusions. For at this point, he needed emotional support from Sadie, but this was not forthcoming, she had moved on. Maxmillian had moved on; everybody had moved on; only Ralph was forestalling change. Life after all, was dynamic, and they are fools who ever tried to forestall the dynamics of change.

"What you doing home so early from work?" she inquired, innocently, and stood at the door. She did not want him to come in; he would disturb the cosiness; If only, if only she thought. Why did he have to be home so early, why did he have to be home at all? After all, she'd been trying to get rid of him, in a subtle manner. But it was partly her fault as well, she thought. None of us can ever end anything. We always want to hold on, and unwittingly, give those who want to hold on the impression that there was still hope.

So she found herself moving aside to let him in. Ralph touched her arm and with a nod of his head, signalled that he wanted to speak to her upstairs. She followed him up the stairs into the living room.

"What now?" she asked.

"I've just left my job," he replied.

"How are we going to survive?" she retorted.

See, he thought she cares; she used the word we, so there is still hope that we can mend the rift in our relationship. There was still a chance, he thought.

But this was only a thoughtless reaction on Sadie's part; in reality she couldn't care less whether he was in employment or not. Feeling guilty that she may have given the wrong impression about them by her reaction, she said to him:

"I have been thinking about going home to Antigua for good." More to change the subject about their still being an issue, for more than ever before she wanted out; as if suddenly she had come to her senses.

"Sadie, girl we're out of here," Juanita called out. "I'm taking the stags with me."

At this Sadie rushed down stairs, she didn't really want them to leave. She was having fun, at least, until Ralph had arrived, and she resented his intrusion, his reliance on her; but the least she could do was to see her guests off.

After all, this was her home and they were invited. Ralph was on his way out of her life and she would sort it out. But she felt she still needed his money.

Roland was at the head of the retreat when she reached down stairs. Juanita looked at her as if to say I told you so.

Maxmillian was uncommitted, but seemed sad. Ralph had forgotten him as he had forgotten everybody when he had first met Sadie. He now seemed obsessed and so far gone that nature could only take its course. That was the way of change, and everybody feared it.

"Wha' gone bad a morning can't get good ah evening," he said, and followed Roland out the door.

"See!" said Juanita.

"I'll phone you tomorrow morning," said Roland, "I'll give you a wake up call!"

Chapter Nineteen

What Ralph failed to realise was that Sadie had already made up her mind to end the relationship. He had already served his purpose. But she knew that he would always be there for his children and that Alexis would never be abandoned. These were the qualities she liked about him, but she had been influenced to expedite his departure from her life. As she closed the door an atmosphere of doom descended on the place; she felt as if she wanted to run away. She wanted to leave with them, but made her way back upstairs. She re-entered the living room to find Ralph sitting on the settee with his face in his hands.

A feeling of empathy came over her, but she knew he was the only one who could help himself; others could only empathise. If he was in a bad way because he had finally begun to realise that Roland was more than a friend, she could only feel sorry for him; she had no regrets because she wanted to see if she was really in love with Roland, with him she had felt complete, satisfied and filled, he wore the trousers and that was the kind of man she wanted, the type Ralph were when they had first met. Now he was a mere shadow of himself and failing badly. She had been there before, when Raul had turned up with two hundred pounds and left, suggesting an abortion. Now it was her turn to end a misalliance, a burdensome relationship. She smiled.

He thought he saw a ray of hope, perhaps, she will change her mind, he thought, that his present untenable position would make her realise that he needed her support to stay in work. That she had grown accustomed to the good life that he had given her was apparent to all. Even Roland and Juanita had commented on how well kept she was. And she still needed a man that worked.

"Want to talk about it?"

"They wanted me to cheat with the portfolios and write up the students' work. I couldn't do it. I told them no."

"Well, what are you going to do?"

"Find another job; I have an interview next Thursday. It's a place in Tower Hamlets, if I get that it will be better because it's nearer; not so far as Barking. Just down the road. It's about twenty minutes or so from here."

"Better from your flat on Falcon Terrace," she said.

There was a hint, but even that he couldn't hear; he felt that her interest in his finding work meant that their relationship was back on track. Ralph got up and looked out of the window facing east. The communal garden was to the left of the window with apple trees and a couple of horse chestnuts in the centre. There was a squirrel at the root of the red ash tree to the far right; he watched as it sprang across the grass and stopped half way across, and dug up a nut from a tuft of grass, held it in its paws and darted across to the horse chestnut trees and disappeared into the branches. He turned and looked at Sadie.

"I'll give you a comfortable life. But you don't care, you don't care at all. But I miss the comfort of your love."

"We all love in different ways; I love my children, my brothers, my sisters, my mother and my father."

It was beginning to dawn on Ralph that this woman did not care; that she no longer held any interest in him. This was a winding down of things; that whatever resentment or excuses she had to leave him ran deep. He was finally making up his mind about her. After she had finished speaking, there was silence and she waited for him to reply. But Ralph had said his peace and could think of nothing more convincing to say to persuade her to stay.

"I don't think it's bad of me to want to finish the relationship. I think it's the best thing for both of us. We weren't getting on and I told you before when I met you that I was still in love with Raul. I hadn't made love to anyone for a long time when I met you. You said you'll be my love doctor."

"I want you but you don't want me. You prefer to do it with other people that don't love you, because it's your life. It's your life, but I feel hurt."

"We can't help who we love," Sadie replied softly. "That's life. I always thought I was in control. I don't know what's happening to me."

There was a peculiar tone to her voice, like a sentiment contradictory and forced. She could not help leaving him and the circumstances meant nothing to her; and Ralph knew at that moment that he had lost her, lost her forever, for good and his heart sank; deep feelings of regret came over him. He had been hurt so deeply before, and here, in this very room where she swore there was no one else; history was repeating itself all over again. He had loved and love being mortal had decayed; their vegetable love had grown, and died: a death by natural causes.

For his part Ralph was beginning to shed his ignorance, he was beginning to understand that he was nowhere in her life, that in truth he had never been anything more than a passing fancy. That she had rejected him long before Roland had arrived. There was no place for him in the drama of her new life, despite the fact that they had a child together. And as more and more he realised his errors, so many emotions were welled up inside him. The way that she had deliberately exploited his resources, as if, like Barbara had done, making sure that he would never have any money. He realised now how little Sadie had cared for him.

Ralph looked at his watch. It was seven thirty.

"Got somewhere to go?"

"No!" he replied.

"I'm glad that we can talk we have Alexis to consider, if nothing else."

There was nothing that he could say to mend the rift. But then again, there was no rift to mend. Love had simply died a natural death. It was not that he had done anything to offend her. It was not as if he had committed a sin, anything unfaithful to make her change her mind about being with him and loving him. It wasn't even that she had decided on a change, and although it seemed pragmatic and based on so many contradictions, it was her life, after all.

"When can I see Alexis?" he said.

"Phone me," she said. "He's with Francine!"

Then she looked at him; gave him her sweetest smile. She remembered he might be unemployed now but could be working in the next couple of weeks or so, and Alexis was his son. And being the most vulnerable in her household she reasoned that Ralph would always keep the home safe; not that she needed to keep him sweet for his duties, she was only about to offer her condolences for their love had died and felt that for Ralph that this was quite possibly his last chance, so she said:

"If you can't be my star, perhaps, you can be somebody else's star."

He felt patronised but replied softly:

"We are all stars."

"Well, I finished with you before I started fucking him."

"No, you didn't," he said.

"See, I know I shouldn't speak to you too much; you can't see things from my point of view."

"Let's face it; you did it while we were together; then you had me competing with the ghost of Raul; now you want to convince me that your behaviour was so right. If human action and the consequences of our own actions are ours and nobody else's business and no one else dare comment on what we do, or contradict our actions, where does it all end?"

"I can't reason with you. You have a bigger vocabulary than mine; you mix up my mind with your words, and I can't think right when I speak to you."

Ralph fell silent. It all seemed so strange to him now. Were his friends right that this was just an upper crust fuck that he thought could be turned into a relationship? Was this the descent into the abyss of the lower depths that his college friends had warned him about so many years ago? That one day he will find himself cast off like an old rag, after he had been drained of all his potential? And what was wrong with his vocabulary, anyway. It was odd to be able to reason at last, and he was told this by the woman who had come to him, had picked him out precisely because he had been educated to think a certain way.

The distance between them had grown deep; so deeply now that she found it painful to speak to him because he had not let her convince him with another lie. For if he believed her now that nothing had happened between her and Roland before that Sunday when he had come to Francine's house when they were having a party and blown his horn and she had rushed downstairs on the road and got into his car and disappeared, then he would be allowing her to warp his judgments and twist his sense of reality. And no one must ever be allowed to do that. Not now; not any more, for if anyone had told him months ago that this was happening he would have sworn that they were lying. But something crossed his mind as he reflected. Didn't Maxmillian hint that her so called shopping on some Saturdays when she left him to look after the children and apparently went to the market at Ridley that she was actually seeing Roland? Ralph smiled.

The more he spoke to Sadie, the more information her attitude gave him about what she had been doing. No wonder she found conversations with him confusing. She had always feared his power of reasoning; his calmness, and matter of fact ways of putting things, like puzzles of a jigsaw: putting things together. That's how his mind worked and she felt a certain pleasure because she knew their child will have such a mind; after all, had she not eaten him and told him that very day that women only did that to men for whom they wished to have children?

Ralph looked at his watch; he knew that it was getting late and that Branton would soon be closing shop and he wanted more marijuana. He got up from the chair and stretched his limbs. It was getting dark.

"Listen, I've got to go now."

"Phone me," she said as he left.

There was no need to follow him down the stairs; he would see himself out and she was grateful that they had the talk. Things seemed a lot clearer and now she could get on with her life, which had been on hold because of his obsession with her in refusing to let go, and because she had been looking after their child.

Chapter Twenty

It was Saturday midnight and Sadie was in her bedroom. She was naked as she looked at her body in the mirror. Her hair was in plaits, some piled on her head, and others falling around her heart shaped face, contrasted well with her breasts, which were not large, but neither were they puny and without shape. Her long arms, her torso and her shapely legs; all of her was desirable, topped by her little presentiment: her pussy, which was nicely shaped with hair at a minimum, and yet not sparse at all. Turning side ways to read her profile, she touched her backside; it felt firm and well proportioned. Roland opened his eyes and noticed her standing before the mirror. He looked around at Sadie's new place and wondered how in the world they were going to finish the rest of the decorations. It was a beautiful place in the south of the borough and he wanted to do it justice. There were so many questions that he dared not ask Sadie.

The sex was good; quite exceptional. The underwear she wore were expensive, so were the body suits that showed that Ralph must have enjoyed her in a special way; a very special way, he thought, for Sadie still called out his name when they were having sex. But apart from the mistaken identity, the mechanics of it was excellent.

Sadie seemed to have read his mind and reached for him; he pulled her towards him and she fell into his arms, laughing. He turned her over on her back and moved hard inside her. She relaxed; he struck twice and then stopped. Then as she began to move under him, he forced his full weight onto her and held her tightly. She bit her lower lip as he pushed deep inside her. They continued to move together for some twenty minutes, and then lay quietly for what seemed to Roland, an eternity.

Suddenly, Sadie pushed her body upwards, placed her feet between his thighs and rolled over on top of him. Roland was shocked.

"I do the fucking!" she said, before he had time to say anything.

"Where did you learn that?" he asked.

"I'm more than a woman," Sadie replied.

"So what's wrong, girl?"

"Do you think we are supposed to be completely helpless; always underneath?"

He looked at her puzzled; now he understood why Ralph could not just let her go. Those lips were soft and dewy – her face, a complete heart. Yes, he thought more than a woman; much more. But resentment began to set in, that meant she had a special love for Ralph; if not now because that love had died, it must have been there before things got bad. Their child was the product of this love. "More than a woman," he laughed.

Sadie got out of bed, turned her back to him and got down on all fours.

"You will have to marry me," she said. "Now that you have taken over from Ralph, you have to make an honest woman out of me. I want to be your wife."

"Then you have to get what only wives get," he replied.

"Yes and whatever we do in our married chamber is ours and nobody else's business, so long as it's not funny. Come on top of my back; put it in here, I want to feel it; you know what I like."

He positioned himself between Sadie's legs and grabbed her around the waist, as if he was angry with her. He thrust himself forward repeatedly until she balanced on her outstretched arms and lifted her behind in the air like a wheelbarrow, looking back at him through her legs. Despite the force of his thrust calmness came over her entire body and her senses became washed with the most tumultuous emotions that she had ever experienced, while she felt a tremor in the prepuce of her clitoris. He had done it again and she took a deep breath and adjusted her backside, pushing it up more in the air to meet his thrusts as she prepared herself to be overwhelmed by him.

"My husband," she said, breathlessly.

He placed her feet over his shoulders, and pushed in and out. Sadie felt a flood of fulfilment as the throbbing spread from the clitoris throughout her entire frame and a tingling sensation began in her eyes and the spot in her forehead just above her nose. There was an intense feeling in her womb as the feelings subsided only to begin again. He carried her walking on her hands to the bed. Then changed his mind and pushing her against the upright chair standing, he plunged deeper and deeper into her, while keeping her back straight.

"You have a strong back," he said, adding, "Stand up straight I don't want it pushed back yet."

"OK," she breathed. "Take it steady, please give it to me; you know how I like it."

Roland slid his hand between her legs and began to caress her as he pushed forward. Sadie began to push back but continued to hold on to the front of the chair. He then walked her away from the chair to the bed and pushed her back forward, resting her hands on the mattress. After some minutes he walked her away from the bed again, pushed her forward, while Sadie bent over spreading her palms onto the floor as she raised her backside in the air. Then he pulled her up straight. She sighed as she felt his penis adjust itself deep within her. Her legs buckled as she felt herself climax, and she continued to breathe deeper and deeper. Suddenly he pulled out; turned her around facing him, balanced her back on the bed; raised her legs in the air over his shoulders and stepped away from the bed. Sadie screamed as the movements were so sudden and unexpected, as if he had penetrated her very being. He stood holding her and she could feel her head getting lighter and lighter as if she would pass out as her nerves began to tingle on edge. Then he pulled out and placed her on the bed and tied her legs in the air on the bars of the four poster bed.

"My Lord," she said. "You put me to shame."

"I've got you!" he said.

"I want you!" she replied. "Please give it to me!"

Hanging there, Sadie waited in anticipation. If there were any doubts that he was the one before, she was certain now. And who is to say that her tastes were immoral, wrong or even bad. At that precise moment she spared not a thought for Ralph; if he wanted to spend the rest of his days inhibited and died a bitter fool that would be his own fault. Why waste time, why not experience the range and intensities of human feelings so that when your time has come to die, you go without holding on to the world. What was wrong with living in the world? She wanted to see what Roland would do next; she was not afraid but just burning with anticipation: she was excited. He had bared her all. Her legs were hanging there and she felt like a bird, trussed for the oven. And why shouldn't she feel like a bird? She reasoned with herself silently. Didn't she have eggs inside her? And couldn't men also be referred to as birds? Love birds?

It was suddenly Sunday morning and the house was quiet as an occupied chapel of silent prayers. She could see the morning light coming in from the window; outside, the birds were rehearsing their morning song. Roland positioned himself between her thighs and struck deep inside her vagina; her body felt a tremor of sensations and she gasped, stretched out her hands and gripped either side of the bed. There it was again, that tingling in her spleen that disappeared the moment it began.

Then she brought her arms together and folding them around his neck, hugged him in to her breasts. Roland kissed her breasts and began sucking the nipples alternately. Sadie felt the entrance to her womb opening and closing as he sucked one breast and then the other, and all the time her legs hung in the air spurned her on to move, pushing her front forward with every stroke of his penis as it pierced her through and through, burying its prepuce deep inside her, chipping away at the walls of her little presentiment, like a laser beam in a glacier.

As a young girl back home she was taught by the more liberated women of the village of Half Way Tree, in Antigua, where she was born, that the utterance of endearing sounds during love making improved the performance of the lovers; that sweet words made love making sweetest, and she believed this with all her heart and mind, for life was performance. And utterance and speech, pleasantries and endearments proved that the man was hitting the right spot, or the woman was giving the right wind, and making the right movements, that both knew the "g" spot was being hit enough times and with enough pressure to reach a climax; while this had been an issue with Ralph who discouraged it, Roland took her sighs, moans and groans, to mean that surely he was striking home, loud and clear, and digging there, right there at the seat of her pleasure, exciting her emotions, heightening her passions, with all the subtlety, all the rhythms and intensities that the human mind could imagine, to make her feel like a beautiful, wanted, adored, devoured and satisfied woman, with a lover who knew exactly what he was doing to her when he did it ; who knew just what she wanted and how she liked it: had willed it to happen to her; a woman who would fantasise often about what he was doing to her now and who had dreamt what it would be like to be consumed, trussed and then carved on a silver platter, eaten like a bird, devoured, piece by piece.

Sadie felt like a love feast as they clung to each other, like twin shooting stars extinguished by their own descent. After they had climaxed together, again, finally, Roland untied her feet, and kissed them; kissed her all over her body; kissed her forehead, her lips and her breasts and, massaged her thighs and then her hands, held her face in both hands and kissed her gently on the mouth.

"Thank you!" she said; turned over on her belly and drifted into a deep, calming and tranquil sleep.

Chapter Twenty One

Coming to terms with the loss of Sadie's love, Ralph took Alexis, the two Aishas, Alexander, Anum and Ali to the London Fields Park at about three o'clock on Sunday. He had been there before, but every loss was different as every death is different, although grief is the same emotion, somehow the bereavement was more like the inextinguishable sparks of a fire whose flames can only smoulder and not be rekindled. It is a fire that will not ignite fully; cannot ignite fully because time and circumstances have changed the nature of its being. It will never be a conflagration that will produce flames strong enough to wash the souls dangling in purgatory to purification. And without purification there can be no catharsis. The children were now divided; and he felt sorry for the two Aishas, Alexander, Anum and Ali. And Ralph felt guilty as if he had no right to interfere in the lives of her children in the first place, or to have introduced his children to hers, for now everything had changed right before their eyes. But three months into the break up Anum, Ali and Aisha still came to him with Alexis. They would all congregate at his place and return to Sadie and Barbara on the Sunday night. He knew they were finding it difficult to cope and he hated himself for it, for he had changed their lives, and now would not be able to alter which other changes that might stand their way as they grow into adults. He was sure, however, as long as he had breath he would be there for them. But now most importantly, he realised that he had failed to break the chain, along with the torch of hope, the pain of desolation and division had been transferred from him to his descendants again. For Ralph was in no doubt that he was an ancestor to all of the children, irrespective of the origin of their genealogy. His frame of reference told him that he was – all of his generation - were cast in that mould, for those who came after them, after they had gone would regard them as such. He was sure they saw him in that same light, much the same way as he saw all those older people that died when he was growing up.

As he pushed her Aisha on the swing he realised that Sadie had broken his heart in more places than one. The children's hearts were also broken; but to survive he realised that he had to be strong for them; he had to show that he could adapt to the new situation; and to achieve stability he had to somehow distance himself from the pain of losing stability, and from losing her love, and not to lose them by self pity or bitterness. And for himself, he had to be strong. At least, he still had them around him and they still enjoyed being together. His Aisha and Ali were chasing each other across the park; Alexander and Anum as usual were alone at the far end, engaged in one of their dream – times in the world that they had created for each other. And her Aisha was on the swing, still addicted to motion.

Three hours had passed since they were in the park and it was beginning to get dark, so he called them up and got ready to walk back to his house on Falcon Terrace. But none of them were ready to leave the park just yet, so he sat down while the elder children took turns in pushing little Aisha and Alexis, on the swings. He sat resigned to the fact that they would be in the park until closing time, occasionally, shouting encouragement to them, or reprimanding them as they jostled each other to push the swings with their two younger siblings.

Finally the park bell rang and they were ready to leave. He cajoled them and walked with them in disorderly fashion towards the south gate of the park where several cars were parked.

As they turned left to into Gayhurst Road, someone shouted Ralph's name from one of the cars, which stood stationery in the make shift car park to the left of the entrance. Ralph stopped abruptly and instructed the children to wait on the pavement as a man some years younger than him approached them. He was about five feet four with closely cropped head and wore blue denim jeans and a burgundy velvet jacket, with black shoes to match.

"Hey!" he said, holding out his clenched fist.

Ralph boxed his hand. "How are you Ash?" he inquired. "Thought you'd be back in south by now. I thought you didn't like it in Hackney!"

"It's not Hackney," he said. "It's the local judiciary: Shoreditch County Court; they are getting rid of us; taking all our houses off us. And guess what they are using? Not guns, and bombs and overt violence against us. It's covert and very dangerous: Money!"

"Yes!" Ralph said. "When it comes to this, the law is more dangerous than guns."

"Yes!" Ashton replied, and added "More terrorising than a terrorist, more dominant than the US; more nuclear than Pentagon; terrible, terrible, terrible!"

And they both laughed; then a pause.

"These are the children?" inquired Ashton.

"Yes!" said Ralph and introduced them after he had finished, they exchanged mobile numbers and Ralph said goodbye, while Ashton, said goodbye to the children and went back to the car.

They resumed their walk home.

Chapter Twenty Two

The time spent in the park with all that fresh air saw them ravenous when they got home. Ralph had prepared chicken, which he had seasoned with an assortment of spices and herbs: cinnamon, nutmeg, jerk, oregano, paprika, basil, turmeric and rosemary; these he had sprinkled on the two chickens, together with lime juice and virgin olive oil, celery and garlic oil, the Trinidadian hot pepper sauce – which he had diluted more for the flavour, rather than the hotness, saw them ravenous. The steamed carrots, turnips and parsnips were the immediate favourites followed by the rotis. The table was quickly set by the two Aishas, and Ali, Anum and Alexander brought the serving bowls with Caribbean coconut rice, the turn corn, macaroni cheese pie, coconut, tanya, coco yam dumplings, Johnny cakes and a large raw salad, with Julie and East Indian mangoes and a large pineapple, already cut into portions for the dessert bowl. When Ali was called on to bless the table; he did a quick recitation: "Ancestors; I bless this table," he said.

"Allah is praised," intoned Alexander, reinforcing the expediency and the humour. And everybody laughed and began their meal.

They ate engaging in conversations about the park; school and general chat about the islands; the world and Africa, and fought for the chess set, and argue about football, with Ralph chiding them from time to time about the dangers of speaking with their mouths filled with food. As usual he reminded them of the importance of music, and encouraged discussion about the different scales and keys that music can be played in, the various instruments, especially the steel pan and the rumba box from the West Indies. Then an hour later after they had finished dinner, Ralph cleared away the plates while they played chess and ludo and monopolised his music set and record collection.

At seven thirty Konrad came to take them home.

As quiet and punctual as ever he entered and the children greeted him in chorus as usual. Ralph and Konrad went back since the early years when the great trek from the north to the south began. About Ralph's height, of fairish complexion, and always neatly dressed, the children knew that like Ralph he came from the north and considered him so close that they give him the epithet Uncle.

As usual Konrad refused food but took the fruit that Ralph had kept especially for him. After a while he was ready and Ralph went with them in the car; first, making the journey to Barbara to deliver Alexander and Aisha, and then at Sadie's, with Ali, Aisha, Anum and Alexis.

Chapter Twenty Three

It was the sixth month and Ralph had finally come to terms with the fact that people do not really lose in love; because in love no one ever really loses. The question is really one of interpretation. Who loses in love? One may lose an arm, etc. But love? To lose what you love. It is not the same as losing an opportunity, a material object, or one's life. There's a wonderful abstraction, he continued turning the thought over in his mind. Some people have lost an arm, a leg, a finger – some part of the body that is their material substance which they had and have survived.

Ralph was surprised when the phone rang. "See I kept on hinting, but nobody would take any notice of me; not even you." He heard a voice say as he picked up the telephone. He knew instantly that it was Maxmillian.

"How are you fixed?" he added.

"Fine," Ralph replied,

"Good, you have my sympathy, but it should only last so long."

"I hear you." Ralph replied.

"Juanita is having a party on Wednesday. Do you want to come? It would be good if you could make it. Come and scrub down a gal off the wall, man."

All through the months while Roland and Maxmillian had been meeting Sadie and Juanita; Sadie had been giving money to Juanita to save up for her birthday party in June. Both Roland and Maxmillian knew this. They also knew that a high percentage of the things bought for the party will have been bought with money which Ralph had given to Sadie. They knew Ralph liked a good smoke of marijuana and that with him there they reasoned that it was bound to be a lively party.

"So what, you coming then?"

"Yes; yeah – I'll be coming," Ralph heard himself say. "Yeah; be there," he added. "Yeah."

"I know it's a week day, but it will be nice."

"Nice!" Ralph agreed. There was a click, and he was gone.

Chapter Twenty Four

The party atmosphere was infectious when Roland and Maxmillian got there; they rang the doorbell, and someone opened the door. They walked in. The front room was filled with music and people were dancing and generally enjoying themselves. The room was dimly lit and Roland's eyes peeled the darkness, looking for Sadie. After their eyes had become accustomed to the darkness they went to the second room; this was not as crowded as the front room – she wasn't there either; she must be in the kitchen Roland remembered she had said that she would be helping out with the food. She was by the sink with her back turned; so he crept up behind her and covered her eyes with his hands. "Guess who this is?" he said. Sadie stopped what she was doing and pushed his hands away, turning around. "You silly arse," she said, "Of course I know it's you!" They both laughed.

"I'll get you a drink," she said, she turned to the table laden with a variety of drinks and poured him a Jamaican rum punch. "You might like some sorrel later."

"Thanks!" He took the drink and sipped it. Then he put his free hand around her waist and pulled her to him. "I'm pulling you." He played his fingers around her waist; tapped and squeezed her; then pinched her backside.

"Ouch!" she grimaced; hitting him on the shoulder.

"What you doing to her?" Juanita asked.

"Oh, only touching her," he replied.

"Why don't you take her for a dance? She could do with a good rub and squeeze."

Sadie grabbed his hand, placed it around her waist and stepped forward.

"Let's dance then."

They danced from the kitchen into the middle room. They danced until the song ended and stood close together, waiting for the next song to begin.

"So what you say, we slip away and run away; abscond. Let's go to Bethnal Green."

"I don't know," Sadie whispered.

He slid his right hand to her spine and felt all the way down to the last vertebrae at the bottom of her spine and pinched the skin.

"What do you say? "He insisted, pulling her closer to him and held her tighter.

"Ehem! Ehem! Ehem. Emmm! Ehem!" She moaned. Roland pulled back and looked at her. "Come on gal!"

Juanita came out of the kitchen, "Where you're off to?" Sadie held down her head and remained silent.

"We're going to her aunt's house to pick up something!" They hurried away.

Chapter Twenty Five

Whisked away from the party Sadie closed her eyes and let her vivid imagination flow; the music in the car was loud. Roland touched her leg as he put the car into first gear and moved off. Seconds later he changed into second and, turned up the volume of the music. She liked the way he looked in his Reebok jogging suit with the jacket over his yellow net merino, pristine white Reebok trainers, with his choppers.

"I want to fuck you," he began. "That's why we're going there. That's what I want to do when we get there!"

She didn't remember their turning into the drive way of his house. Everything seemed to be moving so fast. They were on the settee now. "I want to fuck you!" he said, sitting down beside her. She began unbuttoning her blouse. She got out of the poncho and pulled the long black dress down, stepped out of it, pulled her thong off and tossed it into the arm chair.

"Come on then, big boy," she teased.

Her body shuddered as he turned her on top of him and she was shocked as she found herself riding him. Then he sat up and spread her legs over his, and pulled her back and forth like a seesaw. That same vibration, that shudder ripped through her body and she chorused:

"Lord me God." Then she screamed and began to move frenziedly. Her body was still trembling when she flung away all her inhibitions and began to cry with pleasure. "Lord me God!" "Oh Ralph, Oh Ralph! Ralph!"

But it wasn't Ralph; it was Roland and she soon corrected herself as he plummeted into her with, at once tentative and intense strokes, until she felt soft and overwhelmed by his sudden change of movements, they climaxed together with emotional exultations and fell asleep.

Back at the party, Sapphire singled out Ralph; walked over to him and started dancing and flirting with him. She kept looking into his eyes as she danced, but his mind was occupied elsewhere. He was being foolish, looking to see if Sadie was there. Sapphire danced closer to him and put one arm around his waist. He responded with a half – hearted gesture by holding her as if she was made of shell and that if he squeezed her she would break into so many pieces of egg shell. The rest of the dancers all formed a ring, and she pulled him, joining the circle with her back turned to him. They danced like this for a while, and she naturally expected him to make contact with her but he did not. She moved back, pushing her backside against him, but he acted as if he didn't know what to do; as if what she was doing was somehow indecent. Then the music stopped. And even when the dance was over she let him know that she was available. But still he did nothing; did not make a move, neither did he engage her in conversation. So she left and went into the next room.

Some minutes later she returned and they danced together. This time he danced closely with her, then she danced with her back to him, making groaning sounds; this embarrassed Ralph. And after three dances with her he left and went for a walk; ten minutes later when he came back she had gone.

And he would never see her again. He had lost his chance; his one in a million golden opportunity; for she was younger, more graceful, slim and more delicately formed than Sadie, and more beautiful. He left the party soon after.

Chapter Twenty Six

Ralph had issues, it was as if someone a long time ago had put a spell on him. The night air struck his face as he waited for the train at Walthamstow Central to make it back to Hackney. He had no explanation for his behaviour; he wanted Sapphire. But there were skeletons in his cupboard. He who had helped so many people come to terms with their life issues, himself, lived in denial and walked in darkness as if his own darkness was daylight. He was facing his skeletons now. And he was beginning to miss Barclay and Abba, and wondered whether they had returned from Trinidad; for of all the people he knew only Barclay, having had a cousin who went to that same school in the days of Mas Luke, knew the contradictions.

He found a seat on the platform and waited for the train to arrive, and a blue feeling came over him. It began as vivid as if it was yesterday. He could see it all now: he was ten years old and the girl, she would have been about fourteen, but he was in love with her; in love with her white blouse and blue skirt and black patent leather shoes and white socks; he was in love with her hair and her mouth and her breasts; he was in love with her face. And every lunch hour he saw her with Mas Luke; she would be in the classroom down stairs before he had walked to his uncle's house in St Clare Hill for lunch; and when he had walked back she would still be there with Mas Luke until the school bell rang and she would go to her class upstairs; and Mas Luke at the piano, cocking his backside out and looking back at the boys:

"Listen children: doh ray mi fa so la ti doh; Doh ti la so fa mi ray do o! Listen up children, Ralphie, listen." Mas Luke would sit with his backside hanging over the side of the piano stool.

And the young boys - all thinking that you had to be like Mas Luke to get the girls. That was home and still years after in England, he would not give up. For Ralph loved music - loved the sound of the piano - loved the sound of the tuning fork: "Ping... doh!"

He was in his teens then, after Michelle had put it there. She had insisted that it was a test of love. He remembered every detail now. The piano in the room, similar to the one in the classroom all those years ago, Mas Luke decided since he couldn't have him; he would get him the other way, or was it an accident, coincidence. He had been talking art; for he had supervised his very first piece of written music back at the school, and introduced him to poetry; he had taught him how to read the ledger lines, too.

"This guy will phone me up; he wants me to screw him. He claims I have him dangling. Wait, you'll see. He'll phone in a minute."

The telephone rang and then he had come, because Mas Luke had one of his students there. And while they sipped Champagne, Verdi's Requiem was playing. And Mas Luke:

"Ralphie, why don't you take him into the bedroom and philosophise."

And he had; he had moved into the bedroom and taken him like a girl, like he wanted to take that girl at that flag ship school in the village that sees itself as a town, even more than that, a city. And the girl - boy had screamed and cooed like a turtle dove; opened up like a girl, the soft tissues breaking, yielding, like that girl in the white blouse and blue skirt, would have opened up for him, if only Mas Luke would let nature take its course. But no; he had to bring in that other element; he had to complicate things; for he wanted her like he wanted Sapphire tonight until she turned her arse to him. And so often a parent came to the school to complain against Mas Luke. But no one ever took any notice of them. They couldn't read Shakespeare or Shelley or Byron or play the piano like Mozart...

Whilst occupied in these thoughts the train arrived. Ralph touched his face; it felt moist and warm as streams of tears ran down his cheeks. His eyes were welling up with tears and it seemed to him now that all his life he had been dangling. He pulled the handkerchief from his pocket, dabbed his eyes and the wetness from his face and walked into the carriage which was empty, thankful and relieved that no one was standing near enough to see his eyes were wet; and yet he still felt a little embarrassed, just in case someone had seen. As the train pulled away from the station he cleared his throat and sat down, peering out of the window to his right. The train sped off. Some minutes later it stopped again at St James's Street where a few passengers from the occupied carriages got off; and started up, making its way towards Hackney. He was still reminiscing when it reached Clapton Park. As he looked back more on his life; he realised that he had thrown away so many chances – so many opportunities; not just twice, but several times. The second vital thing that never happened to his life – and which ought to have happened – was the interview at Essex University to take his doctorate. Barbara just would not let him sleep at his flat on his own the night before the interview. She had to be there, taxing his mind. Who was going to look after them: her and the girls? And despite his assurances that he would not desert them, she would not be convinced. She didn't want him to go all the way to Essex. So he had left late and arrived late and Jane Bradbury, head of the department had left her office disappointed that he had not arrived, for she had read his thesis and found a good clarity of mind there. She liked it; it showed talent and great promise. It hurt him greatly and distressed him years later when Barbara had called him a "has been."

Fly, caught in the spider's web, dangling, and had not her boyfriend Derrick, the decorator who had come to decorate the flat he met her in, and later Bower, her friend's husband that she had taken up with, referred to him as a fly on the wall? And didn't Denzal Whiteman, with whom he shared his money, referred to him as a "ghetto boy." Denzal, whose sister would have her young daughter's dirty knickers on the living room table when he had visited with him that weekend in Acton, in the West.

But this was hardly the beginning of his fall from academic grace, or ultimate salvation. He had likened himself to Lucifer for daring to challenge the power of the status quo, because the status quo always protects itself against people like him - people with great promise and who had missed their unused opportunities – who dared to dream to change the world. Ultimately, their down fall was by the hands of comrades in arms, the host of fallen angels – like hopelessly equipped soldiers sent into battle whose lives were cut short, untimely struck down, shot by friendly fire. A feeling of nausea gripped his stomach like a pliers around a cable wire. He could feel it now – perhaps too much beer at that party, or the oily fish that he had condescended to eat, or was it Branton's cheap ganja? That same feeling had gripped his stomach that morning of some unremembered month when as an eighth year old, he ran from the sea shore at the beach at his maternal grandmother's house, after discovering a perfectly formed child rolling in the waves of the Caribbean sea, pale as a scrubbed piglet with all its black hair scalded off – then twirling in shore, resting between the rocks, and, like a white doll, its eyes stared at him, accusingly. The sea was rough; the waves rolling in and rolling back out to sea again. The horizon beyond the water mark – out to sea, the sky reeling. And he had frozen; thought it was Judgment Day, when the sea would give up its dead and that it was the end of the world. He ran in shock, up to his grandmother's house, pulling at her sleeves to see the dead coming in from the sea; and she had come down to the shore as if she believed the end of the world had indeed come, and shouted at his uncle to fish the child out of the water where it had lodged between the rocks, and everything else from that day became a blur, as if unconsciously, he had refused to admit that it had ever happened.

But the police had come and taken the mother of the child, raped by the Portuguese shopkeeper who travelled from Trinidad to live among the villagers, and not wanting to bear his child, as she was already in love with one of her cousins, she was abhorred and had decided to abort the child. Soon after she had to leave, and then everyone was leaving. Things had changed. England was the promise land and the sea wall at the end of the village was the Wall of Jericho.

Yes, he had been harmed as if in seeing the unsightly image he had imbued the sinful act committed by the mother of the dead child, and that in finding the dead child rolling in the waves and told on her that he was responsible for her sudden and shameful departure from her home and all the people she loved. But she had also harmed him; caused him to see death at so early an age, and in such circumstances. He knew now that he had been harmed: hoodooed.

The lump in his throat became larger; from the bottom of his stomach he could feel the froth forcing its way up towards his chest; his nose began to itch, the wind in his stomach pushed its way downwards. The train came to a halt at London Fields. He pulled himself up out of the seat and pushed the exit button. The fresh gust of wind slammed him like a clenched fist in the face. The belch exploded in his throat, and he reeled forward, stepping out of the carriage onto the platform. The remains of half digested food spurted out. He found the wall and leant forward resting his head against the brick work and vomited profusely until tears came to his eyes.

After a few minutes he wiped his mouth with the second handkerchief he carried: the large pretty one that he liked and carried only for style, and walked towards the exit, making his way to the park. Skipping down the steps he turned right into Martello Street, walked under the bridge and entered the park.

As he walked towards Gayhurst Road, his feet began to ache; his chest felt sore so he sat down on a bench at the side path to take a rest. He had hardly noticed the moon, until he saw a shooting star shoot across the sky. The firmament seemed alive with light; the night seemed cool now and despite the slight feeling of nausea, his stomach bad begun to resettle. The moon was not full, but there was enough light from the street lamps at the side roads to light the shadowy parts of the park. He got up and walked to the exit, turned right into Greenwood Road and into Falcon Terrace. He was glad that he was home.

Chapter Twenty Seven

Three days later, it was Saturday. He up early as usual and not had to collect the children that weekend he had monopoly of his music system and record collection. He was building a marijuana cigarette when the telephone rang. Putting down the paper with the drug on the table he raced to the phone.

"Hello!" He said.

"It's me Ralphie," the voice at the other end replied.

"Hey, Barclay," he replied.

"You should see your other part of the world." Barclay shouted...

"It's nice down there, man. Cause you should. I know you is a big man, and I can't tell a big man what to do, but you should see St Kitts, Trinidad, nice man – but for the violence. They should bring back hanging down there; then those bad johns will behave themselves. Chicken they arse – talking 'bout them bad and killing people for nothing – behaving like frigging Yankees. What you doin' next week? Come for dinner man. Abba is here; he sends his hello. Hope you are not a queen. Keep the faith, man."

"What time?"

"Come about four o'clock on Monday."

"Fine!"

"See you then."

Ralph put down the phone and walked back to the table, took up the papers, found the gluey side, licked them and stuck them together. He rushed into the bedroom as the record was scratched and kept repeating the same part of the song; he then turned the record over. He preferred the old LPs to the new CDs, and he had always hated tapes. He was glad that he was in the process of adapting all his old tapes to CDs. He walked back into the living room, sat down and lit the cigarette, inhaling and exhaling; he blew the dark smoke out into a puff and watched as it moved like a cloud of pollution across the room, circled like a miniature tornado and lodged itself in the curtains. He knew that one day he would have to give it up.

Barclay and Abba had already warned him about smoking. And he had cut down on the ganja, for he never smoked cigarettes, apart from with ganja; but never alone. He had already begun to wean himself off it by deliberately holding to his nose the remains of butt ends which he kept in an astray at his flat in Hackney, hidden under the sink cupboard. Its foul smelling stench would make him wretch and he hated the sickening stench of his habit. They would remind him that he had to break the habit from time to time as he was allowing stimulants to cloud his mind, destroy his discipline and influence his talent, whatever that might be. They were given to making jokes like that. They said to him that he was enjoying his slavery by giving the British government taxes to kill him. It was his way of maintaining his slavery they said, because he liked being a victim, and the sooner he realised who was making money out of the sickening habit called smoking that he would stop. He was still waiting for that day of absolute resolve. Ralph could recall the conversations that he'd had with them three years ago before they left for the Caribbean. He had gone to visit them at Adelaide Gardens in Leytonstone and Abba had read his palm for him. Since then he had had recurring dreams about that palm reading session. But he admired them because they were extremely mentally equipped; displaying their backgrounds and pride of place in West Indian standards; even a little old fashioned – just a little.

He liked their quiet and unassuming ways; they made everyone around them feel comfortable and regarded those brought up in England as suffering years of mental stress, having been uprooted at such an early age from the Caribbean. Sadly however, they couldn't fully engage with the majority of adults whom they referred to as "born ya," although they loved the younger children; in fact, they had met his own children and found them the epitome of Caribbean manners – but then they were his children and bound to be influenced by him, by background as well as by nature he was, after all, one of them, a federalist.

They were born in the late forties and early fifties, during the short lived federation, which lasted until Eric Williams, had imprisoned his lecturer and propounded the only mathematical theorem that anyone in the islands have since advanced or equalled: one from fourteen leaves nothing and they all fell down, the federation disbanded because of the conflict of size and which should be the capital site, Jamaica and Trinidad neck and neck, while the others spurned them on; it was the era of the "bad man" that all were conditioned to admire; had singled out this rebellious individual for particular adoration. So much so that when the United States told them that Fidel Castro was a bad man, there sprang up a thousand nicknames in the islands in his namesake, and parents began to name their sons Fidel, even Ralph himself had a god son by the name of Castro, named for Fidel and they both loved Fidel; they had imbued a federal and religious zeal that was at times, more potent than the Zionism of the Rastafarians. Now the name dropping of the capitals of each island, which they were drilled to memorise at school, were like litanies on their tongues. They could still remember the tiny little flags of the West Indian Federation, when a black man couldn't even play for the cricket team, and that also meant Indians.

The generation before were hardy men and women; immediately after emancipation when the stealers of people had been compensated for losing their live stock, the slaves, they fought for a decent wage and the right to walk the streets of their islands and without the food being married: sweet and Irish potatoes with salt fish; rice with peas and with pig's snout; flour with salt beef or salt pork; banana with salt mackerel, and trotters, and salt and sugar going together and, sex from the young girls, the most natural of human acts twined as a commodity, with the right to work, and the famous dictum that filled the Anglican Church pews to overflowing every Sunday morning and afternoons: the word of God is under your head - the son of man is upon you - the holy ghost is in your hole - so wind your arse and save your soul. This was said to the young girls called for confirmation by the white priests of the church, obsessed with siring black descendants. And, they had fought against ten shilling for every ton of sugar cane they cut in the hot blazing sun; they fought against a hard week's labour for payment in a butter pan of sweet potatoes; and no one had applauded their readiness to forgive so readily or so easily, and no one had compensated them, for they were the real victims, not the descendants of the stealers and sellers of people, who had lost their human properties, the slaves. But that was another war, and no doubt there'll be more. For their blood had been poisoned with too much salt and too much initial inbreeding, and too much unconscious incest taking place for a people who have no idea where the bloodlines began or ended.

So Ralph could forgive them their indulgencies, the way the staccato speech of the Caribbean rolled off their tongues: the familiarity, the naturalness of simply being alive and breathing. They took none of these for granted, but were grateful for every minute of the day they lived. It was only a matter of time before that infectious passion for living would affect and transform his own view of the world and of England. Innocence can be shattered with the dawn of new knowledge and knowledge like language is never static. It goes on forever from one plateau to another, even unto the very minute whenever time as we know it shall end. He knew they were positive influencers for neither smoked, were too easily provoked, or used angry and obscene language. They were a race apart from the people with whom he had been interacting with over the past years. So he looked forward to seeing them on Monday. Before that though, he had chores to do.

Chapter Twenty Eight

On Sunday afternoon he found himself near Homerton Fields, where there was always a game of football on a Sunday as far back as when he had first lived in Hackney. Years ago when he was still a stranger, he had made his way there to look at the fair and had enjoyed the trip to what seemed to him then, an entirely new area. He remembered the local people staring at him and how he felt slightly lost, for he didn't know Hackney then, only Islington.

He marvelled at the familiarity of the place and how it seemed now, in comparison to the way he saw it all those years ago, when he was still a stranger. In the past he thought he had fitted in very well, but he wasn't so sure now. While the landscape had become positively familiar, the familiarity of his personal relationships had for the most part, resulted in despair.

He could hear the noise as he approached and before long he saw the spires of the tents that rose not as high as the trees, but high enough to be seen. He approached three large tents on the grass, near the tennis court, and he could hear the jangle of tambourines, the bass guitar talking to the drums, the organ and the guitar and the vocalist calling and answering one another. He stopped at the first tent which was the largest, a marquee; it was crowded with people and the pastor, a man of about six feet four inches tall, was rocking on the rostrum as the singing stopped.

"Amen!" he said and opened his large bible on the lectern. "We thank the Lord for another Sabbath. Good morning Sabbath school."

"Good morning pastor," the congregation chorused.

Jeremy McLaughlin touched the wings of his bible which was spread like a giant, black and white crow, and stared into the congregation.

"This morning our text is from the Psalms."

"Amen," said a voice in the congregation; "Amen to the Psalms of David."

Ralph looked across the pews from where the voice came and recognised a short dark man with a cane. He remembered the face, the high cheekbones and the mole on his left cheek. That was the man from the shop in Kingsland Road, he thought.

The pastor fixed his eyes on the congregation, as if holding the different faces at once in a single stare. "This is the twenty third Psalm of David of the House of Judah, of Ethiopia, as Taharqa would have it." And he raised his hands in the air and shouted:

"Praise the Lord." He lifted up his voice and willed himself into a frenzy. "Praise the Lord! Praise the Lord! Praise ye the Lord!"

"Amen! Amen! Amen!" the congregation responded.

"Amen to the Lord!" the pastor exhorted.

The congregation took up the call, spurred on by a tall, lean woman of fair complexion in the back row, followed by a woman of dark complexion sitting beside her. "Amen to the Lord! Amen to the Lord! Amen to the Lord!"

The pastor stared into the congregation as if he had spotted an unfamiliar face; he looked straight at Ralph, and recited:

"The Lord is my shepherd, said David." "And it is here; here within these pages for all to see. The Lord is my shepherd: our shepherd, and we are, and we are... "

"His sheeps!" shouted the man with the cane.

This pronouncement gave cause to several whispers in the congregation; some querying the grammar in the use of the word "sheeps."

The light skinned woman with the lean face and even leaner body supported him. "Yes, we is his sheeps, yes!"

"Yes! Yes! Yes!" said her friend, beside her.

"Amen!" said the pastor.

"Amen," said another voice in the back row, with a clearing of the throat.

"He is our shepherd, so we shall not want, want, want?" Pastor continued and paused, and taking a deep breath, he shouted at the top of his voice:

"Want to do anything else than to praise him and keep his commandments," and he accentuated this with a movement of his body by raising his hands in the air, and shuffling slightly.

"Amen!" The congregation chorused.

"Amen to the twenty third Psalm of David."

The man with the cane encouraged by the support that he had received earlier becoming more emboldened repeated: "And we is his sheeps."

There were again the hushed whispers: his grammar of course being queried by the more concerned members of the congregation. The pastor raised his arms in the air; this time showing off the brocaded wide sleeves of his preaching gown. "Amen my brother; Amen to the Lord God of Host." And he stood for a few minutes in the same position; his head bent back, looking up as if he was ascending into heaven.

"Praise the Lord!" the congregation chorused. "Praise the Lord!"

The pastor walked to the edge of the rostrum, holding out his arms: "Yeah, I lay down in green pastures because of my Lord, and I am beside the still waters because of my Lord. And when my soul could not be found I did not look into a packet of cigarettes to find my Lord. Yeah, I did not look into the pub to find my Lord; I did not look for my spliff to find my Lord; not into the houses of profanity," and he repeated the last word for he liked the sound of it: "I said profanity, to find my Lord," and then he paused, wiping his face with his silver handkerchief. "But he led me here to the paths of righteousness... that is how my soul was restored."

"Amen, Amen, Amen," shouted a large woman in the front row, clapping her hands.

The pastor looked at her concernedly, and paused; but the other members of the congregation took this as a sign of his approval and all chorused:

"Praise to the Lord."

"We is his sheeps," enjoined the man with the cane. The pastor lifted his arms in the air; then spread them out either side of his body, so that his body looked like a cross. "Brothers and sisters, are you hearing me?" He asked.

"Yes pastor," they chorused.

"Brothers and sisters are you hearing me?" He shouted.

"Yes, the lamb," they chorused.

The organist, who had been quiet, broke his silence and began to play a hymn softly. The pastor moved towards the edge of the rostrum.

"Brothers and sisters," he said hoarsely and paused. "Brothers and sisters, please turn to the psalm twenty three." There was the shuffling of pages as the congregation searched their bibles for the psalm. Then when he was certain that they had found it he read:

"Yea, though I walk through the valley of the shadow of death, I shall fear no evil."

"Now read with me church" he exclaimed, "read with me now." Together they read the rest of the psalm. And after they had finished, the organist began an up tempo version of "Steal Away;" the bass joined in; the choir took to the stage and a tumultuous sound erupted from the make shift church. The sound carried out into the streets; drifted north to Homerton High Street; east to the wet lands of Hackney Marshes; it reverberated south towards the Wick, and west to Clapton Park. The tambourine players took up the beat and dispersed it to the four corners of the earth, so that all who heard would, in their eyes praise the lord.

After twenty minutes pastor held up his right hand with the palm facing the congregation, then slowly brought his palm down facing the floor. The congregation and the music stopped.

He began to read the bible slowly:

"And when he heard say of Taharqa king of Ethiopia, Behold he is come out to fight, he sent messengers unto Hezekiah king of Judah; for the Lord is with us. Lift up your hearts and rejoice. Here ended the first lesson of the scriptures of the Lord."

"Amen," chorused the congregation.

"Now, let us pray," said the pastor.

Ralph waited for them to begin to pray. And while some of the congregation stood and closed their eyes, others knelt to pray; and as they began to pray, he wandered off.

"Hear our prayer Oh Lord God of Ethiopia, God of Egypt, and God of Israel. Let our three nations live in peace." The pastor's voice carried on the microphone followed him across the park as he walked to the edge of the road, turned right, crossed the road at the edge of the wet lands and made his way towards the canal. As he strode away, he still could hear the pastor's voice as it filled the air above the rustle of the wheels of the cars and the rest of the traffic, and the chatter and laughter of the bargain hunters on their way to Sunday Market on the marshes.

It was then that he spotted her, a tall dark woman about twenty five years old, as she walked along the perimeter of the wet lands; her midriff was exposed, flashes of her waist line peeked out intermittently just above the dark jeans, topped by matching denim jacket above a light blue tee shirt.

Her legs were long: they tapered down and fell over her hips; she was tall and medially rounded; her hair was braded, and her face was slightly chubby, but he liked what he saw. What to do, he thought, and swallowed sharply, clearing his throat. He could feel a bulge in his trousers; it was instinctive; he wanted to drag her into the bushes and copulate with her there, right there; tie her to a tree and have his way with her; to hear her moan and groan and scream with pleasure and sensuality as if they were lion and lioness breeding a new pride. Her blue - blackness excited him; he wanted to find a way to tell her what he could see in her, what had made her appear so beautiful to him, but more importantly, what had made her so attractive to him?

"Hello, purple girl," he said. "Can I have you?"

She smiled, her straight row of white teeth showing above and under her dark lips, and her eyes wide and enticing. "When?" It was obvious that she was amusing him.

"Now," he said.

"You can't," she said.

"But I want to!"

"Well, my husband wouldn't like it; he's very jealous," she said, and laughed.

"Not as jealous as I am," Ralph retorted, and smiled. "I'm sure he's got you to himself all this time and not letting you go. Think of it, we are new to this type of jealousy; don't you find it exciting?"

She laughed. "Where are you from?" she asked.

"You will never guess," he said.

"Tell me," she insisted.

"Have you got a mobile?"

"Yes."

"Well then, I will text you," he said, winking at her.

She laughed again and her breasts heaved as she did; the cups rounded and full excited him and he stared at the deep valley between them. He was honest.

"I don't mean any disrespect, but I find you extremely tantalising," he breathed the words out rather than spoke them. "You look good and fit, healthy!"

"Thank you," she said, politely.

"My name is Ralph, what's yours?"

"I'm Belinda."

"Nice!"

"Nice what?"

"You have a strong magnetism; you must be enjoyed all the time, Belinda; you've got everything to do a good time on when did you last come?"

"That's personal," she said, feeling a little uncomfortable.

"Yes, it's very personal; but you see I want to be personal with you, very personal, because I like what I see, and a lot more that I can't see. I would like to have you, at least once, so that I can enjoy you as a woman. That's it; I would like to enjoy your femininity, I would like to screw you!"

Belinda laughed nervously, more in shock than in humour. "You are very bold; do you always say what you mean?"

"Not always; no. But you hit me like a thunderbolt and all I can think of right now is to beg you for some love. Come Salsa with me next Friday!"

"No."

He looked her over. "Chances are I can give you exactly what you need; give it to you good; do the things you fantasise about, but can't get done, but what you really would like. Tell me what's your most secret desire? You can whisper it," he coaxed, putting his face to her cheeks, "and I'll whisper mine in your ear as well. Tell me what would you like done that you've never had done before? I want to drive you perversely crazy. I would like… I would like to experience your lovely body and your sweet little arse."

Belinda laughed; she felt him funny, but in a curiously funny way, because he was making her feel excited. He was certainly not beating around the bush and it was obvious that he knew what he wanted. So she laughed again and smiled at him in a girlish sort of way; she found herself flirting with him. "But you can see me at the market."

"I want to get to know you; meet you somewhere, so we could talk: get to know each other."

"You can always see me at the market."

"How about you invite me to your church week after next Sunday? We could meet on Tuesday and plan to go to church later. You are going to invite me to your church aren't you?"

"Yes, you can come any time; it's in the morning from eleven on a Sunday."

"Good then, so we can meet in the park on Tuesday and then plan a visit to church week after next, then."

"Yes." Belinda said and smiled.

"Here is my mobile number," he said.

They exchanged mobile numbers. Ralph held her around the waist. Her body was lithe and full, though not fat, but with curves in the right places. He knew he was right from the first moment that he saw her that she came from Africa. There is that subtlety of build that distinguishes the women of the continent from those of the Diaspora, he thought. It was a genetic code. After all, as Pervase had often commented they were born and nurtured, not for the masters' table, but like Asian women, for their men.

Ralph walked with her passed the marshes and, when she turned right heading in the direction of the market, he said goodbye, turned back the way they had come and went along the canal. He felt good, for she excited him and he realised that he had not felt like that for years. Although he reasoned that she might change her mind, at least, it had been a pleasant encounter and he felt good. Life was short and neither of them could be certain that they would ever see each other again. Ralph thought about this as he walked along the canal. He always felt refreshed beside water; his thoughts took on a renewed sense of freedom whenever he walked beside the sea, a river, or a canal, even in the rain. The fresh air filled his lungs and he inhaled deeply; held his breath while he counted to twenty, and exhaled though his mouth, took a deep breath again, counted to thirty and exhaled. He continued four times more and then began alternate breathing. Then he stopped, walked to the edge of the canal bank and peered into the water. It was a good feeling.

Suddenly his mobile rang. He rummaged through his pockets, and found it.

"Hello," he said.

"It's me Pervase," the voice said, adding, "What are you doing?"

"Out for a walk along the canal, what's up?"

"What are you doing on Monday?"

"Busy."

"What about Tuesday?"

"Why?"

"These two young things, sweet as hell, want us to funk them."

"You make them sound like mangoes." Ralph could recall from all those years ago, back home when their grandmother would pick her favourite mangoes from the tree, place them in a box with dry banana leaves and hide them in the kitchen to ripen, and how they would hunt for them by smell, and once found and still slightly hard, they would squeeze them to soften them up so that they would seem as if that they were now ripe enough to eat: funk them.

"They are of legal age, so don't worry. You know the one called Nicole; the same one that I've been telling that at seventeen she is too young. She said to me the other day that I was ageist and that I was in serious breach of making myself look a fool."

"That's what she said?"

"Yes!" And they both laughed.

"Her friend wants us to show them a good time as they are leaving for the United States Sunday next. So what are you doing during the day, next Sunday?"

"I'm at work during the day, but will be home about eight o'clock."

"Right; see you at about eight then."

"Yeah!"

"Good!"

"By the way, we'll discuss that other matter when you come."

"Yeah."

They both signed off. Ralph liked that; a nice clear arrangement of words; a transaction done without argument. He had begun to realise what Frank was telling him all those years ago, who, despite the fact that they no longer spoke, despite his arrogance he finally felt that he had a point after he had taken his ganja seller to his god daughter's christening and Frank had objected.

"One day, you'll find out who you are," he had told him, and Ralph had gone quiet. He came from a very quiet family; he could see this in his own children now, when they visited him. There were often long silences between them and an overwhelming comfort and peace would come over him in their presence. At times when he asked too many questions he could see them becoming agitated, as he often would, when after giving account some people would go on and on; and he would end up criticising his children for the very trait that they had inherited from him; with his family, probing was meaningless. They told you what was what and then gave you freedom to think. He longed for that now. That matter of fact way of putting things, of coming across clear, with confidence and with purpose.

Chapter Twenty Nine

Monday came. It was a very British day: the weather was ambiguous. The morning began sunny; but at about twelve o'clock it began to rain. Ralph looked out the window after hearing what sounded like a shower, but it was a slight downpour. Then it stopped abruptly, but continued dripping. A few minutes passed and it started up again. It began with a weeping; then it started spitting; then it steamed for about twenty minutes; stopped; then another down pour, followed by a miniature storm which saw the wind meandering through the trees across the road. The crowns of the trees were dancing as if they were happy because of the rain. Ralph smiled. Then the rain stopped for about ten minutes; only to start up again this time a heavy shower came crackling over the roofs of the houses, the sound of water gushing everywhere; in the streets there was a miniature flood as water gathered in the gutters.

He looked out onto the street again. People were rushing to their destinations, and he wondered if the rain would ever stop. Barclay and Abba were expecting him. As he moved away from the window, the mobile rang. It was on the table beside a pile of books; he picked it up.

"Hello."

"It's me, the girls want the date brought forward for the coming Sunday." It was Pervase.

"Can't make it" Ralph said. "See if they can make it Saturday."

"OK," said Pervase. "I'll see what they say and call you back."

The rain stopped suddenly; the sun came out and Ralph imagined that it was warm outside. The wind had died down now and, whereas once the crowns of the trees shook wildly, they just swayed gently in the almost still breeze. He put on his socks, found his shoes and decided to go out.

Stepping out he felt chilly; the sun was lukewarm and the air was cold. Luckily he had put on a tee shirt under his jacket, so it was chilly but bearable. He did not figure on staying out too late so he began to make his way to Leytonstone. He would take the bus at Mare Street, and so he made his way to London Fields. It was a familiar walk; he had met Ashton at the gate a couple of days before, but did not expect to meet him there. At least, not at lunch time

Ashton's car was parked in the make shift car park near Gayhurst Road. As Ralph approached he turned and blew his horn, winding down his window. Ralph walked over to the car; he opened the door and Ralph got in.

"Caught you loitering again," Ralph joked.

Ashton laughed. "Guilty." They both shared the joke.

"What's up, where you going?" Ashton inquired in a matter of fact way.

"Leytontonstone," Ralph replied.

"Want a drop?"

"No, it's all right," Ralph muttered.

Ashton looked at him, shrugging his shoulders.

"Su huw come nobody seeing yu any mure?"

"I tired a peple man," Ralph lapsed into patois. It was expected; everybody did this when they wanted each other to know that they were very serious about anything; it was the language of the emotions, and everybody knew the significance once the English had become broken.

"So whappen, yu turn anti-social now?"

"Yeah man!" He answered affirmatively. "I tired a people dese days man. I wanto get outa England!"

"Yu is nat de ongly one," Ashton said, winding down the window on his side. "Dem downt luve wi. Dem gotsomeem gainst West Indians."

Ralph smirked. "Dem got someem gainst everybody. Every dark skinne betta gitwise. Dem garne weird, ehem, ehem."

"But why dem turn weird so?"

Ralph looked at him incredulously. "Su whey yu dey dese laast dayes, man? Yu downt see sence the bombing an tings, Babylon garne mure rasist den before. You no see dem dawnt warnt gi we work any mure?"

"Yu really tink so?" Ashton asked inquiringly.

"Dats because yu downt warnt to bring hume de bacon." Ralph said accusingly. And they both laughed, because they knew what was being implied. Ralph nurtured the moment and continued thickening his accent.

"Yu see hif yu di bringe hume de bacon; git yuself a nice lily white gal an hact mure lek you ave blueyeyes, yu wi be cuul, cuul, cuul, lika h'ice."

And they both laughed out loud, slapping each other on the back.

In the middle of the laughter, Ashton suddenly became playful. "Tel mi, yu think Treva bring home de bacon?"

"Yes man!" Ralph replied quickly; making it sound more comical.

"Yu tink Wrighty bring hume de bacon?"

"Yeah man!"

"And whatabout Hernan?"

"Cho!" said Ralph kissing his teeth. "All dem bwoy dey bring hume de bacon lang, lang time; somme a dem heven bring hume de bacon wid de hag 'ead."

"Cha!" said Ashton. "We is in serias truble, yu knuw, serias truble, bad, bad, bad truble, wi West Indians." They both nodded agreement and fell silent.

After a couple minutes Ashton cleared his throat.

"Yu hearbout dis sista dat use to 'ave lacks take up wid de bese man, and set table wid de Rastaman pickny dem wid pork and tell dem say dem ave fe ete dis fram nuw arne?"

"No," Ralph said. "Mi neva 'ear bout h'it."

Ashton began to chuckle, which then ended in riotous laughter. Ralph joined in and they continued laughing and then stopped.

"Bwoy, we situatian bad yu knuw."

"Yeah man," Ralph said. "But dornt worrie habout hit, Rastafari cuming soone." And they both laughed satirically. "See neva minde," Ralph continued, "Jest teka likkle a de ealing erb and Jah Jah wi put tings right."

"Rastafari," Ashton blurted flippantly. And they continued chucking; after pausing, Ralph wiped his eyes and cleared his throat.

"Di yu ear bout dis Rastaman in de early yeares wen tings was almost right?"

"Which Rastaman dat?"

"De wan dat tek dis yung ting a yard fe shuw er Rastafari, an dem say im pull hout im business fram und im and say, see im ya, see Rastafari ya."

This time they didn't laugh as much. "See huw stupid we kan be; every progress we mek, we slide two stepe back. We tuu damn fuul," said Ashton.

"And we live in a countrye dat doant luve wi."

"Tuu right," replied Ralph.

Suddenly Ashton started the car engine and put it into gear. "You might as well let me drop you to Leytonstone," he insisted.

"Cuul," Ralph replied.

Ashton turned right into Richmond Road and left into Mare Street, making his way towards Morning Lane and followed the W15 bus along Homerton High Street, passed the Marshes. It wasn't long before he pulled up outside Adelaide Gardens. "There ya are brov," he said. "Now get lost!"

"Listen, phone me," Ralph said. "Let's meete; wi can talk."

"Cuul stay cuul." He said and drove off.

As Ralph walked away and waved goodbye to Ashton, promising to keep in touch, he weren't to know that he would never see Ashton again, that within forty eight hours Ashton would be dead, his body found dangling at the end of a rope lassoed around his neck and tied to the branches of an elm tree, with his hands tied to the outlying branches and his feet crossed, bound together like a crucifixion. And no fellow motorists, passing the A45 - an off road of the M1 Motorway, would be available to give witness or assist the police with their inquiries. Neither had he any idea that as he prepared to leave England for the Caribbean, the Coroner's Office would recommend that Ashton's body be kept for six months, giving the medical hyenas ample time to scavenge for body parts, so that his remains would dangle from one laboratory to the next. As if to demonstrate that throughout his life he had been dangling. The cadaver had a tea towel covering its loins and a crown of ivy bush around its head, and beneath its feet was a caption that either he or his crucifiers had written: Behold the saviour of the Blackman! Behold the Lamb of God that taketh away the sins of the world.

Chapter Thirty

The front door opened as Ralph walked up to it and was about to ring the bell. It was Barclay. "Come on in Ralphie," he said. Ralph stepped in the door. "Good afternoon," he said. "Thank you." Barclay walked back into the kitchen, calling out to Abba. "Abba, Ralphie is here!"

Ralph joined Barclay in the kitchen as he began to stir the pot on the cooker. "It's all sea food, apart from the vegetables - no mammals in this pot my man."

A conch shell was being blown upstairs. Ralph looked at Barclay a little surprised. Barclay looked at him as if nothing out of the ordinary was happening. When Ralph stared back at him for confirmation as to what he was hearing, Barclay just shrugged his shoulders and carried on preparing the food. The conch shell began to blow again. The sound became nearer until Abba appeared at the bottom of the stairs.

"Ah! I saw you coming," he said.

Ralph smiled. He could not help but like Abba Mohammed - of East Indian descent, that is most part of him appeared to be from there, he was darker than Barclay, whose mixed descent was obvious. The two were well contrasted. Barclay had glowing silvery curly hair and Abba with jet black, wavy hair. Ralph looked at them both and wondered if they weren't related; Abba was slightly taller than Barclay, yet to Ralph they seemed more like relatives than friends, although Abba came from Trinidad and Barclay from St Kitts.

"Ehem," Abba cleared his throat, "I saw you coming."

Ralph looked at him; it was like the dream.

"I saw you coming," Ralph recalled as the words echoed in his head.

"I saw you coming along the road; I was asleep, then I woke up trying to play my conch and I saw you coming with a friend. Where is your friend?"

"He only dropped me," said Ralph.

Abba looked him over. "You should have brought him in and introduced us."

"Sorry," said Ralph, "Next time."

"Somebody harmed you; you need healing. You could have been a rich man. But they robbed you."

"Read his palm," Barclay said. "Give him a reading."

"Oh yes," Abba said. "He's been tampered with." And he started playing his conch.

"Give the man a reading," insisted Barclay. "He thinks we are queens." Then turning to Ralph, "Are you sure Mas Luke never got you? Don't think we don't know what used to go on in that class in that school, you know. For someone brought up from your background to have escaped Mas Luke, you must have been lucky. Are you sure he didn't get you? "My little cousin was in that class and he has four children and a wife and he is OK."

Ralph felt uneasy; he remembered Adrian whose grandparents lived in the beautiful house next to the school. And Adrian was always invited him over for lunch. Did he ever go? He couldn't remember. He knew that Mas Luke usually took lunch there, but could never remember going over. His cousin Raul would never have allowed him to any way. He was grateful; even though as the youngest he would have to go to the shop at the end of the valley to buy the lunch and they could get anything they wanted. And Raul had let him know from the start that as the youngest he would have to get the lunch. Uncle Alfred would pay the shopkeeper at the end of the day. Did he ever go to that house? Was there ever a day that his cousin didn't attend school? No, and even so, he would have had to go to his uncle's house to listen to the calypsos or the classical records on the radiogram, or the BBC World Service on the radio. And then there were the big cousins who had left school and were waiting either to start work in Basseterre or to go abroad to the United States, or England, or to join the police force and go up the islands to work and have children so that the blood lines didn't just stay in St Kitts; they felt they had a mission to spread the seed of the McFarlane's everywhere.

Ralph sifted his mind for a memory. No, he never went to lunch in that house where Mas Luke took lunch. May be he got Adrian, but not him.

He was taken home another time by those part Portuguese boys, but nothing ever really happened. There was no penetration and when they discovered that he was related they let him go; they had kidnapped him in the old infant school and taken him to their house in Old Road , but were in mortal fear when the neighbours had called them and told them who his father was. The man who owned the biggest shop in the town was his father's cousin; the old lady was related to his father's mother; so they had come back into the house and told him to go home or go to school; so he had never been molested in that way. It was something else.

Somehow Ralph felt that he had to say something and was surprised when he caught himself almost defending Mas Luke. "He was an excellent pianist," did he really say that? He checked himself. He may not have been molested physically, but psychologically, he had been. Somewhere on the inside something had snapped as a child in that school and Barclay knew it; there had been some tampering, so that every time a woman turned her back to him he had found it indecent. And hadn't he taken Sandilina young girl years before, unknown to himself? And didn't he find her attractive then? But had abandoned her because he felt guilty about the relationship? There were so many questions to his life; so many contradictions that he had to face up to and no longer be in denial about his disparate situation. And he was scared, petrified of the future and completely puzzled by the past. Every time he tried to make sense of his life in that school, he felt as though he was dangling.

"We all knew that he was a good pianist; he used to play the organ in church every Sunday, that was good practice," Barclay's voice boomed. He smiled. "But it's the other matter that we were concerned about; all of us with little cousins and brothers and sisters in that class."

He was right Ralph thought. Didn't Mas Luke tell him the night that he introduced his admirer to him and had him take him into the bedroom and do him, didn't he boast about his daughter back home and his woman in Handsworth. And wasn't his woman beautiful, and didn't he say she understood that he liked men as well? Ralph felt agitated. If only he could undo that night, erase it from time; it was still very faint in his memory, but it hurt to see that Mas Luke had won the other way. Since he couldn't get him the way he wanted, he would spoil him, anyway.

And Barclay knew; just as he must have known with his cousin Danny. The intake of nineteen sixty one for the grammar school entrance had been spoiled. Never mind the Shakespeare and the Milton and the Keats; never mind the Mozart, the Tchaikovsky; they had been under the spell of a libertine Svengali. And he wondered how the girls fared. How did Claudette, Cynthy, Pauline and the rest of the girls turn out? Were they like him, dangling? And were Ira and Hilary, boys with unisex names, were they too dangling?

"Well, how's it been, since we left town," Barclay inquired.

"Not much," Ralph said. "As you can see things are still very much the same. More awkwardness, I guess; more racist; we still can't get work, but we are here. We don't even have a nationality – if you can recall that our passport is arbitrary and can be taken away from us at any time."

"Yes, it's an insult when you can spend forty years of your life in any country and people still refer to you as an immigrant."

"Yes, this is probably the only country in the world where nationality is seen as a colour."

"You cume ya yung and born ya betta cume outa de peple dem countrye and lef dem to giton widit," Barclay extolled.

Abba who had not said a word after his initial greeting, never said a word, but just smiled. Ralph was shocked by the change in Barclay's accent. He had never heard him speak in anything but Standard English before, so he looked at him and then at Abba. Abba once again smiled, but never uttered a word. Ralph felt embarrassed by his own reaction and also smiled.

"You see," Barclay continued, addressing Abba, "they have a similar attitude to the natives; they are as English as they are. They always think they know people – always know what's going on, but they are wrapped up like toffee in pretty little packets, their world is so secure that they feel they have it all figured out."

"Life is unpredictable," said Abba. He cleared his throat. "And we are like the ocean; like the sea. Unpredictable and life is not always what the surface of things tells you. Like if you listen to them; it's not what they say, it's how they say it. And sometimes, it's even who they say it to."

Barclay smiled, and stirred some more herbs into the food on the cooker. "And sometimes it's even where they say it. Don't you understand the many things they say to themselves, that's if when you hear what they say; you know it's not directed at you, if you're wise? It has its own audience." He paused, looking over Ralph. "Hello sunshine!"

Both Barclay and Abba laughed, and Ralph joined in. Barclay continued. "See, you take things too seriously you and your lot; the Asians and Africans don't. You lot don't want to come home; and we've been warning you all these years to plant your feet on firm ground, instead of sinking sand, but no, you all want to be English, as if you can fight a people for what's theirs. Come home and enjoy life; it is time to come home. Call it a day; let it go; you have so many beautiful islands to choose from and you're here fighting them for their little England. Give it up, man!"

"It's true," said Ralph, "I don't think they need us."

"They need us," Barclay replied. "They need us here to clap them when they do some great feat, like Simon Smith and his Amazing Dancing Bear. Don't you know the record?" "We are their captured audience; we make them feel good; it feeds their sense of inherent superiority. We are here to make them feel that they are superior, and to show the rest of the darkies that what we can't achieve, they can, until they are ready for them, and we are here as a buffer between them and the Jews."

"Let me see your hand," said Abba.

Ralph laughed and gave him his hand.

Abba took it and made a ululating sound. "They've been after you for a long time," he said. "But oh, look what we have here; a rescue, but you must do right. Your grandmothers are all disappointed in you. You used to deny them, but you are alright now. You will have a great big mansion home and your children will call you blest, while the people will call you father of the nation. You will be responsible for the bringing together of the islands and you will be revered as a great religious and political teacher for all times. The expectations of the past will be revived and you will recover what you have lost, you will be great again. That's a good hand."

Then he took the left hand. "This is the hand of the heart; the colon is good; the spleen is good. Good stomach, good liver, pancreas, kidney not too good. Stop smoking!"

Ralph became uncomfortable; he wanted to hear something about the heart. But Abba just stood there, holding his hand, still reading the palm. His lips were moving as if silently reading a book. "Oh, it's a pity," he exclaimed. "Tut! Tut! Tut!

It's such a pity," shakes his head. "Spiritually you are good, but there is a blot in your heart. Its spiritual, it's not physical; you need spiritual protection and, even there, you will still have to be careful. You need to go home and drink sea water."

"My parents are expecting me for Christmas," he said. "But I have to sort out their house first. They want it divided into two flats."

"Oh! look at that," Abba exclaimed.

Ralph became more attentive. He was afraid that Abba would find something wrong. Now he knew. There was a hole in his belly; but it wasn't physical. He had forgotten how to touch things without stifling the feeling; without being too obsessive about it. He felt slightly drained and wanted to sit down. Abba let go of his hand.

"Your mother was a spiritualist."

"Yes!" Ralph said.

"I know that she was, and you're not too far off either. If that thing with those boys didn't happen to you, you would have been a rich man by now. But you still can be; only that you can be a sage as well."

Ralph knew that he was talking about the company that he had formed with Donald Thumb, Denzal Whiteman and Kelville Shorjohns. They had gone along with his every plan until the company had several real estate properties and then had conspired and eased him out of its operations, after he had been the prime force to bring them in and who had developed the company. A sudden sadness came over him.

"Food's up," Barclay said. He turned off the cooker and began taking plates from the cupboard. "Come on children," he joked. "Daddy's serving dinner."

They sat down to the meal and Abba said grace, supported by Barclay. That was another angle to them that intrigued Ralph. He didn't realise that their spirituality, although not religious in the conventional sense of the word, would manifest in these ways and that they did observe grace at the table, and before they began to eat, all three one by one went to wash their hands. Finally, they sat down to decent conversation and their latest collection of soca music.

Barclay poured himself a glass of red wine, which he reckoned was good for the health and offered Ralph a glass, which Ralph poured himself.

Barclay took a sip of his drink and cleared his throat. "Do you know they are costing the development in the Leeward Islands a lot of money for building materials?" Trinidad seems to think they have a monopoly of the market for bricks and concrete, and St Kitts and St Lucia have to pay them an arm and a leg; Dominica as well. Doesn't say much for local trade, does it? CARICOM. Carry go, bring cum!" There was general laughter.

"Seems to me that the governments can't make up their minds about this free trade area thing," said Abba.

"I think it's the way of business to make a profit," remarked Barclay, "But there needs to be some duty to the region by the business sector; if you dry your customer unduly by over charging him, you're only cutting your own throat, and in the end you can't sell because he can't buy any more, and you're bankrupt because he is as well. They need to learn some business sense, but otherwise we getting there. Don't forget we were only slaves and indentured labourers just the other day. We're getting there."

"Don't worry Ralphie! Abba said consolingly, "Come home and you'll be alright," and he added affirmatively, "we're getting there!'

"I tell you what we're going to do; we'll open up another factory in Dominica," said Barclay.

"So what about the job in Tower Hamlets? I thought you had an interview before we left?"

Ralph placed a portion of food onto his fork, put it into his mouth, chewed it slowly, swallowed it and cleared his throat, gently. "That didn't go well; they weren't really looking for anyone, really. They already had somebody in the job. I can't think why they had even bothered to advertise it. But I have an interview at Havering next week."

"You'll get that one," said Abba.

"How was the interview at Barking College?" Barclay inquired, gently.

Abba cleared his throat and coughed gently, and took a sip of water. "I've heard of that place; you got to be really connected to get in there, I hear."

"Yes," said Barclay. "I have a friend from Pakistan who like you is in education. He was telling me the other day that when he answered that he had a few CRB checks, one of the interviewers remarked that she wasn't surprised the amount of jobs that he had had; and even before the interview he had to give account of the dates of his jobs." He stopped and paused for a moment. "I wonder if she had asked anyone else the same questions; somehow I don't think she did. Any way, he knew he wouldn't get the job, and he didn't get it."

"Yes," agreed Abba. He had a similar experience with Peapod Trust; he had three interviews there and didn't get the job. "I advised him that the next time they are advertising a post for the president of the United States that he should first change his religion, and become a born again Christian Jew, that way he'd stand a much better chance of being employed by them or getting work."

They all laughed. Ralph forked the last portion of food off his plate, put it into his mouth and chewed it slowly. Then he sipped the last of his wine from his glass. Barclay promptly topped up his glass. Ralph looked at him concernedly, but grateful.

"You're the guest!" He said.

"Thank you," Ralph said.

"Don't worry about anything Ralphie," said Abba. And he too finished off his food. "I'm looking forward to sweet," he added, and walked to the kitchen returning with a dish of rhubarb pie.

Ralph looked astonished; he did not realise that he would find such a treat at their table. Barclay noticed his astonished look. Got up and went to the kitchen returning with three mangoes. Abba noticed Ralph's face and started to laugh. Soon Barclay joined in.

"Don't worry children," said Abba. "Uncle is sharing the dessert."

They all laughed as they dug into the dessert of mango and rhubarb.

"Don't forget what our motto is down there you know," Abba said, and smiled.

"I think Jamaica get it exactly right," said Barclay. "Out of many one people." And he laughed: "Think how sweet our women are man; think of it like sugar cane."

"Yes," agreed Abba. "But some are sour like limes; sour oranges. You mean the ones who just understand the scientific age."

"Yes again," replied Barclay. And he winked at Ralph. "He's a cub of Marcus Garvey and a nephew of Mahatma Gandhi; am the Nigger of the Narcissus," and he laughed.

Abba smiled, and turned to Ralph. "But Ralphie," he cleared his throat. "You have lived in a racist country for so long that you are clinically traumatised. You can get mango here, but rhubarb at our table comes as a surprise." And he turned to Barclay. "See, he needs to take a trip to the islands; our people from Canada: the Canadians and the United Statesians come down often so they don't lose the ambience of oneness. These English blacks when they come home their women want to run back here because they can't treat their men like they do here. People tell them they can't do that down there. They are not allowed to undermine their men, so they can't stay. It's best that some of them stay here. They might bring discord."

"Ehem," Barclay agreed, and there was finality to the matter. Then the rum punch came out and the volume on the music station went up and they ended up slamming dominoes onto the table and voicing arrogant, threatening and challenging threats to one another, and Abba won the first six games, and Barclay the second. Then they took set on each other and then on Ralph.

"Who have de double six?" insisted Barclay.

"Me have it," responded Ralph.

"Dash whay dat," Barclay teased.

"Dat ded," Abba said quietly. "Game block; count two." The others turned over their dominoes and the game started again. Later as Ralph was leaving, they were all in good spirits.

"Next time bring your friend to get a beating Barclay said." They all laughed.

Volume 3

Chapter Thirty One

They were at salsa; Nicole the seventeen year old wore a cut off jean mini over her leotard; topped by a red blouse, the tails of which were knotted just above her belly button, as she preferred to refer to her navel. "Here's my belly button," she had told Ralph as Pervase drove up to their gate and they got into the car. She preferred to sit with him in the back seat, while Anita, her twenty one year old cousin sat in the front with Pervase, similarly dressed, except for red shoes and Nicole wore black. Nicole had her hair tied in a yellow turban, while Anita's was tied in black. They looked East African, but then one could never be absolutely certain about the true origins of all black people whom they met these days. So this didn't worry them. Besides being Caribbeans they would be up to anything; even if they were Martians as long as they had pussies what did it matter, any way, and girls were girls and the rarer the sweeter.

"Kiss my belly button, coz," she had said to him. Now they were at salsa and she was dancing, swinging her hips from side to side, turning and making those quick steps. She loved swaying and swinging her hips. He would go behind her and keep turning her, then bring her to face him. And when they moved closer together she would make those moaning sounds. Pervase was in the middle of the floor with Anita, doing much the same moves, but her swaying was slower, more accentuated and wilfully designed to set him aflame. Ralph wandered how he had been paired with Nicole, and then remembered that the choice was hers. That is the girls had chosen; and there was a mystery to it. As if it was back in the old centuries in Africa when relatives only married among themselves, and cross cousin marriages were the order of the black world. There was something seminal about the choice, and Nicole was unpredictable as any explosive device.

They faced each other after twirling their hands above their heads and linking; she moved in close and bit him gently on the neck. Ralph felt an upsurge of heat run through his body, and he tickled her; this made her press her body to his closer and she moaned as they broke apart. Then he pulled her back to him and she could feel the friction: long, slow, hard, soft and stroking movements as they ground their bodies together. Her mouth opened intermittently as she took in air, and a glowing feeling ran down the trunk of her body as he pushed her away again, twirled her and brought her in close; her breath was slow and seductive as she breathed into his ear. The song began to end. They pressed their bodies together, without moving away, and Nicole froze as if she had climaxed. She had wet her clothes, and held on to him, refusing to let go, for fear that she might fall over if he moved away, or attempted to twirl her any more. And they both were panting.

"Now change partners," the instructor ordered.

But they were in no state to follow suit, so Nicole stood against the wall. Ralph fixed himself, for he was hard as a rock, and searched out Pervase. As he approached Pervase handed him the car keys and Nicole having recovered some of her composure joined him beside Pervase and Anita. Anita smiled at Ralph as he made for the exit, followed by her cousin.

They raced across the car park together, and as they reached the car, Ralph fidgeted and couldn't get the door open. This took him some seconds and finally they got in and he headed for Marks Warren Quarry; he remembered he had seen it on his way to the Toll Gate Salsa Ponderosa. He put the key in the ignition, started up and drove off; reversed and headed in the opposite direction.

Nicole removed her bra and leotard and pulled her jeans down, and smiled at him as he drove past Marks Kildare, passed the entrance to Marks Gate and into Marks Warren. He passed the barriers and the zinc fence and arrived at an open field, turning the engine off. Nicole sat on his lap facing him; Ralph pushed back the seat. She caressed his head and ran her fingers down the left side of his body, pausing briefly at his heart, then down to the crease in his thigh and held his penis through his clothes; then she took his hand and placed it on her throbbing labia. "This is my Libya," she laughed. Then she held her right breast and put it into Ralph's mouth, and as he licked it she kissed him hard on the lips, forcing her tongue deep into his mouth. She liked the taste of celery that lingered faintly on his breath. It was then that she inserted him into her, and began to rock to and fro.

Ralph suddenly realised that he hadn't time to put on a condom and stopped.

"What's wrong coz; don't you want to?" she said.

"Yes, but...

"Then shut up and do it; do it now." And she began to move again, pushing her breasts into his face. The fruit had been tasted and Ralph reasoned that Nicole must know what she was doing. This was planned, he told himself. The girls had chosen.

"Do you think it's every day that I do this sort of thing?" she asked, panting. "And I suppose you're thinking that I should be a virgin?"

"No," Ralph replied. There was silence as they consumed each other willingly, and stopped, rested for ten minutes and started again in the same position, without any further words being spoken by either of them. After an hour had passed, Nicole got out and stood at the edge of the field with her hands on the bonnet of the car, arched her back, and looked back at him as he had got out of the car to follow. Ralph entered her body from behind and forced himself into her, and after they had become exhausted they both slumped over the bonnet of the car and drifted into a trance like state listening to their breathing like tides of the sea, coming and going; and saw deep within the consciousness of their race, ancient and seminal memories: waves coming in, breaking on the shore, then by the drag of the earth's magnetic force, atoms of white water splitting against green rocks; shell, pebble and shale caught in the drag, retrieved by the ocean. As if they could hear the hum of the sea resounding with the call of ancestral voices, plaintive as the blues, murmuring in their ears. After some minutes they awoke to the clash of thunder in the skies; lightning flashed like a trailer across the horizon; the thunder roared voluminous as drums, and as the lightning flashed again, the thunderclap reverberated and echoed like a thousand talking drums, beats made holy beneath baobab branches, and a downpour of rain started, wetting them slightly. This excited them and they made love for another ten minutes in the weeping rain, until it began to fall hard, and became unbearable and, after she had climaxed. Ralph pulled out of her and they ran into the car, winding up the windows, laughing. The rain fell in bucket loads as they drove back to the salsa class. Pervase and Anita were waiting for them when they arrived.

"Had a good time coz?" Anita asked Nicole.

"I came!" she replied. And she held Ralph's hands in hers, put them to her lips and kissed them.

Chapter Thirty Two

It was Friday prayers and Sheikh Ahmed Ahmed had been to see the mullah Mamadhou Aziz Shabaaz, his sister had been missing for three days, and he knew that physically, she was safe as Yasmin had told him where she was likely to be. And his cousin had also confessed where she had been. These were her very words before the family. The uncles had met several times with the aunts to discuss the annulled marriage between Yasmin and her cousin Nazir, who, three months after he had married Yasmin, had also married Sharifa, yet another of his female cousins. The marriage had to be annulled by all parties coming together and deciding that all was lost between the couple and that there was no possibility of reconciliation. If this did not take place; the "I divorce thee" thrice could never be enacted, and the couple would remain married, even though all physical contact had since ceased and there was no compatibility between estranged husband and reluctant wife.

Yasmin was determined that her cousin would be spared this turmoil of feelings as she had been promised to Nazir's elder brother Muhammad, who invariably accompanied Nazir on his wild trips to Birmingham, only to return saturated with the unpleasant odour of cigarettes, khat and alcohol, demanding both food and sex simultaneously. To make matters worse, while she struggled to work to build a career and to take advantage of the opportunities for a better life, he insisted in having babies and the possibility of living off the child benefit. This she hated as she had seen so many of her people become doctors, lecturers and newscasters since they arrived from Africa. It may be that some day the continent will be in better shape and they can all return home and live good among each other as they used to before Arabic insanity had began to rule. It may be she reckoned that it was the fate of African women to produce better men that will heal the continent of its fractures and sort things out, as if it was ordained by history to restore the rule of women. Therefore, like her brother Noor, she wanted to go to university and she wanted her little cousin to go there as well and get a degree and get married to a man of culture, who neither smoked nor drank.

They had decided three years ago to reinvent themselves and came up with two nom de plumes. They would call themselves Anita and Nicole. It was easy for them, once they had decided to move outside of their community, on occasions to find friends among other Africans, who saw them as quite like them, but they came from Somalia when they were young girls so being British was part of their way of life, and all over the cities there were the younger generation becoming partially integrated within their new country. Their community elders felt exclusive and kept themselves apart from other blacks; some even insisted that they were Arabs and influenced the young people to see themselves as such. They seemed not to have had any consciousness of the Kushitic origins of their language. Some even denied being Africans.

They had been expressly instructed that on no account were they to build any relationships with people from the Caribbean. For some reason unbeknown to them and the community that they were instructed to hate, they had no idea why they were so disliked by their people, who seemed to tolerate everybody else. But they had seen white girls walking with them to and from school; Indians and Pakistanis and other minorities talking to them, and this had intrigued rather than abhorred them. They had also seen Somali boys with them, and even with some of the girls, and lately they had learned that some Caribbeans were Muslims.

So that late evening while they waited at the bus stop at Vauxhall and Pervase and Ralph had stopped, offering them a lift as it was raining, they had reluctantly accepted and both got in the back of the car. Ralph was quiet. But Pervase had laughed and engaged them in polite conversation and when they had reached Battersea the rain had stopped and they, out of courtesy had agreed to keep in touch, so they gave them their mobile numbers. This was a year ago, in which they had spoken to them on their mobiles but had largely ignored their calls and kept their distance, until one day, Pervase had met them at the British Library, where they had gone to research tropical medicine as Yasmin wanted to be a doctor. And he had invited them to salsa.

Yasmin had recounted the full story in presence of the mullah, who seemed even more saddened than the family for this unholy encroachment upon two daughters of the faith. Yasmin on the other hand, felt less alarm for the very community they had been instructed to dislike, but she never could see any good reason for hating any one.

This was not the first time that the mullah had been called upon to sort out the problems of his two communities. Many Asian families were also uncomfortable with their daughters having misalliances with Caribbean young men. He was sympathetic and being of a sociological background, evolved a social theory that interpreted their anxieties towards such relationships as symptomatic of their diminutive cultures. They were cultures in which old rituals had become so fossilised that they carried out actions and held purported beliefs in old worn out habits, which they no longer understood, but nonetheless, insisted as their cultural prerogative, which were at heart resistance to change. They were not alone; all human beings shared this fear of change.

"I will put out feelers and find out where she is," he assured the distraught brother. The uncles had refused to meet him. For all they knew he could be part of the same conspiracy, and being Caribbean they distrusted him. "I will put out feelers and see where in Essex, she is."

And Yasmin had shuddered, for she had had to confess that they had been calling themselves infidel names like Anita and Nicole. Her cousin seemed to like this man, and would probably do as he instructed she thought and allowed herself to smile, despite the severity of the situation. Somehow the mullah reminded her of Pervase. Perhaps if he knew her situation the marriage could be annulled.

She had gone back to Pervase that night and slept with him at his house. Since that fatal night when they were raped by the two Cuban soldiers on the SS Havana, which had docked at Djibouti, after they had been smuggled from Mogadishu, where the Arabic terrorists had won the new offensive against government troops, they both hated sex, and the very idea of it sickened them. Yet there was some interest in it, for they had bodily desires. This desire to experience it, and the experience of rape, had confused them both. This was eight years ago when she was thirteen years old and Mulki was nine. There was also the fear that Mulki would be disgraced like her for not being a virgin on her bridal night, and through no fault of their own.

Memories of her wedding night were revisited in her mind as she recounted the shock of Nazir when she had explained to him what had happened on the ship, when the sailor had lured them into the hold and taken them there and they had cried the night, and during the day, and could not be consoled by the boys who said that it wasn't really their fault and that they shouldn't worry about it.

Yet they knew that it did matter; mattered to them and to the community into which they were born, and in any country where it had merely transplanted itself on foreign soil. It mattered that they would have to explain. And when they had tried to tell the captain, he seemed too busy to take action and in the end there was no justice.

The ship's doctor had instructed the nurses to examine them thoroughly, and they were tested and although, physically they eventually were healed, there were mental scars that ran deep, so that until the night of the salsa class, they had a secret resentment against men.

Yasmin had since tried to have sex but couldn't stand her husband touching her after he had disgraced her by recounting to the uncles and aunts that they had married him to a woman, not of the seed of Adam, and that this justified his taking another wife. And this he had done.

And Muhammad had even tried to take Mulki outside the marriage bed; inquiring if she also was not of the seed of Eve; and being inexperienced she had allowed him to partly have his way; and in allowing him partial access to her body, he had concluded that she had something to hide. Eventually, the two brothers had compared experiences and it was no longer a secret that neither were virgins. This had made Mulki wonder if any man would ever want her, until they began to attend nightclubs and became confident from the provocative dances that were done at discos. In this way they had rediscovered their sexuality. For during their brief encounters with sex, they had never experienced an orgasm.

Now lately they had come to know it as that intense quickening of the heart. The exquisite beat of the pulse, the sharpness and sweetness of breath and other sensations. Now she remembered the following day and she still hadn't left his house in Vauxhall.

There were flashes of light as Pervase instinctively understood the nature of her desire from the movements of her eyes, her body and the sounds that she made; he was masterful, yet gentle and she was surprised because she was enjoying it.

She was on her back and he devoured her with slow steady rushes, and she responded wildly, then finally stretched out her right leg and curled the left under her as he had told her to, and when her throat became dry and she had begun to swallow lumps of saliva and breathe swiftly through her nose. He stopped, pulled out of her and instead of plunging swiftly back inside her, he moved forward slowly, very slowly, and ever so slowly, and entered her again. She found herself inhaling short breaths of air, and when he kissed her, she moaned in response to the deliberately slow penetration. When she moved her backside back and forth in a rocking chair motion and her heart began to beat so hard that he could hear. He instinctively knew that she wanted him to beat short, sharp strokes into her, and as she came she squeezed her thighs together, stretched her body and closed her eyes tightly, blocking out the daylight as it streamed in through the gap under the bedroom door; and for the first time in her short and sorrowful life she experienced that intense human emotion, a force like the feeling of flight or dying and she cried out under her breath, "I'm coming again coz."

Was this the reason for the hatred: the taboo? Well it must be, and what sweetness it gave her. Unlike her culture where women were made vessels of flesh and tissues to be filled by men, she had been a full partner in this act. She did not commit the dishonest sin to lie still and pretend that she didn't enjoy it. Neither did she fulfil the fossilized tradition, which was a lie, that she expected no satisfaction from it. She had been encouraged to express her sexuality and to be as vocal as she wished. She knew at that moment that her entire life was being fulfilled, filled by a black man.

Sheikh Ahmed Ahmed began to question her. She stared back at them blankly as if she had lost her senses. She gazed intently into the mullah's eyes as the hot tears flowed down her cheeks. She felt like a fish on a hook, wriggling to shake itself free from the line, and they didn't know, couldn't know it, but right there before them she was wet underneath, as if the sperm placed there eight hours before had shaken itself free and like a drop of water from a stalactite had dripped down wetting her underwear, and she ran from the room in a flood of tears.

"So this is what Caribbean men can do to our girls," Sheikh Ahmed Ahmed, inquired softly. "Only if it's true love," Mamadhou Aziz Shabaaz answered. "They have an insatiable and phenomenal appetite for African and Asian women," he continued. "It's not a fairy tale," and as if suddenly remembering his own origin, he corrected himself, "When we make love to them. We can't stop; they give us what we call white liver," he concluded, absentmindedly. "It's an ancient addiction; it goes back thousands of years."

Sheikh Ahmed Ahmed began to crack his fingers. What nonsense he thought, these people have no culture; they lack thousands of years of grooming. How could any girl, any woman with any sensibility and thousands of years of culture find herself enamoured of such a person. The white man's statistics had said that they were not intelligent; that they were largely criminals like the Irish and the Australians who were transported from England; they were transported from Africa for stealing and were slaves. How Mulki could bring disgrace upon her family and if she had a child by this man that child will have the blood of a slave in its veins; their blood mixed with slavery.

"The uncles are threatening jihad," he said. And he remembered an incident in Battersea Park a year or so ago, when a beautiful young Asian girl had entered with one of them with their child, which looked remarkably similar to a Somali, and the other Asians had looked on her as if she had suddenly contracted leprosy; they spoke to her but you could see in their attitude that hint of pathos as if she had been bewitched. Oddly enough the whites who saw this felt offended by their reaction to the couple, and their body language spoke volumes. A remarkable people the English he had thought, and then he had remembered at least seventy percent had a sprinkling of British blood any way, that they were hybrids: slaves, coolies from India, pirates and thieves. Now weren't they warned not to form any relationships with these people? Weren't they told daily to keep away from them? Now he might have to disown his only sister and this cousin who had gone missing for three whole nights.

"That might be unwise," the mullah said. "Our faith forbids unnecessary violence, and as I hear, this man is a scholar and a Muslim."

The other man suddenly had a brain wave. "Are you sure this man is not one of your relatives?" he asked, part accusation, part inquiry.

Mamadhou Aziz Shabaaz laughed. Then he became very serious. "My brother," he said, "are you thinking that perhaps, I can't help you, because if you are I will simply tell the uma at east London that you find me not in a position to help," he said crisply. And he could remember a similar encounter with a Bangladeshi family in Tower Hamlets ten years ago, who were similarly abhorred by a Caribbean suddenly, taking up with one of their daughters. Really, he thought these people are trying my faith. For he could not recall a similar crisis if a Caribbean girl had taken up with a Somali or an Asian young man. There might be concern, but certainly no attempt to paint a picture of doom, disaster, outrage or dishonour. He felt in a unique position and slowly it was being brought home to him why these communities saw the Caribbeans as unworthy creatures. Their ancestors were slaves and they feared the purity of their free blood being diluted with the legacies of slavery. Being Muslim he could only blame the white man.

"Being Muslim doesn't mean that I can't have jihad against him," was the retort.

"Well, if you must see jihad as a cure; you would do well to remember that like you they have African genes and as you know all our peoples are mentally unbalanced, that would be unwise."

Sheik Ahmed Ahmed was silent. He had heard of Trident, the special police force for Caribbeans killing on Caribbeans. It's true, one of the legacies of slavery was their madness; the criminal element that they had warned their young people about; especially their young women. And yes, they were bad Africans who stole and were sent away. He smiled. "Tell me what to do!"

The mullah was reassured. He could see sense prevailing at last. And he was convinced that the impact of the white man on these cultures had bred suspicion and distrust among the dark races of the world. His intrusion into their world had resulted in humiliations, and provided unmistakable legacies which still divided them. It was the nature of Islam to heal these wounds among his peoples and bring them to common ground before common sense could prevail.

"Leave it to me; I'll visit you again in a couple days." And before he left they prayed for themselves, all Muslims and the sins of the world.

Chapter Thirty Three

Mulki stretched her legs out to let her toes touch the foot of the bedstead and smiled. It was the most beautiful bed she had ever seen or slept in. A beautiful four poster with white nettings, and a mixture of silk hangings, canopy included, with chains, beads and bells, so that whenever you moved on it, it made a musical and percussive sound. There were long silks at the head and at the foot of the bedstead and six large pillows at either end. It was the end of the May holiday and Ralph was not at work, but had gone to a meeting in East Ham. She wondered why he had left so early and was still there, why when she asked him to take her he had told her that he wouldn't be long. It was nearly three o'clock and although his dinner had been prepared and waiting for him he had phoned at half past two and told her that he had been delayed. She had just taken her burkah off when he rang again.

"Where are you now?" She inquired.

"Still at East Ham," he said.

"When are you coming home?" She asked politely for she was a good Muslim wife and did not wish to offend her husband.

"Soon, baby," he said.

She laughed, ending it with a giggle. She loved such endearments.

After speaking to Idris she went to the kitchen and made a cup of green tea and ate an apple. She was sad about leaving her family but she had been able to speak to her brother on the mobile which Ralph had bought her. But she could not phone Yasmin as they had taken her mobile away. She felt sad about her cousin. It was now a month since she had left their home to set up her own, and the uncles and aunts, while still in despair at the disgrace that she had caused could not force her hand in any way whatsoever. She was a married woman now, with her own home and a husband whom she both loved and respected. The age gap didn't bother her because she was a believer in Allah, and she was aware that Ralph had gone to East Ham to meet a very important man who might reconcile her two families.

The bed was so comfortable that she could not help but reminisce about the past four weeks. Things had moved at an accelerated and invigorating pace. That night after the salsa lesson Ralph had taken her to his parents' house in Guidea Park, as it was love at first sight, she had showered for a good thirty minutes . Then it was his turn. After he had emerged from the shower, she dried his body and massaged him from head to toe. He showed her the beautiful clothes and jewellery that he had bought over the past two years and put down for his new wife and she was intrigued as everything fitted her so well.

Having decided that they would make love, a prayer was offered and an enactment of marriage was performed. She then dressed in a beautiful, greenish blue linen skirt that he had bought and set aside with the gold bangles and ring.

And they both pledged three times that they considered themselves husband and wife. Then she changed into a beautiful silk sari. He watched as she unclothed herself from this.

Then he massaged her all over and, afterwards, he had spread her out on the bed and tied her feet to the foot of the bedstead with those pretty silks; tied her hands to the head and performed that most exquisite of acts that she had heard of and, for which she held a secret longing, as all women do, but until that moment was uncertain that she would ever experience. Yet, it was being done to her. She remembered Muhammad demanding it but whenever she had asked about it being done to her; he would say he couldn't do it. So as he refused her desire, she had refused his. It was only fair, she thought.

At first she was afraid that she would die with pleasure as he stimulated her "Libya," as she had called it; then her "peninsula," and then her belly button and, by the time he had eaten, devoured and kissed her pussy, her nerves were at such an edge that she couldn't stop her body from shaking. The deprivation of being unable to touch him at first was unbearable and she had begged him to loosen her hands but not to stop. And he hadn't, but her hands were loosened, so that she could hold his head and caress his neck and direct the right amount of pressure by putting his head at the most right spot. The scintillation had made her scream and she was glad that the music was on so that the neighbours wouldn't hear her bawling out. Then he had turned her over and kissed all over her body and massaged her toes, her calves, her ankles and caressed her backside, rubbing it and smoothing it down, kneading it until her whole frame was on fire with passion. And after that he rode her passionately, with the percussive sounds made by the beads and bells as their movements shook the bed. In moments of scintillating passion she had consented to be his wife another six times, making it nine times each that they both had spoken the marriage oath: "I marry thee; I marry thee; I marry thee." And in the morning they had rushed to the registry office and got married. He had kissed her belly button. Since then she had become devout and they both attended Friday prayers regularly; she joining the sisters and, he the brothers in different parts of the mosque.

It was three o'clock. Idris Suleiman, accompanied by Ismel Shah, rang the door bell at number nine Lakeland Lane, in Forest Gate. They were expected and didn't wait long before the door was answered. Ismel had already briefed Idris on how the interview might go.

"This is only a preparation," he had told him at his home in East Ham before they had set out for the meeting. "Only Allah is the final judge; no one else," he had reassured him. They had not seen each other for eight years, but they still communicated as if they last saw each other yesterday, as if they had been in contact every week or at the least every month last year.

A tall Caribbean male appeared in turban, long sleeve white tunic and baggy trousers. He greeted them according to custom and invited them in. They responded and entered the house, where they were ushered into a spacious, genteel, and simply decorated and furnished living room. He disappeared for some minutes and returned with cups of black tea, which he placed on the coffee table, and sat down. They sat in silence for another few minutes before Sheikh Ahmed Ahmed joined them.

"Salaamun alay - kum," said Mamadhou Aziz Shabaaz.

"Wa alay - kum salaamun," the three other men chorused.

There was a pause and the mullah took a sip of his tea and looked at Idris studiously.

"May Allah bless our meeting," said Idris. "Al-Hamdu- lil-laah

"Inshaa - Allah," chorused the other three.

The mullah took another sip of his tea; the others followed suit and waited for him to speak. "This is a delicate matter," he began, and paused, looking at Idris, "a delicate matter. This concerns the sister of our brother Ahmed Ahmed here. And now, I understand that she has become the wife of our brother, Idris here."

"Yes," said Ahmed Ahmed.

"Now is she married under the Sharia?

"Both," replied Ismel.

"But not yet eighteen?"

"No," Ahmed Ahmed replied.

The mullah looked at Idris. "Brother Idris," he said. "What is it you want out of this meeting?"

Idris looked directly at him and turned over his first sentence in his mind before he spoke. "As a way of going forward, I would like to apologise to brother Ahmed Ahmed, for not asking consent to marry his young sister. I accept that things were rushed. But I do not think that it would have made any difference. The outcome of conflicting interests would have been the same. After all, I am the descendant of slaves and of impure and captive blood and this is a taboo amongst the less enlightened African and Asian communities against us. They feel that we are not worthy to lay with their sisters and produce children with the legacy of slavery that may call them uncle."

Ahmed Ahmed became incensed, and got up to leave, but the mullah quickly poured him another cup of black tea.

Ismel looked intensely at Ahmed Ahmed and smiled. "It is partly true," he said.

"What do you say of this?" the mullah asked, turning to Ahmed Ahmed. "Is this true that you would object to this brother because of … because of the misfortunes of history," he stammered.

"There is no such thing in Al Qur'aan," said Ismel. And he turned to Ahmed Ahmed, "I have known brother Idris for years, and can vouch for him. If you argue that she is a bit young and he is older, it would make some sense. But a girl is a woman at fourteen in our culture, and that is not legal in England, and that is sensible. But she is seventeen brother, and of legal marriageable age, and she is now his wife. What can we do?"

Frustration was getting the better of Ahmed Ahmed. He couldn't object on grounds of age or culture, or religion. Either way he reasoned, the others would see his objections as stemming from age old prejudices. He realised that he had to adapt. He had one final card to play, and that was the thousands years of his culture, which seemed at the moment totally separate from everybody else's, and the criminal element among the Caribbeans.

"We prefer to marry someone from our own culture, according to the custom of our clan. That way we know the person and what to expect. I don't know how many bad people might be in that family so I have to be concerned, and there are many criminal elements in the culture here. So we have to be careful."

Idris looked at him intensely as he finished speaking, but said nothing. It was apparent that he didn't think what was said worthy of his reply, so he set his jaw firmly and resolved not to speak.

"That might be so brother, but you have to adapt to change," the mullah said. "Look at your own country," he urged.

"That is why we have to be very careful."

Ismel was getting restless. He had come across the caste system in India and its dire consequences: The Muslim – Seikh conflict; the Kashmire - Kashmire and India- Pakistani Kashmir conflict, the North South India conflict and a host of other conflicts in which people had divided themselves only to pick a fight. But this was ridiculous; he was beginning not to like Ahmed Ahmed as much as he did when they first met.

But Ahmed Ahmed had another concern, the matter concerning Yasmin. He would come back to the dishonourable act with Mulki later. "Then there is the matter of his friend; the other one with my cousin, Yasmin."

"Yes," said the mullah.

"Well, it seems to me that she has been bewitched. I don't know what was done to her, but she keeps crying all the time, and that one hasn't even respected us by showing who he is, or what his intentions are."

"No doubt, Idris our brother can persuade this person to come forward," said Ismel. He smiled as he finished the sentence, in an attempt to warm towards Ahmed Ahmed, with whom his patience had been growing thin some minutes before.

"Good," the mullah agreed. "But what does our brother Idris say?"

"With the grace of our most revered prophet, Muhammad, the ever merciful, I am sure that our brother Idris will be able to persuade his cousin to come forward and give the proper respect to the family, and to us, as we are to solve the matter."

Ahmed Ahmed, put his half cup of tea on the coffee table. He wanted to hear outcries, outrage, and acceptance that their honour had been breached. If this was the old country he thought, these two foreigners would not be so tolerant and complacent. He was convinced that had it been their sister or daughter that they would not be sitting with so much forbearance. That they would take sudden and violent action for their family's honour. If only he had his way, he would take action; the family would take action the clan would go to jihad. Outwardly he appeared calm; inwardly he was fuming like Mt Kenya on fire.

Chapter Thirty Four

Ralph had not reverted for the sake of emotion. He was always a highly strung, but a spiritual person, even at that school in the village that saw itself as a town, even a city, and where his mother's father was born. They had baptised him in the Seven Devils as he had later come to call the first path of his spiritual enlistment. But he had always one problem, he could never perceive man as God, and to his mind Jesus, with blond hair and blue eyes, looked more like Lucifer than the Lord of Host, with those strange looking pale men that looked like Captain Drake, Henry Morgan and John Hawkins around him. He had seen pictures of the Last Supper as a child and, at first it had terrified him as one of the men looked more female than male. He had finally found solace in Islam, and now with this man whose sister with whom he had fallen in love, despite her age, he was beginning to feel the way that he had not felt for the past months, that he was dangling.

He finished his tea, and the mullah held the plate of cakes towards him. He took one, thanked him and began to nibble at it, letting the taste slowly permeate the pores of his tongue. It was not too sweet; it was mango cake with ginger. He remembered the taste of mango in his maternal grandmother's house back home, so long ago and smiled, taking a deep breath.

Ralph had two nicknames for the Christians he knew: Seven Devils and Jehovah Wickedness. Now he was developing a name for the type of Islam that he was encountering in Ahmed Ahmed. He called it fake devotion, and turned over images of Ahmed Ahmed as a terrorist in his mind. Besides, what was wrong with some men? In searching his mind for an explanation, the old Caribbean term of pussy watchmen, seemed too mild. He wanted another term. Yes, he thought finally: any man with a morbid interest in which penis goes into the vagina of their sister, daughter or cousins, simply wanted to fuck their female relatives by proxy; that was it fuck by proxy, that was the explanation, and he looked at Ahmed Ahmed and smiled.

He swallowed the first chew of the cake and laughed softly, so as not to alarm the others or show disrespect in any way. He was wishing that he had married Helena. But would he have had such beautiful children? Would he have known so much love? Yes of that he was sure. Her love, but not perhaps, the kind of love his children had given him, not from their children, the kind of love that Sadie's children had given him, not that intensity; not the same feeling that Mulki had given him, with so much tenderness and surrender. After all, Helena was white. He was alarmed by his own thoughts as he was beginning to despair, or searching for excuses to justify his negative feelings of late.

"I'll bring my cousin Pervase to the next meeting, provided the family realises that I have no intention of sending Mulki back for good to live among them. She can visit, but I don't think she wants to leave her marriage."

But Ahmed Ahmed did not expect such resolve. Who does this son of a slave think he is talking to, him? Didn't he know that he had powerful friends in high places, that he could and would ruin him? "I think she is too young to know what she wants," he said flippantly.

"That might be so; that might be so. But what if she comes back to you; will you be able to keep her in the way that she has become accustomed? I hope that if she does come back that you will be able to keep her in good health and good spirit, Inshaa-Allah." And he laughed softly, and began to chuckle. The others joined in - even Ahmed Ahmed, began to laugh.

"Well, we are at least finding Allah in all this," the mullah said, "if we cannot, we are lost; look around you my brothers, do you see the other communities here indulging in the three "Ds?" dishonour, so he kills his daughter because she decides that she will have this other Muslim as husband; he kills his daughter because she has brought disgrace upon his family, and the Caribbeans: he shoots his cousin. No his brother because he apparently disrespects him. The very person he has referred to all of his life as "Blood." "Blood claat?" And he paused and then adding, "May Allah forgive me!" He held his forehead.

Idris laughed; Ismel chuckled. Ahmed Ahmed was stunned. And the mullah - one for laughing at his own jokes - especially his serious jokes, recovered quickly and was in mirth, quite beside himself with laughter.

The other two had heard of the strange classical reasoning of Shabaaz. They knew that he had in the past disrupted meetings when the ministers had come to the community with ideas about keeping the young people in check. These politicians had done so without doing proper research and had felt the wry humour of the mullah. Aware of his more humorous side they were beginning to be disappointed with his seriousness, until this sudden outburst. Although a quiet man, it was known that he had a sense of humour. "Now my brothers," he said after managing to control his laughter, "What common ground have we?" And he proceeded to tell them, "That we are all black men, and if we do not learn to put aside our differences we shall produce a Mao tse Tung, who will teach us what it means to have to build order from utter and complete chaos. We need a grip on things."

Ahmed Ahmed was offended. Black men, he turned the name over and over in his mind and couldn't see himself as such. But surely he is Somali, the black men were the Nigerians, the Ghanaians - even the Egyptians, but he was a Somali, an Arab. And Ismel didn't look black to him either. He pulled back from the edge of his seat the moment he heard that word used to describe him. He must tell his people about this new concept: that they were black men and women now that they had arrived in England.

And that he had met a mullah, who used bad language. One of the Caribbeans who had become a member of their religion, that served black tea and mango cakes with ginger, and had a picture of the Ka' ba on the wall of his living room. And he must also write home to his parents to inform them that he wished he hadn't come to this country or brought their daughter here as she was now married to the descendant of a slave who had become Muslim. How everything was upside down here? Crazy country!

Idris looked at him; he felt sympathy for him. He realised that he was not typical of most of the men of the community who had recently arrived in England. He had met so many of them: Eritreans, Somalis, Ethiopians and a few Egyptians, Libyans, Algerians, Lebanese, Yemenis, the Congolese, the Sierra Leonians, Ivory Coast people, black Portuguese, white ones, Italians: black ones, white ones, and in between ones, French, all types, the Filipinos, Brazilians, Spanish, Poles, Albanians, Estonians, Georgians, people from Kosovo, Bosnia, Greece, Cyprus, Turkey, he held a discrete eye for Chinese and Japanese ladies, Vietnamese, Koreans, Mexicans, of all descriptions, but they seemed very well disposed and friendly towards the Caribbeans.

And while not wishing his daughter to take up with any of them as partner, would accept as a Caribbean hybrid that it would be her choice, and would have to admit that if any of their women ever looked on him favourably, and the chemistry was there and everything else, he would rise to the occasion, with respect. And get to know their ways and innovate a little of their music and food into his own, "out of many one cuisine."

He had always been interested to learn new languages and at one point when he worked in Surrey, his friend Yusef was teaching him Somali. Now Mulki would help him with the vocabulary and the grammar. Perhaps Ahmed Ahmed needed reassurance, he thought. A compromise would be best for all concerned, and he loved Mulki, and this was her brother and he wanted the meeting to finish as he had a book to write, as with Mulki he had begun to write poetry again. And any way, despite the fuck ups in bringing all these diverse people here, in his own way he loved England, especially Birmingham where he grew up and Leeds where he spent most of his school holidays and ate Yorkshire pudding with his rice and peas.

"I see you have a plan," the mullah said to Idris.

Ismel cast a cautious look at Ahmed Ahmed as if signalling not to interrupt; a look that ended with a smile. He cleared his throat, and took a mango and ginger cake from the plate on the coffee table. "I think the biggest grievance that the family may feel is that Mulki was hurried away in the night and eloped with brother Ralph," the slip of the tongue was deliberate. So he smiled again, correcting himself, "Sorry, I mean brother Idris, and then of course there is the delicate question of circumcision, and of course, some recompense according to tradition for the elopement and untimely marriage of the young sister." He winked at Idris and smiled at the other two men present. Then nibbled a piece of the cake and swallowed it, and took a sip of his tea.

Ahmed Ahmed warmed to the deliberate slip of the tongue by Ismel calling his new brother – in - law Ralph and he too smiled. Finally, he thought this is what he wanted them to address.

The mullah realising a break through was imminent, it was his turn to clear his throat and smile. But he wanted the two opposing forces in Ahmed Ahmed and Idris to wait, so they could meet in middle ground now that they had established common sense, and besides, they wanted to bring the dispute to a close. "Allah is great," he intoned.

"Praise is to Allah, and Prophet Muhammad, the Beneficent, The Most Gracious. Peace is upon him," all four uttered. Then it was Idris who carried the discussion forward.

"I understand that brother Ahmed Ahmed and the family are very disappointed in that this was in their eyes an elopement. But the opposite is true that there has to be a problem within for there to manifest contradiction without. But putting that aside, I apologise for my actions, which were due to loneliness. I have been without a woman these last two years and my spirit was moved by Mulki. It was her intelligence which first attracted me." And he paused, clearing his throat.

The mullah looked into the tea pot on the coffee table and sighed; it was almost empty and the remains of the tea were cold. "Brothers, excuse me, please," and he took up the tea pot and left the living room. Ismel took the chance to change the subject to get the two opposing forces to relax more and turned directly to Ahmed Ahmed,

"So brother, how is Battersea?"

"Oh, it's not bad; we have two Adhan."

"Good, good," he replied, shaking his head. "And the women, they have their own part; they are good?"

"Very good," Ahmed Ahmed affirmed. He was grateful for the small talk, as the whole affair had been distressing. He was warming to both the mullah and Ismel now as they seemed to be moving in his direction in a sensible and reasonable way. But he was still uncertain of Idris; he didn't know how to place him. He had heard that he was a scholar, but at the moment he seemed to him more withdrawn than scholarly. That is he could not conceive of his scholarship within the main stream system. Perhaps he was a religious scholar, he thought.

When Shabaaz returned, he placed the fresh pot of tea with newly washed cups and a fresh plate of cakes, all of which he carried on a tray on the coffee table. He poured four teas, offered a cup to each, and taking the last one for himself, offered a cake to Ahmed Ahmed. He thanked him and took one. The mullah clasped his palms together and sat down.

"As you are aware, my brother, to have sex is not a sin among us. It is the conditions under which we have such pleasures. As we are aware, unlike the followers who see Esu as God incarnate, or God the son, or whatever? We are aware that it is human to love, and sex is a gift; a precious gift, a treasure. Therefore, marriage is the condition that we adhere to. But I believe Ahmed Ahmed is saying that Idris took his sister, not only without his consent, initially, but also before they were married."

"That is exactly the point," Ahmed Ahmed agreed. "It is a very good point," said Ismel. "However, we have to move on. After all, we do not deny the body; we are not Christians who would tell you that Jesus never used the toilet, but that he was human, and that he never experienced the divinity of human sexual intercourse." He paused and smiled. "No disrespect meant, of course."

The mullah nodded; Idris smiled. Ahmed Ahmed thought a strange thing that a prophet had never experienced sexual intercourse, but smiled as well. This was something that he would look into later. But at the moment he liked what he was hearing; the legitimacy of the law; the justice of thousands of years of culture and grooming.

Idris cleared his throat. He had already agreed a price with Ismel hours ago, who as a good brother had agreed with him that there were points of right and wrong that he would need to address at the meeting. After all, he had said to him:

"Don't forget that with all our peoples, it's not a question of procedure or points of law. Our peoples differ from the establishment here in principle. It is never whether there is time limitation or the right court or the right argument being pursued. It is always the question of right or wrong, or both."

The delicate matter that at seventeen Mulki was already an Ayyin would not be any part of Idris' argument. That was the past, and he would never use it against her any way. Love meant more to him than honour. So he smiled, cleared his throat, took a sip of his tea and asked if he may have a cake; inquiring what they were.

"They are coconut cakes" the mullah said.

Idris smiled as he put the plate towards him, took one and smelt it. It was fresh and spicy with a hint of nutmeg and cinnamon. "Thank you." He nibbled the rim of the cake, chewed and swallowed it, and took a sip of his tea.

"I am willing to pay what in parts of Africa they call a lobola to the family, that is a sum of one thousand pounds; to assure them that Mulki will have five thousand pounds in her bank account, which I have opened, by her eighteenth birthday; that I will accept that I was not entirely right and that it may have seemed like elopement and, once again, I apologise to Ahmed Ahmed."

Ismel winked at him and smiled, turning towards the mullah. "I think the gravity of the matter from the family's point of view has been graphically brought home to brother Idris."

Ahmed Ahmed was still somewhat unsure. He never expected such reasoning from the abductor of his sister, who must have been a virgin before he deflowered her as her boyfriend, and then as her so called husband. Although he was coming round to their way of thinking he still had nagging doubts. There was the other matter of his circumcision, which he felt too embarrassed to discuss.

Ismel looked at Ahmed Ahmed and smiled.

"You are very lucky that Idris has a very good mosaic background. He is circumcised; does not eat haram; not even halal meat, does not smoke or drink. You must understand that children of the middle passage do not convert to Islam, they revert to it. When their religion changed they had no choice and no one has ever looked into the turmoil of turning fish eaters into lovers of pork. When one of them reverts it is a glorious day for Islam."

"Good point," said the mullah. "As they say in Jamaica, give a man his shirt tail and beat his back." And he laughed, holding his sides.

The others laughed too. Ahmed Ahmed less inclined than the others, but the saying sounded something remotely like one of the sayings in his own culture.

"It is a glorious day for the Carolinas when an event like that happens."

The Carolinas meant nothing to Ahmed Ahmed in relation to Islam, but he smiled, nonetheless, and muttered inquisitively. "The Carolinas?" he asked. He turned the word over and over in his mind. He had been there for at least an hour and a half, and he was getting tired again and as he became tired the old suspicions began to creep back into his mind.

"The Carolinas: islands off the coast of the United States where the slaves established their hegemony as Muslims. That's an old legacy of slavery. Many of the slaves came not just from Ghana, Nigeria South Africa; they also came from Sudan, Egypt, Mauritania, Chad and an awful lot from Senegal. The griots for example were all Muslims. That's how the music came west. All we have is music - no culture," explained the mullah.

"But they are getting there," retorted Ismel and burst into laughter.

The mullah laughed, wiping his eyes with his handkerchief. Idris laughed. Ahmed Ahmed could see the funny side of it, and laughed, although, somewhat restrained.

"Oh yes, some came from India as well; some from South America," the mullah said. "Lots of crazy people," he added.

"And of course there are Arabic inscriptions on a rock in St Vincent that shows Abu Bakr, a prince of the time of Sundiatta, arrived on the island before Columbus even got there. But the conquistadores wrote history and award themselves magnificent trophies and their account is the only one that has credence. Everybody else's is referred to as legends," said Ralph. He laughed infectiously, which made the others join in.

"That's a good point," said Ahmed Ahmed. He was surprised that the words came out of his own mouth.

"There we have reached a consensus," the mullah said, "A common ground, at last." And they all laughed. In between the laughter he continued.

"So we shall meet again soon, brothers" he said.

"Yes," said Idris as he drank the last drop of his tea. "I'll get Pervase to come along the next time and am sure we can sort out something more amicable: he has a degree in chemistry, you know."

Ahmed Ahmed was a little alarmed. Surely there was no need for lies. How could he have a degree in chemistry? Surely the newspapers couldn't be lying, that these Caribbeans, especially the men weren't up to it when it came to education. Or was it perhaps, the present school leavers and not the first generation? Perhaps it was the present ones, he reasoned quietly to himself. Any way he was glad that it was over.

"We have to meet next Sunday, "Inshaa - Allah," said the mullah.

"Inshaa - Allah," chorused the other three.

"May Allah bless our meeting," he replied. "Al-Hamdu- lil-laah

"Inshaa - Allah," chorused the other three.

They finished off their drinks and got up to leave.

The mullah walked them to the door patting them each on the back affectionately. He put his arms around all three as they approached the door to leave.

"Don't forget my brothers; the man has his democracy - his capitalism. All we have is our devotion," and he raised an index finger pointing and shaking it and gave a little chuckle, "all we have to unite us is our prophet Muhammad, Peace is upon him. All we have is our Islam!" he said, kissing them at the door, as they took their leave in kindred spirits.

Chapter Thirty Five

Idris looked up at the second floor, the living room lights were out. He wondered if she was all right. He had phoned immediately after the meeting and she was there; happy to hear his voice, to hear that things were better than they were yesterday, and happy that he soon would be home. He pushed the key in the lock, walked into the house, climbed the stairs stealthily and entered the apartment. He heard the toilet being flushed and her voice singing. He imagined that she was washing herself. He knocked on the door, "I'm here," he said.

"Don't come in," she said softly.

He walked away from the door. "I'm getting my dinner."

"Don't please, "she said.

"OK, I'll just chill then!"

He walked into the living room and turned on the television with the remote. Then switched it off in frustration at the television programme, about some corrupt country in Africa called Zimor in which the local dictator was hounding the opposition. The leader of the opposition looked more like a villain and an opportunist to Idris, but the west had unofficially appointed him to run the country, and much to their consternation, the elected leader had refused to step down. He was apparently taking white farms away from the white people there. He tuned his guitar, took a music book from the shelf and played the first two bars of "Purple Haze."

Mulki heard the music and her ears pricked up. She loved music of all types and wanted to know if it came from the television or the play station; hurriedly she finished her ablutions and realised that it was Idris playing the guitar as she walked into the living room. The music caught her ears and she started to dance. She remembered the salsa class and the first day they went, which although only a month away seemed to her like a life time ago. But she never imagined that life could be so complete, so simple and uncomplicated.

Yet she grew a little sad when she remembered that while all around Africa, and perhaps, the world, but she couldn't concentrate too much on the world, although that was part of her concern, but while two black people of different countries were about to have dinner in a quiet part of London, you had men with guns and children with lethal weapons running wild like stray dogs in Africa, disrupting the lives of the ordinary people and displacing them. Meanwhile the United Nations peace keepers were offering soap to children for sexual favours, with an African as Secretary General of the United Nations.

And, although she knew that Idris would never hold it against her, she remembered the two Cuban sailors who had raped her and Yasmin, so that they would go to their husbands' beds as Ayyins.

"That sounds good," she said.

Ralph looked up and smiled at her. "Hello baby."

She laughed, walked to the kitchen sink, washed her hands drying them, placed the food in the microwave and turned it on. This done she rejoined Idris in the living room. She loved the way his fingers moved smoothly across the fret board and when he picked out the notes to the chorus of the song she was certain that if she hadn't already done so, she would willingly have given herself to him. And then she recalled the griot, the kora player in Mogadishu, who had made Yasmin cry with the beauty of his Senegalese music. That music summed up for her all the tragedies of her country Somalia, and the pathos of Africa, and she marvelled why a place of so much beauty had been set upon by Europe, the mighty continent, then the most powerful military might in the world, partitioned, and whole cultures and people destroyed, and then prop up and instigate a century of madness, in which warring factions murder and displace the ordinary people so that there is chaos everywhere. On days when Mulki felt like this her heart would break, for then it seemed to her as though there had been years of conspiracy and crimes of humanity committed against the black race by whites and by Arabs. As if these two warring factions among the races of the earth held an ingrained jealousy against the most beautiful of Allah's creations. For he had created the black race in a thousand - and - one images, and instilled music in their souls, so that above the races of the earth, Allah had given them hearts of pure gold.

She brought in two trays of food and placed them on the table. In the old days Idris would have been fussing to help her, but as a reformed personality, he had realised that women in general hated men who patronised them by always rushing to help with minor little tasks, instead of concentrating on the major ones which needed help. So he let her bring the food in. There was also no necessity to wash up either; if she needed him to, she will ask, and it would be done. For years Caribbean men were labelled as misogynist; he could recall Bower, accusing him of such in relation to Barbara, after he had reputedly stuck a cigarette in his wife's face. Apparently it was the season of legitimacy, when like the helots of ancient Sparta, white women in relation to their black mistresses had been disenfranchised and became hereditary enemies of the state, and therefore, white husbands with black mistresses were legally bound to deny their human dignity.

That was a long while behind him now.

He rose from the chair, went to the bathroom to wash his hands, came back and sat at the table. She brought the food in, then he said grace and they began to eat. He swallowed the first fork full of rice, with vegetables and looked at the fish, with brown stew. It was better done than what he had ever achieved, and he was a very good cook. His grandmothers had taught him. He turned it over with the knife and fork and saw how evenly fried it was, still with moisture in it though.

"What's wrong?" she asked.

He smiled, a satisfied grin on his face, but he ignored her question. He leant forward and whispered in her ear. She hit him, playfully on the shoulder.

"It's your birthday next month and I don't know if you want to have a party at home with your brothers and uncles or a neutral place. My cousin Pervase knows a little boat along Thames, it's run by some guys from Mauritius, you'll be at home there, all black people with wavy and curly hair," he laughed.

Idris had come of age as Ismel had once told him when he was floundering about his Caribbean upbringing: "Class is permanent - style is a migratory bird, which eventually loses its way in the hurricane." And he had laughed until tears came to his eyes.

Mulki laughed out loud and struck him on his shoulder. He put his fork down and rubbed it, claiming that it was broken.

"Don't be silly," she said.

So he laughed; took up the fork and resumed eating his meal.

He could not help realising that there were those unfortunate black people like Indians who maintained that they were brown, despite the fact that the complexion of an Indian may range from pale to the blackest hue. Idris laughed about them now. Then there were the unfortunate blacks who talked about nine ether hair, six ether hair and light complexion as diluted blood, he considered them ludicrous too, and although they sometimes held sound ideas, they had become like their masters the white man; they held right knowledge and the truth for the entire race, or races of black people and were preoccupied with the differences rather than cemented their similarities.

But they came as messiahs, each and every one of them, in their own confused state; came to save the race, or races of black people. That whites called themselves white was also equally ludicrous - but on the other hand, it was their choice. That black was a political term as was white seemed ridiculously clear to him. He simply used it as a point of reference, not proven scientific and absolute reality.

He smiled, he was glad he was a Muslim with a Muslim wife, who although young, understood his intellect. So he carried on eating and complimented her on the food, which is what she had been waiting for all along.

"Thank you," she said, and smiled.

He looked at her lovingly.

She stared back at him. "What?" she asked.

"You," he replied.

"What about me?"

He smiled and paused.

"What?" she exclaimed.

"You," he replied.

Mulki laughed. She had played this word game before and knew that it could go on forever. She remembered being introduced to his cousin Frank, who upon meeting Kathryn his young wife who was born in England, took her to see the Caribbean one night and told her that she could spot it from London Bridge, and she had been in mirth and complained to her mother that her husband, had taken took her to London Bridge to show her Jamaica. So she smiled and stared back at him. She had lunch with them, even though Idris and his cousin weren't on speaking terms.

"I want you," he said.

"You got me: you're my husband."

"I know," he replied. "But I still want you."

"You can have me later," she said, and laughed.

"Cuul," he said.

"Iskerwahan," she asked.

"Mega'ar," he replied.

She took a fork full of food and chewed it, swallowing. "Why do you always have to ask me, why don't you just take it?" She was teasing him.

"That's because it's like food and its best to ask for it; in the old days we would say: please, can I have some pussy?" "Me and my cousins we were brought up to ask for what we want." And he smiled, resting his knife and fork, "please can I have some pussy?"

Mulki laughed. "No!"

He cleared his throat. "Your brother said to tell you hello."

"That's good - is he fine?"

"All the family send their love but Yasmin is now living in Birmingham. They want to meet Pervase and I have agreed to pay them a lobola: ancient African custom; and I've promised to make sure that you are financially secure. The meeting went well, and I 'm happy about the arrangement for your birthday party. It's up to you."

"Good; Inshaa- Allah."

"Sub – haanallah."

"May Allah bless our marriage," she said softly.

It was almost weekend and she knew the children were expected, she reminded Idris to collect them. The children having been to the home several times were fascinated by her and her country of origin, and of course, were looking forward to spending the weekend with their father again. Mulki had begun to teach them the language of her country. Idris had encouraged this, including the history of Islam in the Americas, which went back since the first slaves were sold in the Americas. She soon learned the history to extinguish the light of Islam in the Americas so that it died out until it was revived by the martyrs Noble Drew Ali, and Wallace D. Fard.

Mulki soon came to appreciate that she had married Idris knowing nothing of the history of the past and had begun to realise more about the world, and how human beings interact, but even more tragic, was the unknown history of Africa, the continent of her birth and lately of the magnitude of Islam, a religion into which she had been born, and had always suspected that she knew very little about.

Chapter Thirty Six

Pervase had just returned from Birmingham where he had taken Yasmin to stay with Raj. Both he and Raj had attended Handsworth Wood Grammar School, and had kept in contact over the years. It was a friendship that had been forged for mutual protection since the day when Idris as Ralph and Frank and a couple of their friends went to Hall Green baths to fight with the local skin heads who were harassing Raj and his friend who had only just arrived in Britain, and one of their cousins who was over on holiday. They were into beating up "Pakis," and it didn't matter to them that Raj, Gurdial and Piara and Sunni, one Hindu; two Sheikhs and one Muslim, weren't from Pakistan. And not one of them was born in the subcontinent, but in Kenya, in East Africa.

And after that a series of incidents occurred in which the skin heads had harassed Idris at the age of twelve for going swimming in Hall Green where he had met a girl his age who liked him and he liked her, and it didn't matter to either of them that she was white and he was black. They liked Jadine as well, but had to come to the swimming baths several times to stop him from being beaten up by the skin heads as they lived close by. So theirs was a relationship spanning forty years. Being a solicitor, Raj had drawn up the necessary papers giving Abby the house in Handsworth Wood and the better part of their joint account to bring about a quick divorce. Pervase was therefore free to marry Yasmin, which they did at New Street Registry Office.

Parked outside the mullah's house, he took the three envelopes from the dashboard that their uncle Alfred had given. They were sure that they contained the one thousand pounds each that he had gone to the bank and withdrawn, to give to the family of his newly acquired nieces. It was the right thing to do. In the old days in St Kitts, their uncle had remarked there was the tradition of "writing in," as they called it. In that the young man or the parents of the young man would write to the parents of the girl that he wanted as wife and once accepted the marriage was arranged. Things had changed over the years, he thought, but here was an opportunity to show the Africans that there was still a semblance of culture in his little small island. In the Mother Colony of the British West Indies, where both the English and the French had established their first colonies in the Caribbean, like leeches upon the backs of the Caribs, but some good had come of it. Even out of slavery. At seventy he was still a proud man.

The two cousins arrived outside the home of the mullah that Sunday at exactly three thirty and parked outside talking. It was a sunny day and they both felt good. Were it not for their Seventh Day Adventist upbringing they would not have gone to meet the family. Pervase recalled some fifteen years ago when he had dressed up and gone to Ovid's parents' house in Cannon Hill, having been invited to dinner by her parents as they had got wind that she was seeing a little small island boy. He had recounted the story to his friends at Mount Pleasant Youth Club.

He had rang the door bell and the mother, very cordial and civilised invited him in. The meal was familiar: rice and peas and chicken, but the absence of Yorkshire pudding and macaroni cheese pie. No rhubarb for dessert either. He knew something was wrong. Ovid looked as if she had been crying, and sat between her parents around the dinner table.

"And where would you like to live if you got married?" They asked. "Ina England?"

Pervase had answered in a negative manner. After all, he had only just arrived in England four years before, and the thought of leaving all his new friends and going back to the Caribbean was frightening for a thirteen year old with all his closest relatives recently arrived in the Mother Country.

"And would you consider living in Jamaica, hif you get married?" "You h'unnerstan?"

So a word like "if" being considered too simple for the occasion became "hif" followed by "You h'unnerstan?" He knew what subtleties were at play when a Jamaican carried the "h" or placed it where it ordinarily wouldn't be. He knew that in St Kitts, they substituted "w" for "v" when they wanted to test your understanding, and ended every other sentence with "You unnerstan?" So they tested your hearing as well as your ability to reason on their terms. So water became "vater," and vanity became "wanity." All new words newly made up to suit the occasion.

And "You unnerstan?" Caribbeans of that generation were always testing you, so he begun to despair. He had gone ashore in Jamaica on his way to England as they had cruised to England, and he didn't want to go back there in a hurry, he wanted to experience all the different islands in Birmingham.

Suddenly there was a change of tack. The mother rose as the father questioned him about his education, and then she sat down again. He wanted to be a chemist, and he wanted to go to the United States of America. He really didn't know why he had said that. That was the time when the United States was very unpopular among the Caribbeans in England. That made Mrs. Bailey's blood pressure rise. All she saw were the riots and black people being beaten by police with dogs, on the news and whole cities burning. And she remembered that song about a strange fruit growing on southern trees, blood at the root and blood on the leaves and some charcoal body burning, or hanging from a tree, and her beloved daughter being caught up in it. She rose from her seat, watched by Ovid in her Sunday best dress.

"Stamp h'it h'out, stamp h'it h'out h'Archie," she cried out. "Noo, h'I will 'ave none a h'it!"

At which point both children began to laugh uncontrollably, making matters worse as she had taken offence. Mr. Bailey took them into the Holy of Holies: the living room. Told them that they were still too young to marry, that they needed an education first, and then perhaps they would have his blessing; then took them back into the dining room to finish off dinner.

He had left a lasting impression on Pervase all these years and with Idris who had never met the man. But in his hearts of heart Pervase wished that he had married Ovid, at least, the feelings and sensations would have remained the same, and they would have grown together and it was love at first.

All those years had been squandered by a generation too blind to understand that in England it is best to marry when the sensations are new, when love is fresh and the impressions are vivacious. It didn't give him any peace to learn that Ovid had later taken up with Lance, whose parents came from the same island and had three children while they remained unmarried.

He reasoned as they waited outside the mullah's home that in adherence to some hidden agenda by the Mother Country they had missed their chances. They had left the greater part of that generation that came here in the fifties and sixties dangling. For didn't Raj remain married all these years to Sita, and wouldn't Ralph had married Sofia?

They waited in the car until Ismel and Ahmed Ahmed arrived, who, when they arrived waved at them, parked, got out and walked up to the front door, ringing the bell. The mullah was upstairs performing his prayers when his daughter Salma came to the door, followed by her mother, who was dressed in a sari.

She was a fairer version of her daughter, healthy looking and a woman at peace in her marriage and content with her status in life. They had recently returned from Trinidad and her skin had a beautiful gold to it. The girl was about eighteen, a darker and smaller version of her mother, with sheen of coolness to her skin. A glorious crown of black curls fell over her temples and two thirds the way down her back. She had exquisitely high cheekbones, pencil eyebrows, long eye lashes, deeply set black eyes and beautiful aquiline nose, with flaring nostrils and a small sensuous mouth that hinted at a strong sensuality. Her breasts were well tapered; they turned upwards and then in, and her trunk was slender and wiry, but with meat. Her backside, her other face was rounded, but long in a way as if the genes had become so fused that there was even perfect balance in the way that she stood, sat, walked and looked. Her legs were long with ripe calves and she was beautiful with a hint of other worldliness about her. To Ahmed Ahmed she seemed as if she came from his country in Africa. Ismel, who had picked him up from Stratford Railway Station, knew better. He could see the curiosity on his face as he looked at the mother and then at the girl.

The two cousins got out of the car and joined the other two men greeting them, and acknowledged the two women.

"Hello," Helena Shabaaz, said. "My cousin is upstairs." She liked to remind people that her husband was in fact, a cousin, the child of her Guyanese uncle who had slipped away from the Essequiabo, and traced her father to Arima in Trinidad, with his child by a Creole girl, whose father wanted to kill her uncle; the mother had died in child birth, she was fifteen and the father was convinced that he, an older man had put a voodoo spell on his daughter, or else how could she have taken up with a coolie. In those days it was the norm for an Indian to cutlass his daughter, but to commend his son if he had taken up with a Creole girl, as the less enlightened among them disdainfully referred to the Afro Caribbeans at the time, while the others referred to them with equal disdain as "de Coolie people dem." It was even given out as scientific proof where these indentured labourers were housed in the long houses throughout the Caribbean, "That ten coolie weighed one pound." And while the unenlightened of the former slaves applauded the

British Empire in not accepting their marriages as legal, they both bore the brunt of any challenges to the status quo.

"Hello sister, "said Ismel.

"How is Zainab?" she asked. "Tell her to come to Trinidad, she would like it; we have roti we is de best at that better than any Indian – we have dalpourri – that good too – oh yes and de pepa sauce – you couldn't get anything better in de Caribbean – you don't have to say it – you know we Trinis is de best."

Ismel laughed. Ahmed Ahmed was even more curious and bemused. She stepped aside, turned to her daughter, "Salma, tell you father your uncle Ismel and tribe people them is here. Come in please" and she ushered them into the living room.

Salma disappeared upstairs, and did not return. Helena busied herself in the kitchen and prepared refreshments for her guests. She took the rotis filled with vegetable and fish out of the oven and placed them on a plate. Then scooped the sweet pumpkin out of the sauce pan and filled little cups with it. Then she took the guava cakes sweetened with honey from the cupboard and placed them on a plate which she placed on a tray. She took the mauby and sorrel and ginger sherbet from the fridge and placed them on a tray. This being arranged, she walked to the passage and called Salma. Salma came running down the stairs and as she came down stairs her mother clapped her on the bottom.

"Ouch," she grimaced. "Ma why you hitting me for," she cried out. "Daddy," she called out, "Ma is hitting me bamsy again."

"You don't think I need help, what kind of man will want you if you can't do little things like help with guests?"

The girl ran passed her mother and into the kitchen. "I don't intend to have no man; all they do is spoil your body," she said.

"So what you going to have, women? What stupidness you talking child – you must have a husband. Your father doesn't want any boyfriend marriage – you know - and if it's a boyfriend - you better make marriage fast." And she followed her into the kitchen.

Salma rubbed her bottom as her mother inspected the tray of refreshments. Satisfied that everything was decent and in order she handed it to Salma. Salma took it and walked to the passage. Her mother followed and opened the door of the living room for her and she walked in. "Excuse me," she said, putting the tray onto the coffee table, smoothed down her dress shyly and backed off. She was aware of their eyes on her. Uncle Ismel and his friend from a long time ago smiled, but the one looking like a Dougla kept on staring and never averted his eyes, not even when he saw that she was nervous, as if she reminded him of some one. Perhaps he is just intrigued she thought. She met her father at the bottom of the stairs as she made her way back to her room, with her mother in pursuit and complained to him again that Ma was hitting her on her bamsy. But he just smiled, kissed her on her forehead and stared at his wife in mock disbelief. He knew the relationship between the two women in his life was good. Helena was the kind of woman that he had always dreamt of as a young man, conservative, but with a hint of the rebel in her and spoke more with her hands than her mouth. She'd hit you if you were comical and made her laugh. If a joke was really funny and she couldn't control her mirth and if you were too cheeky to her. These slaps on their daughter's behind he knew were affectionate and jokingly disciplined and more like caresses and excuses to touch her, as if she was still a baby. Little wonder then that she only wanted one child, and a girl to be her friend for life. So that when people asked either parent about male descendants they were promptly informed that Salma would give those male heirs and that was enough for them. Salma was an only child who spent her time visiting friends and relatives and was studying medicine at Kings College. She was self - centred, self - contained and never would imagine sharing her parents with another sibling, especially a boy.

She attended monthly mosque with her mother and participated in the majority rites of her faith, wore a hijab, occasionally, but enjoyed herself as a free West Indian and, being of Afro-Carib-and-Carib-Asian descent: a Dougla, she considered the term more aptly fitting to her than many of her peers.

The women went to her room where they were sorting out the photographs of the recent holiday to Trinidad and Guyana.

"Good afternoon, my brothers," Mamadhou Aziz Shabaaz said as he entered. "Thank you for waiting on me," he smiled looking at each present attentively. "Allah is great!"

"Allahu Akhbar," they all replied.

He sat down, looking intensely at Pervase.

"This is my cousin Pervase," said Idris.

"Pleased to meet you," said Pervase.

"My pleasure," replied Shabaaz. They shook hands.

Then Idris turned to Ismel. "This is Pervase."

"Hello," said Ismel. They followed suit.

"My pleasure," said Pervase.

"Ahmed Ahmed - this is Pervase," said Idris.

"Pleased to meet with you," he said.

"The pleasure is mine, respectfully," Pervase replied. Both men shook hands and when the mullah sat down they followed suit.

Mullah Shabaaz poured four glasses of the mixed sherbet and handed his guests one each and then sipped his. He liked the taste and smiled and that cheered him up even more. There was enough nutmeg and ginger and cinnamon in it, but this did not overpower the taste of the lime. That's the way his father Santosh used to make it, and it brought back boyhood memories of his first days in Guyana and later, Arima in Trinidad. He liked life better in Trinidad, where the Muslims had established themselves as a force to be reckoned with; not like Guyana, where the Hindus dominated and even his own grandmother still maintained the old traditions of breaking plates if people ate out of them. At least in Trinidad, things were more social, so he had adopted Islam as his uncle Saleem had and then married his first cousin.

His Creole mother was of Yoruba background and her mother, who was still alive when he got married had encouraged him to look beyond the gossips and accusations of incest, for some of the Creoles, "Coolie incest," for they had forgotten, and would liked to have forgotten that such traditions were part of the culture of Africa, and that some families among them openly practiced it. Their relationship had simply been a natural progression.

Idris helped himself to a cake and the others followed him.

Ismel complemented Shabaaz on the sherbet, which he assured him, was now hardly ever made in India – he said India, but actually meant Pakistan – which is where he was from, but used India as people from the Caribbean even though they had heard of partition, still referred to the whole of the Indian subcontinent, generally, as India. Somehow, they employed another term when speaking to others, but only for particulars would they ever give voice to Pakistan, Sri Lanka or Bangladesh. Ismel knew this from his various conversations with Helena Shabaaz, whom he rightly considered the voice of the community.

He was also aware of the antagonism which some Carib Asians held against India and that at least fifty percent of the blacks in the Caribbean had some Indian ancestry but would rarely admit to it, he wandered if Salma's children would have the same love – hate attitude, for both Africa and India, and more seriously, in times of stress a full blown hatred of Europe. He knew that England was referred to as "de Bitch," the United States with England as "De Whure an' de Beast o' Babylan," that Tony Blair was "Lucifah," and any Tory leader "Saitan," and various other names depending on the hurt and how deep it felt at the time, and the police: the institution and individual constables were still referred to in quiet corners as "de Babylan;" while racist white people were given a singular which in Creole grammar was a plural "de Beast." All Asians were referred to as "Cha cha," which

The Way an Apple Falls | 227

was alarming as it was confusing and derogatory, because it also meant uncle. The Somalis and Ethiopians were referred to as "Coolie Africans," and other Africans as "Bubu;" the latter appellatives by the far less enlightened. So while the rest of the communities held and spoke derogatory things about them, they also had a well sorted out and stratified hierarchy of the social order as they saw it. After all they were human beings and just as capable of cruelty as anybody else, but all this were in great humour: tongue in cheek, reflective as well as reflexive. These were just retaliatory measures because they knew others said things about them. Their favourite phrases were that other communities held them in "derision."

"The matter at hand is very important for us all men here. We need a solution to the matter to rest between Pervase here and Ahmed Ahmed, and Ismel here and Ahmed Ahmed". The mullah cleared his throat and helped himself to one of his wife's guava cakes, it tasted good and he chewed it slowly and then swallowed.

"I am sure Allah has blessed our first meeting," said Ismel and smiled. He had already briefed Idris on the way that the talk should progress and now he looked at Pervase and smiled, "How is it you have an Arabic name," he asked and added, "no disrespect intended, but it sounds Muslim"

"I don't know; I think it was the first word that came to my mother's mind when I was born."

"I have met so many of our people with such names," the mullah commented, "It only goes to show that we are really one people."

Idris laughed. "Some months ago I met this young lady from Jamaica and her name was Shazia, she said she didn't know why she had a name like that." They laughed.

After a pause, Pervase clasped his hands together, squeezing his fingers and smiled. "Firstly, I would like to thank mullah Shabaaz for making his home available for this meeting; and secondly, I would like to apologise to Ahmed Ahmed for the situation that I have caused by falling in love with a member of his family. I would like to assure him of my good intentions." Ahmed Ahmed smiled and acknowledged the apology by shaking his head in the affirmative.

"And what is the remedy, that you propose?" the mullah inquired.

"For my own part, our uncle has agreed that one thousand pounds is reasonable as compensation; and the same was agreed for Pervase to pay as compensation to the family. We pay it under the system of lobola," said Idris.

"That might be difficult for Ahmed Ahmed to accept under Sharia. I do not know how he feels," said the mullah, and he looked at the other man inquiringly. "I know the Madhhab of East Africa considers the Shaf'ite dominant. And I have looked into the Hanifite, but he was the grandson of a freed slave, so Ahmed Ahmed might object to such a preference," and he smiled innocently.

"I am here to be told what to do by habit as you see fit and Al

Qur'aan, which I believe, you will not go against. So tell me what to do," said Ahmed Ahmed.

"Good," the mullah replied, and looked at Pervase.

"I support Idris in the amount of money and in the principle as agreed," said Pervase.

"Do you accept?" The mullah said, turning to Ahmed Ahmed.

"I think it is a good start," Ismel interjected. "And as I am aware that Pervase is also circumcised and follows the dietary laws of Moses, a compromise here would be good, and as soon as we can agree." He looked at his watch.

"Do you accept the settlement?"

"Yes," replied Ahmed Ahmed, "accept in principle, but there is still the need for Yasmin to return home, and she has a husband, and she has done a bad thing in…."

"But this young man who is her husband, can he keep a wife; can he keep two wives and did he reason with her as to another marriage? I don't know and that is not my major concern. You must annul that marriage if you accept this one thousand pounds," the mullah said.

"Is that part of the condition?" asked Ahmed Ahmed.

"I don't really care; you can do what you like," said Pervase. "As a slave descendant whose ancestors were more than probable Muslims sold to the west by other Muslims, I exempt from certain restraints that anyone from Africa might want to place on me in religious matters. I consider the whole entire continent spiritually tainted and you are fortunate that we see it in our hearts to forgive you; you have made a muck of things in Africa; you have very little governance; you cannot rule as Africans; you beg the white man to solve your problems. I am convinced that you sold my ancestors for a pittance because they were too intelligent for your small understanding of the world, now look at you; how you prostrate yourselves with begging bowls, no," he corrected himself "begging baskets, because nothing ever stays in them, before your former masters then have the temerity to call us slaves."

Ahmed Ahmed got up to leave and had to be talked into staying by Idris, Ismel and Shabaaz. He was not violent or angry, but quite beside himself, agitated, and disappointed as things seemed to be going so well. Idris apologised for his cousin. There was silence for about five minutes.

After the calm, Idris handed the mullah three envelopes which contained a thousand pounds each. The mullah took them, thanking him. He counted the money and handed two and a half thousand pounds to Ahmed Ahmed. Who thanked him, taking the money a little reluctantly?

Pervase looked at Ahmed Ahmed. "I am sorry about my outburst but you must understand us, we have difficulties being sold as objects – like animals, pets and household goods – and then to have the very black people who sold us – calling us slaves and keeping us in derision," he said.

"I understand," said Ahmed Ahmed.

"Well," the mullah began "we have reached a compromise: the marriage of Yasmin to be annulled so that Pervase can marry her within a month; the families to accept the ties that they bear with each other, Pervase to revert to Islam," and he looked at them "anything else brothers?"

"I think that should be all," said Ismel.

"I think so as well," said Shabaaz.

Chapter Thirty Seven

The telephone rang and rang, it kept on ringing. Idris was half asleep. Mulki was already up and performing her ablutions. Idris turned in bed and could hear her running the tap in the bath room. Perhaps it's Pervase he thought. He knew he had to get the telephone, but as he got out of bed it stopped. He got back into bed; it started to ring again. This time he ran back into the living room and pounced on it. "Ralphie is that you?" said the voice. He recognised Calvin's voice immediately.

"Yeah, it's me" he replied.

There was a pause and he could hear Calvin swallow over the phone; his voice became hoarse as he said: "Uncle and Tanty been involved in an accident. They're dead." Idris cleared his throat and swallowed his saliva; then his mouth suddenly became dry; his heart started beating fast, then faster and faster, and when he felt as if he would faint he crept to a chair and sat down.

"You have to give instructions," Calvin continued, "You have to send some money down."

"Yes!" Idris agreed. His mind was racing. The flat in Hackney had only just been sold and the money transferred to his account. He had three hundred thousand pounds in his Nationwide Accounts, both the Flex and the Savings Account had one hundred and fifty pounds each. The

Barclays Account of his parents had two hundred thousand pounds in it. His thoughts were racing and his heart was beating ever faster. He had only twelve thousand pounds in his Abbey National.

"Thanks for calling me," he said and put the phone down. "Mulki!" he called out. She came out of the bath room, in her dressing gown, and knew immediately that there was a death in the family. "I am sorry to hear," she said. "And your parents; I'm sorry Idris," she repeated.

"That means I have to leave in the next twenty four hours; you'll have to stay with Yasmin in Birmingham," he said. She looked at him in disbelief. "You're going to your island and you are leaving me with Yasmin, is Yasmin my guardian then?" Then she smiled, "It's my eighteenth birthday next week and I am a woman - a married woman," she emphasised and recalled that Kathryn had warned her not to let Idris ever go home alone, because he would be prey to too many offers by the women, and business deals by local business men, who only intend on making quick money out of returnees. "Don't forget," she had warned her, "men are all the same, when it comes to pussy, they would do anything; especially when the hot sun hits them, and the sea and sun rub on their skins, they would lose everything, even their balls." So warned, it was very unlikely that Mulki would ever let him go home alone. Surely, she thought, he hasn't got any foolish ideas about women not going to funerals or graveyards as part of Islam, and that she would want to stay in England while he went to his parents' funeral.

Idris looked at his young wife; her face was set and stubbornness seemed stamped on her countenance. He had not seen that look on her face before; a look almost of defiance, which made her look even more beautiful than he had ever seen her. "OK," he said, "I will have to take you then." Mulki ran towards him and linked her arms around his neck, she kissed him and squeezed him and would not let him go. "Thank you," she said, "I'm so happy to go with you, but I'm so sorry it's on account of this; I couldn't bear being here alone with you gone" and she kissed him again on both cheeks. "My parents would never leave each other and go off alone, I couldn't stand it here if you weren't here with me and you need your wife beside you to say goodbye properly to your parents."

The telephone rang Idris raced towards it and picked it up. "Hello," he said.

"It's me Pervase," said the voice at the other end. "I got a call from Calvin some minutes ago, I heard the news; I' sorted out ten tickets, but I need some money off you."

"Where are you Idris asked?"

"At home in Birmingham."

"I can transfer five K into your flex this morning," said Idris.

"Fine."

"Ok then, meet you and the others at Heathrow tomorrow at six in the morning."

"Fine, say hi to Mulki;" "Hi Mulki," he shouted as Idris took the receiver from his ear and held it out for her to hear. "Hello Pervase," she called back.

"By the way; I'm taking Yasmin with me and I thought it's reasonable so I bought Mulki a ticket as well – Uncle Alfred's idea; he wants them to see the Caribbean."

"Fine!"

"Tomorrow, then!"

Idris called Barbara and then Sadie as he made his way down stairs to go to the bank. They were expecting him to collect the children for the weekend. However, they offered their condolences on the death of his parents when they were informed and agreed to have Konrad collect the children for the airport the following day, to attend the funeral of their grandparents. They converged at the airport and took irregular seating arrangements. The children kissed Mulki when they arrived; but when they boarded sat with their father, while she sat with Yasmin. This suited both cousins as they had many things to catch up on and felt as if they were wandering into familiar experiences. Although, the experience of the Cuban sailors was a long way away now, they both, occasionally, felt revulsion for the act that had been inflicted upon them. However, they were excited by the company, and the caring, but care free ways of their new family. They both resolved to send postcards to their cousins as soon as they arrived in the Caribbean. The announcement for departure and instructions came over the public address and then they were off.

In flight they awoke intermittently to find themselves over the sea, heard bits of conversation between sleeping and waking, the chit chat and laughter of other passengers and family members.

They were surprised at the similarity between their new family and the one that they were born into; their husbands no longer belonged to them exclusively, but everybody belonged to everybody else. Pervase's twins sat with Aunt Rosa, and James with Pervase and Idris. And speaking to each other in their familiar language they discussed this, and admitted to each other a little jealousy as their husbands were not even given the opportunity to sit with them.

They had finally met Uncle Alfred. At seventy he was slim, with a head of grey hair that curled without a bald patch all over his head. They were reminded of the old men in their village south of Mogadishu. His wife Nadine, a dark skinned woman about the same age sat beside him. She had been equally courteous to them both, as was their son James, his wife Jane and the twins, Emile and Emilio. Jane sat, not with her husband or children but with Aunt Rosa. Jane had suggested that they should all stay for at least a year. As a painter she saw the possibilities of being inspired under the tropics where she knew light was more vivid, and besides she loved the outdoor life. Aunt Rosa, in comparison to her brother Alfred was fair skinned, a pensioner of sixty four, and had raven black hair, a slight frame and looked East African. Aunt Rosa's two daughters Nadia and Rosaria sat with Uncle Alfred. They had heard so many names being called, whom they would meet once they had arrived in the Caribbean.

Chapter Thirty Eight

The airplane taxied on the runway, the fields of sugar cane with their pretty flowers growing either side, some three miles away stood in the hot sun, shaking their heads of yellow flowers. The two cousins awoke, wiping their eyes with the soft tissues that the East African looking stewardess had given them on the West Indian Airways flight into Golden Rock Airport south of the city of Basseterre, the capital of St Kitts.

Yasmin looked out of the porthole and sighed, joyful that they had arrived. She had telephoned her cousin Ahmed Ahmed, and the rest of her other family members briefly and had promised to see them when next she was in London. She felt slightly disappointed in letting him down, as she had no idea that she was only passing through on her way to the Caribbean. She would send them a card. She was surprised when Pervase had told her that they were going back to London, and was anxious to see Mulki. She had no idea that she would be driven to Heathrow, and then boarding the airplane with Mulki and other members of the family who were all there waiting. It was a surprise for her, but Mulki having overheard the conversation between Idris and Pervase, knew that she would be coming. They had sat together on the airplane during the whole flight. And fell asleep as they reached the Leeward Islands.

The twins Emile and Emilio thirteen years old were excited and anxious to alight from the airplane and were being scolded by Jane. Aunt Rosa, quite unashamedly, was crying, taking the hand of her brother. They had developed a fondness for her during the flight. Then she stopped; wiped her face and dried her eyes when she heard the national anthem of the twin island federation which was being played over the radio, on the airplane, now that they had landed. They were rushed through customs.

Out of the building they were met by Frank, Kathryn and Calvin. There were kisses all round and brief introductions of those who hadn't already met, but knew of each other. Aunt Rosa linked her arm in Frank's and walked proudly to the Jeep; Uncle Alfred strolled behind, taking his time as if savouring the moment and the air. Mulki introduced Yasmin to Kathryn and they rode with her in her car, with Jane, her twins and their grandmother. Frank and Idris were still not on speaking terms but he got into his car any way. So did his children. Nadia, Rosaria, James, Pervase, Alfa and Rashan went with Calvin in his car.

The three vehicles headed for the family land at New Yellow Crescent Estates, Idris had renamed it by proxy.

Although Frank had paid for the upkeep, the deeds east of the river belonged exclusively to Idris who had choice of name, but the other finances were in Frank's hands as had been arranged by Norris, Idris' father, and Idris, never one to compete with this particular cousin, allowed the arrangements to remain that way, at least, for the time being. But all the family knew that there would have to be a compromise of some sort; especially with the recent deaths of Idris' parents, and Uncle Alfred was down to arbitrate on the matter.

The drive through New Fountayne and East River took twenty minutes. North West of the island, New Forest was a sprawling town on the Atlantic coast, where the sea was rougher than on the Caribbean side. It was rounding the dangerous bay, Arawak Point , where the sea came up to the road in little streams as it was stopped by the promulgation of rocks that had been placed there to break up the waves as they rushed inshore, when the sea was unusually rough or in the hurricane season, that Idris' parents' car had slid into the sea and by the time someone on the lonely stretch of road had called the emergency services they had already slipped into unconsciousness, as the car had hit a large rock, leaked petrol and exploded. They were eventually pulled from the vehicle, but the burns and the shock had been too much for them. They had both died simultaneously and were confirmed dead within an hour of being taken to the hospital in New River.

As they approached New Forest, they could see a yellow and black sign post which read: The New Yellow Crescent Estates. There was an electronic gate and a lodge; two men spied them with binoculars and waved them through. The cars drove off the main road and entered a private road that seemed to stretch forever. They eventually arrived in the middle of a large estate yard, with two large houses left, where the road became a path, turned right and carried on into the dusty distance, passing a mound. They got out of the cars and the sound of a river could be heard gushing its way through the tail of a rainforest to the far right, where there was a mango walk. Both houses were enclosed within iron fences and rolling green lawns.

Other members of the extended family emerged from the houses and helped with the luggage. They organised sleeping arrangements and disappeared leaving Calvin to report the funeral arrangements. It was as if the visitors had no say in the matter; the family at home would be in charge of every detail, including what time they ate and where they would go. Idris felt like time had not moved on for forty years in the minds of the family members at home. They were in charge and everyone was expected to do as they were told. The extended cousins would serve, but they were not servants. They were organisers, as they were when he was a nine year old boy and attended that school in the town that saw itself as a city.

While the others went to bed, Pervase, Frank, Calvin and Idris stayed up for the next hour, sorting out the finer details of the funeral which would start at twelve o'clock the next day. They planned who would ride in which cars and the arrangement to bring the bodies from the undertaker in New River, as they were to be buried on family land, like in the old days. A tradition which had died out in the family, but would be revived now that they had regained their former social position. They would be churched at New Forest and then interned at New Yellow Crescent Estates, where a mausoleum had been newly constructed. With the finer details outlined they joined the others, who were so jet lagged that they weren't disturbed as they stepped quietly upstairs and went to their beds.

The following day was Friday and Calvin who only took instructions from Frank and had it confirmed by Idris organised the women and children. His wife Bernice made sure that they were all appropriately dressed, assisted by her sister Arlene; various other family members arrived early in the morning; organised the tables and chairs outdoors, placed the utensils and plates around the lawns and finished off cleaning up the two houses. Idris could barely remember that the two houses were joined by an underground basement, and when he was taken down to the cellars where his father had stored barrels of banana rum, sweet potato wine and various other cordials, he was astonished by both the storage and the link between both properties. They had only lived in the north east of the house, which consisted of two large libraries, two sitting rooms, two studies, two bathrooms, four separate toilets, a large kitchen and a giant dining room with a giant dining table, made of mahogany wood imported from Guyana. He had already begun to think up ideas of joining the two properties by building in between them and had to abandon the idea. As usual, his parents had thought of everything.

By eleven o'clock they were all ready to leave for the undertaker Ross and Ross, at New River.

Three black limousines halted outside the twin house, as Idris had began to call the properties. Unlike on the air plane, this time Alexis, Alexander and Aisha, sat with Mulki, Yasmin, Rashan, Alfa, Kathryn, Jane and her twins in the first limousine. They were joined by other family members who sat in the back seats. Aunt Rosa, Nadia, Rosaria, Uncle Alfred and Aunt Nadine, took the second limousine, with other extended family members. The third limousine was taken by Idris, Frank, Pervase and Calvin.

It took thirty minutes to reach New River, the hearses were ready, as arranged, and the coffins were covered in flowers, and bouquets arranged into messages of farewell. They set out almost immediately the procession arrived outside the funeral parlour; it took ten minutes to reach the cathedral at New Forest. Idris knew that his parents had converted to the Seventh Day Adventist Church, and thought that they would be churched at the denomination of their choice; for he knew there was a local Adventist church at New Forest. This was therefore a surprise to him. Frank had decided, with the support of other members of the family that they would be taken to the cathedral at New Forest. Being a funeral, he said nothing; they knew he would not openly question such a decision under the circumstances.

He was in two minds for he could remember the great church with its well maintained cemetery, and its gothic interior. What had always struck him were the twenty or so royal palms which lined the pathway going up to the church when he was a boy. And his great- great grandmother was buried there. Somehow it really didn't matter which church they attended while alive, they were always buried as Church of England, for some reason the church of England had claimed their dead; Idris looked out of the window, after searching Frank's face for an explanation for the choice of church, but he just kept his face straight, looking ahead, as if lost in his own grief, and it seemed to Idris then that something in their history would have England claim them forever.

Pervase on the other hand, whispered some inaudible comment to Calvin, who just shrugged his shoulders and grumbled a reply. At which Pervase went quiet, and they continued the rest of the journey in silence. They arrived at New Forest and approached the cathedral from the East Gate. The reverend, Roland Bradbury, a gaunt man with a profusion of auburn curls and a polite manner, was waiting; the doors to the cathedral were wide open. Idris could remember the last time he visited it some twenty years ago. The catafalque was taken inside. The viewing took forty minutes, there were presentations with all the family saying their farewells, and the testimonies passed. Soon they were out of the cathedral, much to the relief of Idris and back on their land, where the internment took an hour and the feast began with live music and steel bands.

There were tears; the elder children who had seen their grandparents five years before they died had suddenly realised that they would not see them again and this realisation, together with the occasion had seen them crying. They suddenly wanted their grandparents and not photographs of them on display. Idris, who had not cried, left and went for a walk along the river, beside the mango walk. When he returned he ended up dancing with Mulki who hadn't danced since the night of the salsa. All the family expected him to perk up and so he did.

This brought Pervase and Yasmin, Calvin and Bernice, and other members of the family onto the floor; even Frank joined them with Kathryn.

The music lasted through the evening and Calvin, under Frank's instructions brought the activities to a close by paying the band members and, explained to them politely that the family needed to rest, due to the busy schedule of the day's activities. They all retired, tired and exhausted, but safe within the fold of the immediate and the extended family. Aunt Rosa after tears wiped her eyes and finally spoke over the microphone that they had arranged for family members to continue their tributes.

"They had a good send off!"

Chapter Thirty Nine

"The benefits of living in England are not as good as here. I want to sell up; I mean the house in Guidea Park should fetch a decent sum and I know I have to share this with Pervase and Frank, Nadia and Rosaria and Calvin, but I can live here once production of potatoes and bananas, and other produce are marketable."

"You've said an important thing: marketable," said Frank. He paused and looked at the group of family members around him. "I'm going back to England to live, and I can sell the house and the flat there, if that's what Idris wants." He smiled for he knew that he had refused to acknowledge his change of name before. "But he has to be absolutely certain that that is what he really wants to do; I'm not rescuing anybody once there is a change of government and things start getting bad."

Pervase laughed out loud. "You make it sound like some banana republic in South America or Africa." "This is the mother colony of the British and the French West Indies."

Frank was on the back foot. "I'm only giving a scenario; its hypothetical, but things can go wrong everywhere. I know things aren't quite what they should be for us in England, but there is money in it."

Uncle Alfred put his handkerchief to his mouth and coughed, cleared his throat and excused himself. Aunt Rosa smiled and patted her brother on the back. Their brother had died and his wife, whose family lands also, adjoined theirs, had been left to their son. Hence their son, who had changed his name, had inherited all the adjoining property; held joint inheritance of their legacy with their children. The house or the twin houses were more his than any other living relative. He held a unique position in the scheme of things.

They also knew that both leading nephews were the antithesis of each other; were they able to sort out their differences they could be good partners in any business venture; but sadly, there was this rivalry between them. Frank had always had difficulties with the revolutionary streak in Ralph, who now called himself Idris and had instructed everybody to call him by that name. Frank also found Pervase a handful for him too, who in his brother's view held equally revolutionary ideas about life. They had both become – or as they had put it "reverted to Islam." As if their unconventional European radicalism wasn't enough, the Africa thing had suddenly resurfaced as it so often did in Caribbeans of their background. As if the eccentricities of Europe weren't, sufficiently, confusing. They had to complicate matters.

Aunt Rosa caught Frank looking at his two peers intensely, as if trying to bring back images of them when they were growing up as teenagers, and visited her during the school holidays in Leeds. That was a long way away now; and in the Caribbean, rather than being immigrants, they were landowners and a part of the means of production. A far cry away from London, where they were social stereotypes: part of the horde of the disadvantaged: immigrants.

She was sure that not even Frank for all his bravado about England believed one word he was saying. The writing had been on the wall for West Indians in England for a long time. They had served their purpose. They had never claimed unemployment benefit when they first arrived in England, she reasoned that they were left dangling; dangling to find shelter, dangling to find work, dangling to eat; dangling to keep warm, dangling to survive racist attacks, and when the new immigrants had arrived they were given all the assistance that they were refused, because the British government had robbed Peter to pay Paul; they knew that Paul would be coming, so they had left Peter dangling all those years of unclaimed unemployment and child benefits.

So she cleared her throat and listened for a logical break in the argument. As if she was a little girl again growing up on Nevis, which wasn't far away, and still part of their enigma, for they held lands there as well – and in Anguilla, which had left the trinity, the federation of the three small islands - when she would watch the skipping rope twirling above her head, and with just – in - time timing would jump in and go with flow of the motion.

Uncle Alfred returned, put his hand up as if he was still at school, raised a finger and smiled. "I will rent my house in England, but I won't just stay flat footed in the world any more, I like Canada too." And he clasped his hands and rubbed them together. "Now if Idris wants to sell his properties there; well good luck to him, why should anyone remain flat footed in the world today?" He paused again as if looking for defiance, "But one thing I'm certain, he can't sell this place, not to government, not to tourist board or tourist prospecting for citizenship, not to anyone. And I don't think he would try to either. That's what Frank, you should be concerned about. No matter where you go or how you would like to see yourself, you will always be West Indian; don't ever forget that!"

Frank had retreated into hypotheses again and it was decided that while he would handle the banking side of the lands west of the river; the east was to be Idris' to do as he wished. Idris offered to share management of the east with Pervase who would maintain parts of the south west as his own; several hectares were afforded to James, Nadia Rosaria and Calvin; several plots in the east to other members of the extended family.

The meeting closed with Pervase selling his part of the house in Birmingham to his brother. Idris decided to sell the house in Guidea Park, and Frank agreed, reluctantly that as a property developer he would effect the sales. The meeting closed and Pervase and Idris went for a walk along the east of the property to plan sites of development for their children. They had not told Yasmin or Mulki that they would not be returning to England to live permanently. They decided to spend a year at home and put themselves in the mind set to realise their aims and immediately began to put their plans into action.

There was a mound east as they passed the bridge which spans the river, and the ruins of an old manor with well kept gardens, this was the ignomy, for while the gardens were well kept the old manor house with a history which began in the seventeenth century was falling apart.

The manor overlooked the river where the rainforest ended; they could hear the tumble of water as it flowed over the turbines that had provided electricity for the estate since they were boys, flowing beneath the cliff. Idris reminded Pervase of the days when he would come from Anguilla to spend time on St Kitts before the adults had a bout of the "going to England travel sickness" as if they had suddenly become bewitched by the romance. Then they fell into silence, taking in the sound of the river that headed from its source deep within the forest of Mt Liamuiga.

After the pause, Idris was first to speak: "Whatever happens, I would like a mosque built on this site. This would be good spiritually and for tourists; people assume too much that all tourists are either unbelievers or Christians."

"It's a good idea; we could dedicate it to our wives to commemorate their foresight to rise to the challenges of history."

"Yes," Idris replied, encouraged by Pervase's support. "For example, this prince in India once he had converted to Islam, built incredible monuments, and all over Asia you have examples of that; Mogul Shah Jahan built the Taj Mahal for his beloved wife Mumtaz." They reached a large boulder east of the gardens and sat down for a rest. "What ambition stirred the Romans to build roads and bridges that would last thousands of years? What ambition could have burned in the heart of Qin of China to bring together the diverse elements of such a vast land, and to this day influence the course of history?" He paused, picked a leaf from the hedges along the path and smelt it. "And what ambition stirred Cicero to write "De Officiis?" He paused and swallowed, clearing his throat, "Tell me, and are we stones without sentient thoughts? Is the black man an animal that he has no ambition, other than to applaud the great feats of the white man, who restricts him in his burning desire to impact on the world rather than be impacted on?" "Is it any concern of the Chinese whether we see Christ as God or not, whether Africans want to build pyramids again, or control their future?"

"No," was the reply. "They have not made it their mission to restrict anyone. They are democratic; they mind their own damn business, and not masquerade as world rulers, but be careful, that you do not hate yourself; we can't afford to hate ourselves," he warned.

"I don't hate Europe, I just don't trust it. That's different to hate," Idris replied. "There are things which are simply human and I admire some of their ideas: such as the command of reason; action as obeying that which is reasonable, while moderation: freedom from rashness, defines the definitive act of duty; I haven't spent all those years in libraries in England to emulate tyranny; I cannot be tyrannical. It is my dislike of tyranny and sense of duty, which move me not to forgive slavery."

"Good," said Pervase, shaking his head.

"If I can't put down that dream here on this land, would you do that for me?"

"Yes," his cousin replied.

"And the idea of markets in each village, would help to establish culture, here as well," Idris continued.

"Which is what we don't have here," he laughed. "We want to stop importing food and farming again."

"Yes," Idris agreed, and laughed, adding, "But we're getting there."

"I know - I wonder how Ismel is doing?"

"Ismel would be good here." He paused as if thinking silently. He could hear the river tumbling on its way to the sea. "Are there any Kittitian Indians left in St Kitts?" Idris asked.

"A few left."

"That's good."

"We're so small. I never would have thought that they have an enclave."

"It's only by natural selection they are still here." They both laughed. Then it was Pervase who paused this time listening to the river gargling its way to the shore. "Out of slavery has come unexpected things; I would never call them great, because human beings are expected to do great things; out of that restriction we have still triumphed, and even in the great errors of going to England, we have continued to make history, not because of the errors, but in spite of them, that too is human; the human spirit at work. Like when the slavers heard our ancestors sing, were they not moved by their music, and when they said they were ugly weren't they moved by their beauty?"

"Yes, but they did not understand the longing in their souls'; love of music, pride of dignity; their clans; their families; their tribes; neither did the slavers appreciate their humanity, and that I do not forgive," he said with a finality that shocked Pervase, and added, "And I mean the slavers; I do not forgive them."

Pervase laughed. "It's a pity we can't speak to Frank like when we were youngsters. There is only the rapport of statistics and figures: numbers and property between us; have you noticed?"

"Yes, I know, I think his sense of duty is like the old mulatto idolatry; were it not for Nevis and Anguilla, St Kitts would be like the Dominican Republic: the hater of its own blackness here in the Caribbean."

"There is something I must show you after Frank goes back to England," Pervase said.

"What's that?" Idris asked inquisitively.

"Don't worry we should spend a few hours at that cathedral in New River looking around the old town," said Pervase.

"Yeah," he said.

They headed down the mound, turned left at the bridge and made their way back to the house; as they neared the house, Idris stopped. "Tomorrow is Mulkie's birthday!"

Chapter Forty

Idris and Pervase woke up the following morning and left the house quietly with their wives. They drove to Harbour View and gave the women money to shop for presents for their family, and housekeeping money, even though it was highly unlikely that they would need to spend money on groceries. There were fresh vegetables off the land and fresh supermarket groceries were being delivered to the house every day; fresh fish was bought from the fishing boats along the coast and extended family members brought fish to the house as several relatives owned boats. The family was self sufficient in almost every way, apart from clothes, so the women were encouraged to order ready-made and tailor made clothes. They wore the hijab on visit to Harbour View.

They needed more money so they went to the Eastern Caribbean Bank to sort out the Accounts for the Estate, as Idris' parents were officially managing The Old Manor House, as it used to be called before Idris had instructed Calvin to change its name. He presented a copy of the will, and changed the signatories to their new names to which they had added to McFarlane so their children would be entitled to own the land jointly with the children of their cousins.

The deed polls had been drawn up by Skerrit and Skerrit Associates, the law firm where Calvin worked, so everything was being put into place to live on the island. So they both became McFarlane – Suleiman, joining the old surname with the new, McFarlane being the new name, because they had only reverted.

Idris had half the Nationwide account transferred to the inherited bank account, which now amounted to one million Eastern Caribbean dollars. Half of which he divided equally among his children. The remainder, he transferred one hundred thousand to Pervase, according to the will, and placed the rest in the Estate's account, for Frank to sort out. After all he was good at these things; liked handling money. The rest of the other one hundred and fifty thousand pounds from the Nationwide he transferred and placed in a joint account with Mulki. He would instruct Frank to sell the house in Guidea Park and that would be it. They then took their wives to the Emporium: a network of shops and stores where they would be helped by customer service, and told them to meet them at the Pelican Inn for lunch.

Afterwards they went prospecting for a retail property as they wanted to run a restaurant - something for their women to do - and a retired home for Aunt Rosa and Uncle Alfred, and for themselves, even for Frank. Then they had lunch at the Pelican Inn. An act which was against family tradition, for they only ate from the village school as children; eating from strangers in the island was considered poor; only the poverty stricken it was misconstrued, ate from everybody. But that was of course, when St Kitts Nevis was a closed society, when if a tourist ever took your photograph, you demanded it back, because the snap had taken your soul, it was a part of you and didn't belong to anybody else. But now things had changed and while it was

The Way an Apple Falls | 255

considered good taste while abroad to eat out, it was an insult to the extended family were you spotted eating out upon returning home.

But they always were revolutionaries. Frank wouldn't do this they thought and both began to laugh. The women were returning from the shopping spree, and were joining them at the table where they found them laughing, in pursuit by three young men whom the store had provided to assist with their shopping. This was Harbour View, from where on a clear day you could imagine that you saw the North east islands of Sabad and Statia. The United States had, with its investments and good Caribbean foresight, turned the old town into a commercial paradise. Idris and Pervase were impressed by the customer service there, despite the wearing of their hijab, their wives were given respect.

The women joined them at the table, and the waiter, immediately, took the shopping away and placed them in keep of the customer service, where they would collect it after finishing their meal. This had become standard practice in Harbour View, where you could sit eating and looking out to see the waves break on the shore, and have all cares taken from you, where you were well catered for in every way.

Mulki smiled as they sat down; Yasmin laughed softly. They had become accustomed to not having their men to themselves, but now that it was to be Mulkie's birthday celebration, they were grateful for these private moments together. They knew that there would be a good celebration as once again Calvin had organised it. The women were not surprised at the arrangements - it's as if Idris and Pervase expected him to take care of such things, despite their leaving the house so early in the morning without having the breakfast, which had been prepared for them, by the extended family. Now here they were alone with them. They enjoyed the domestic order of the estate, the conventional natures of Kathryn and Frank, Uncle Alfred and Aunt Rosa, but also liked this place. That security was there, counterbalanced by this unfamiliar place, with so many strangers where their husbands had instructed them to meet for lunch after leaving them at the Emporium.

They ordered sweet potato cordial, and iced sugar cane juice before the meal. Idris and Pervase ordered pumpkin and mango juice, and a plate of salad, with chocho, popchoi and lettuce, chopped cabbage, and slightly bitter spinach – type leaves, which they called mesambe. Slightly boiled, this complemented the cucumber, tomatoes, and wild spinach, which was blanched. The meal reminded them of their own food at home. They nibbled the salad lightly and engaged in polite conversation.

"Did the shopping go well?" Pervase asked, addressing them both.

"Mulkie wanted to buy the whole store, and they would have given her if she had the money," Yasmin joked.

"Anything for my wife," said Idris.

They all laughed.

Pervase laughed and winked at Mulki, then at Yasmin. "You sounded just like Frank then." "Do you know he sometimes sounds more like Frank than I do; yet we're more alike than Frank is to either of us?"

"I've noticed that they walk like each other," replied Mulki. She laughed, "And even Kathryn mentioned it to me."

"Maybe when families are too much alike and can't get close, they get to resent each other; our two brothers are the same: Noor and Ahmed Ahmed are always not on speaking terms." Yasmin laughed. They all joined in.

The waiter came after they had half finished their drinks and brought four large bowls with incense water and towels to wash their hands. Then they assisted them to order, by explaining what the items on offer were. The four diners conferred and eventually, Mulki and Yasmin ordered baked fish with sweet potatoes, a plate of assorted vegetables, and a further salad. Idris had raw fish fillets, brown rice, banana dumplings and corn on the cob. Pervase ordered steamed fish and steamed vegetables and a raw salad. The resident steel band began their Bob Marley showcase, with all the diners applauding between numbers.

They had been away from the estate since the early morning, had a meal, relaxed with music, in a very inspiring environment, a socially clean and stimulating atmosphere, and were ready to leave. While they waited to catch the attention of the waiters to pay the bill, Mulki and Yasmin wrote the postcards to send to their family back in England. Idris and Pervase, inquired about the presents they had bought for the family, they could not return without buying presents for every one: it was expected. Caribbeans care less about waiting for you to share breakfast than receiving presents, after a shopping spree. Any spree had to include them, if only in proxy, but they expected their reward. They were both relieved when finally the customer service brought the shopping, assisted by three attendants.

On the way out Idris asked to see the manager and realised that starting a new restaurant, would be out of their depth, especially as they would be competing with such quality service which seemed to be extended throughout the island. Pervase volunteered to pay the bill, but was told that it was on the house. They did not realise that the sweet potato cordial, the pumpkin, mango, and sugar cane juice came from their land east of the river, where Frank had installed equipment, and that the barrels in the cellar at the house were samples, with which he had supported his uncles' endeavour.

"It's on the house, because we expect to be doing more business with you. Frank told us that you would have the final say," said the manager.

"But we can still pay," insisted Pervase.

The manager looked at him. "Mr. Mc Farlane. It's a pleasure to have a member of your family eat here." He laughed. "Frank never does - nor does Calvin, even though he works in town."

"We know they are old fashioned," Idris said, and chuckled softly.

The manager smiled. "Maybe the rest of the families will change: the returnees," he said politely and smiled again, nodding his head.

"Thank you very much," they both said.

"Perhaps it will change," said Pervase.

They tipped the customer service, and the waiters, instead of paying. The shopping was brought to the car and they thanked them and left.

Chapter Forty One

They arrived home to find everyone in the kitchen, seated along the giant dining table. The decorations for Mulkie's birthday had been put up; the food already prepared and the local steel band and children from the extended family had already arrived. The steel band was on the lawn warming up. The shopping was brought in by the two young men from the old village of Tabernacle, where the Nevisian, who had married their great grandmother Susan, had first settled. Idris and Pervase had not met them before. But they did not object when they almost wrestled the shopping from their wives, nor were Mulki and Yasmin surprised. They were being cared for. Once again, this had been arranged by Calvin. Frank and Kathryn smiled as they gave way.

The shopping was placed in the library next to the kitchen, and the two young men immediately disappeared.

"That's Freddie and Paddy," Frank said to his brother and his cousin."

The two men looked puzzled. "They are Aunt Clara's sons," he said, and smiled.

Two young girls entered the dining room from the kitchen carrying two trays of drinks, which they placed on the giant mahogany table. They disappeared momentarily and returned again with more trays carrying drinks and cakes. "Those are their girlfriends, Jackie and Tales," he whispered to them. "Nice eh," and smiled. "Have you met Milton and Patrick? They were shadowing you in town."

Mulki and Yasmin were served iced cold drinks, by another couple. Pervase and Idris looked around for their children, Alexis, Alexander, Aisha, Alfa and Rashan, and found them, greeted them and took their places at the table and play fought Emilio and Emile. They were tired. But Frank had suddenly become one of their favourite human beings in the world; perhaps he was coming around slowly to their way of thinking. They could see that he was enjoying the fact that they might be in trouble, but in a good humouredly way. They winked at each other. Perhaps Kathryn had given him some good sex lately; no wonder he's coming round to reason, they thought.

Aunt Rosa whispered to the two young girls as they returned to take the trays away; they proceeded to take the trays into the kitchen and returned. Then Mulkie and Yasmin were approached by them and accompanied upstairs.

Uncle Alfred stood up. "James tells me these two tourists went into Harbour View today and attempted to buy out the Emporium," he said, loud enough for James to hear.

"I told you no such thing father," James said, with good humour. "I'm not one of you spies." And he laughed, "Mama," he called to his mother "tell your husband am not one of his spies." There was general laughter.

"I could remember your grandfather, put on a beating on me for eating out in Basseterre - all old fashioned talk about people poisoning people with mongoose meat," and he heaved, laughing.

All the family could see the comedy of it all.

"Mind dem people don't poison you, for what you have." "We is McFarlanes - we don't suppose to eat out," said Aunt Rosa.

It was then that Idris had a brain wave. Instead, of beginning a whole new restaurant, why not buy the Pelican Inn? Since McFarlanes are not expected to eat out, they could eat in their own restaurant, occasionally. He would discuss this with Pervase after the celebration. And if Frank could transfer Pervase's half for the other house in Birmingham, this could be a joint venture. The manager seemed friendly enough.

Chapter Forty Two

Having been publicly scolded by the patriarch and queen mother of the clan, they stole to the east wing to have a shower and dress. By the time they had returned the party was a hive of activities. Their wives were waiting for them. There was dancing downstairs and on the lawns. The steel band which could be heard miles away was even more melodious as they got closer. There were children everywhere as if the entire clan had suddenly invaded the island from the United States, Canada, and up and down the islands where there were many cousins.

When he finally rescued his wife from well wishers, Idris was slightly intoxicated with non alcoholic juices, all very healthy for both body and mind. Uncle Alfred had insisted that the real alcohol was entirely for his old friends who had come to see him. Aunt Clara had finally resurfaced to patch up their differences and brought her husband Harold, or the "old goat," as his brother in law often referred to him. He offered several drunken toasts to the wife of his "nebhew who had nuw converse to his lamb, and his bountiful wive, and he 'visked ha, a present stay in Sinkit."

To which he drew tumultuous applause from the revellers, especially from the children, who had warmed to him the moment that he arrived at the house. And as for his other "nebhew, de wan James, may 'e haw many mure

Portugee pickny dem cause outa many cum wan, and Pervase should purvey 'is juse, while Frank wus lek 'is namesake, justa frank parson." Then he would raise his glass and conclude his last sentence with "Amen," smashing it, as libation of the remains of his drink to the "deceases."

For this latter act, the children were ushered from the dining room and onto the lawn to hear the live reggae and steel band compete.

"Let him smash dem," Aunt Rosa said. "Don't stap him!" And she laughed. "Lord look at we crosses, dat we sista gu pick up a Wiggley, so fast wid she self tu get married. She will pay fu it; I knows she get money outa Norris and Blanche, before dem dead."

Idris and her other nephews were realising that the longer she stayed on the island the more localised her accent became as did her humour. They were beside themselves with laughter.

But it was Ram, who held sway; especially when he commented on the "vexatious beauties of Jane, wid skin de culur of wan custad apple innards, and titi dem, ripe lika Wingfield graff mango, dat hang dung fram de tree so grasefullie; and de ladies fram Smallia in Afrika, wid de yeyes dem lek de seede o' de sapodilla, wid hips o' Spanish ash, an skin de culur o' marmeapple sap dat vi pruduce de strang brede dem o' de future." And as for Rosaria and Nadia, he recommended that they should "gi support to deir cousins 'ou bringingin de nuw bluud, by gi 'in succour to Milton and Patrick, cause vha ole sweetnes garne fram de bluud ha fu replase, a little cousin an cousin ting an haliday fling might du dem all de wurl o' guud." On this he offered them the local moonshine, which he referred to as "love juice" as this will help their "inhibitions," and tried to coax them into drinking it while trying to join their hands together, much to the embarrassment of the young people, who nonetheless took it in good sport. As for Kathryn, he pretended to stalk her by saying she was "lek papaya yellowing fram greene, 'vid de best titi to launch shippe ina de islands, a seen plenty nuff."

"I don't want no more Royal Family," said Aunt Rosa. "Sit down man; si doung an' behave yuself, ar leve de premises. We rayal aready. Yiu ole bull yiu, yiu tink a fuget wen yui use tu ask me questian?"

With this accusation Ram sat down, laughing.

"Yiu laugh," said Aunt Rosa. "An' yiu is me fuss cousin, nat even second nar thud; yiu ole bull yiu. Behave yiu self ar lef de premises." But the revellers just laughed.

At the end of the evening, a new army of helpers arrived to clear away the plates and paper cups, mostly relatives in some way or another. Aunt Rosa and Uncle Alfred seemed to know of them and who their parents were. Then they settled down to dancing. As it was Mulkie's birthday she became the centre of attention as they sang her happy birthday, then to her embarrassment she was expected to wind down. She had never been accustomed to such a ceremony before and at first found it difficult, as she was shy. But she knew of this kind of dancing all over Africa so she started to wind down, joined by Kathryn who had warned her that the night will have to end with her dancing. But she had no idea that she was expected to wind her behind like an unmarried girl before all and sundry. She looked at Idris for rescue but realised it was beyond his power to intervene.

"Come on Miss Lady," shouted Ram. "Wind down girl; show we what you can do!"

"Never mind him," shouted Aunt Nadine. "He loves looking at women, just dance."

But several of the young girls joined in and tutored her, and Yasmin joined in. It eventually became a women's rite with the men wandering off to get fruit or rum punches from the big tent, so she lost her shyness and had a good time.

Then after some respite she called her brother back in London and spoke to him and other members of the family on the telephone and called Yasmin who spoke to them and they were invited over for the end of the following year, and accepted the invitation, which was not surprising as they had sent them the best post cards that they could find, all the expensive ones; some even of different islands. And everyone at the party had shouted greetings to them over the telephone.

Chapter Forty Three

It was the next day and Aunt Rosa was in a righteous rage. She had awakened in the small hours of the morning to strange noises and heavy breathing, accompanied by sighs, which came from the guest rooms at the west wing. She had no idea who the culprits were, but she was certain of the act. The young people thought that she would be out, tired and lost to the world, were fornicating on the property, and in her presence. At first, she had no wish to know who the culprits were; she needed to purify the atmosphere. It had always been taboo for the young to engage in sexual intercourse in presence of their elders, and that meant under the same roof in the old days and she saw no reason why modernity should have changed the rules. Not while she was alive. They all knew it was anathema and a sign of disrespect.

That night when Ram had tried to coax the cousins to dance, Nadia had played the part. She accepted the suggestion as humour, but was reluctant to take the idea seriously. During the course of the evening, however, she had danced with Milton, and found that she made groaning and moaning sounds on the four occasions. Intrigued she danced with him a fifth, a sixth and by the seventh time, she never went back into the dining room, where her mother was but stayed outside on the lawn, as if chained to him. She could not let him go. She had promised to go to his room, and when at four o' clock, she heard her door scratched, she knew it was him.

So unfulfilled the past months before arriving home and tempted by hot sun, sea and mountain air, the past few weeks, her legs buckled as he rushed her and they made love passionately until, they heard some one's footsteps approach the door and called Rosaria. She knew it was their mother. At thirty four she was childless, like her twin, and neither of them had children. Back in England, they both held down steady jobs, unlike their more educated cousins Idris and Pervase. But they had somehow managed to own properties. They had offspring; so did Frank, who had become wealthy beyond his wildest dreams, while they remained unfulfilled.

That night she was itching; she knew she needed a man, and asked Rosaria to swap rooms so that if their mother came and called out she would not risk being found out by answering. It was always a familiar response, taught to them from the age of three. She would put them to bed early and later go to their respective doors:

"Nadia!"

"Yes mama."

"Rosaria!"

"Yes mama."

Then she would walk away, contented that they were safe.

Frank was not much help with such things, his aunt reasoned. He wouldn't know what to do, and as for Idris and Pervase, they had been sleeping away from their wives; they were too busy shaking off the people who were paid to watch over them, and were busying themselves with other diversions by looking up old school friends, with their channelling their energies into other activities, she figured that it was highly unlikely that they would do that with her under the same roof, in her house. This was utmost disrespect in her house. In fact, as long as she lived, it would be more her house than anybody else's. The deeds might not be in her name, but she was Aunt Rosa, so it was her house, according to family values, which was beyond any written constitution, as yet concocted by man: blood was thicker than water. Anything else was white man's law.

When Calvin arrived, Mulki and Yasmin thought that offence had been taken by some taboo they might have broken the previous night. But any doubts by them were borne out by Aunt Rosa, not even consulting her nephews under the same roof.

Aunt Rosa knew who the culprits were, and that one of them would not be living under the same roof she was certain that it was a visitor, and someone with Wiggley blood; not just a mere McFarlane. It had to be a hybrid.

Calvin went straight to Rosaria and got the truth, after her mother had threatened to bring in de Connors de 'Obeah man, from Sandy Point, to make a divination. It was as if Judgment Day had finally come, as if there was weeping, wailing, gnashing and chattering of teeth.

It appeared to Mulki and Yasmin, that while their husbands and Frank had more money than Calvin, Calvin's authority was unquestionable. It carried more weight in issues of moral conduct. Milton had been brought to the house that afternoon and could be heard screaming in pain, while an unknown figure administered six strokes of a tamarind rod to his stuffed trousers so that he wouldn't mark. Then Nadia was put across a bench in the outhouse at the foot of the garden; this punishment administered by a woman, whom they had never seen and who disappeared after being paid by Calvin. That brought an end to the matter, until three months later, there was a wedding and Milton and Nadia got married, and there was another celebration at the house.

Chapter Forty Four

Three months into their stay and Frank had used his contacts to sell all their property in England, and every few days he would inform them that he was returning to England. Yet he was still on the island. At the second meeting, Frank had transferred the money for Uncle Alfred's house; Idris' parents' house in Guidea Park, Aunt Rosa's house, his lists of properties and Pervase's half of the house in Birmingham into the entire assets of the Estate. It dawned on Pervase and Idris, and the other family members that Frank had no intention of returning to England to live, perhaps, for a holiday, but certainly, not to live.

James had surprised him by authorising the sale of his house by proxy spurred on by Jane who had become inspired by the islands and had started to paint again. More than anyone else, she definitely wanted to stay, as she had put it, "at least forever."

Idris and Pervase had completed the mosque, east of the river. Calvin had developed a park where the local children played cricket, and other teams visited to play Uncle Alfred's teams of youngsters, of which there were three.

This had been his retirement gift from Calvin.

Frank had developed the production of vegetables on the west side of the estate; shared the responsibility for the production of cordials in the south east with his cousins, and collaborated in the purchase of the majority shares of the Pelican Inn, where by special arrangements the family ate once a month.

Chapter Forty Five

The year had passed and it was spring again. Spring in Nicola Town is more spring time than anywhere else on earth. At least, that's how it seemed to Idris as he stood on the ridge remembering that May morning when Anna, his grandmother took him to see heaven.

In spring days as a boy long before the gold rush to England had begun, he remembered children pledged to wear a young green leaf every spring morning, and once they had made their pledge, whoever was seen without it, their match had the right to chase and beat them until they had picked one from a shrub or a nearby tree, just as long as they had a green leaf; and the leaves were always young, bright or silver green, dark to light green, or green and new, and the fragrance of green leaves and cedar wood filled the air. In Nicola Town, you always knew when it was spring time, more so than anywhere else on earth.

Idris had returned to the mountains in the middle of the land, far north, where the steep valleys swept down into Nicola Town. But on the ridges above the valleys there were fields of gold, where young Caribbean pepper mint, African daisies, purple and pale – violet lavender stretched for miles, and which stood in contrast to the yellowing coconut fronds that hung from the tall stilt - like trees. He stood in awe as still they stretched to the very edge of the ridge and recalled that Anna had singled him out for the trip to the edge of the world, after he had discovered the aborted infant rolling in the waves at the bottom of her garden, by the sea. This setting had been haunting him since that day, and every time he thought of Anna, he thought of it, and its extraordinary beauty had stayed with him and haunted him all those years away in England. For he could see now that England could never be his country, and Anna had buried his umbilical cord and placenta beside the river on her land, at the foothills of Nicola Town. He had been in exile all the years.

He had visited this spot a thousand times in his mind when he arrived in England as a boy and had cried every night awake and in his sleep. Like so many children of that era, he did not give his consent to become an immigrant in a strange land; he was of the generation who were indoctrinated by glitz and silver dreams, so insubstantial that for many they had burst like bubbles and faded into the thick air of smog and fog. Time had tied their feet and forced them to fly, but only a few who had learned the art of flight, had also learned how to protect their fragile wings from the evil eyes of time. And for some, circumstances had clipped their wings; he was one of them.

He stood in contemplation as Milton stood back away from him, so that he could take in the vibrations of that place where he had once been healed, and thought of Anna, and believed that by summoning up those memories that he could heal himself again. But Anna had died when he was a child in England and he had never cried. But now tears were welling up in his eyes and he just stood there, feeling the wetness and the warmth around his eyelids, but made not a sound. There on the ridge he realised that whoever saw pleasures in exile was not telling his story, for there could never be any pleasures in exile from the old women, his grandmothers that he loved and whom he never saw again.

This plateau levelling out before him had finally replaced the landscapes of the city of coldness, a land brittle with ice that circumstances had forced his generation to endure, to hypnotise themselves to call beautiful, and to leave true love behind. As if their own landscapes, like their lives back then held no intrinsic values, no inherent beauty that ever quickened the heart, or forced any sentient thoughts to mind; no love that ever quickened the pulse or raised the spirit as he felt now. And he was grateful for Calvin and his wisdom, for unlike them, Calvin had never left their grandparents to forage for love in a strange and donkey land.

Calvin understood his cousins very well; they had been uprooted like young saplings from a nursery and transplanted in a stony and terrible place so he cared for their needs in every way; it was he who had the confidence of the Tegrania, the black Caribs, and had then assigned Milton to take Idris there. Idris had refused to bring a camera. He didn't want pictures, he was home and wouldn't be going anywhere outside of the Caribbean to live ever again: racism had traumatised him.

Milton looked at his watch. "Coz, its twelve thirty." He knew they were meeting Pervase and Frank at the cemetery in New Forest, to see their great - great – grandmother's grave; take the children swimming at Sandy Beach, and then a picnic at the Citadel; they had to be home before evening. Calvin had made up the itinerary and had given definite times for each item. And he had been on the good side of him since that unfortunate incident when he had allowed his passion to get the better of him. Standing back, he now had the opportunity to study Idris.

This nephew of his mother's seemed more peculiar than the other two who had been to England; he had been observing how he faced east for long periods, without moving as if there was something in that cardinal point that preoccupied him most, that took all of his concentration. Now he was kneeling, and going through a prayer ritual. They were all traumatic cases he thought.

He smiled, at least they are not violent and loud, he thought by way of consolation, but there was pain in their lives.

"Coz," he said. He was becoming a little impatient. He would have to answer to Calvin, who might want to disgrace him again by having him beaten by one of those hill people, who hardly ever came down out of the hills to civilisation. Calvin had this association with these strange shadowy people: the Tegremanias. No wonder people said he had joined the de Lawrence, thought Milton.

After his third call of "coz," Idris finally stepped back from the invisible object of his devotion and they wandered off. Milton drove as fast as the traffic would allow, and they arrived at New Forest at one o'clock.

Chapter Forty Six

New Forest had been a tidy little village in the nineteenth century, which had that peculiar looking church, called a cathedral, ten shops, two cemeteries, a swimming bath, and a primary and a senior school, and about a thousand living souls in residence. Their grandparents never grew up there, although their great - great - grandmother Susan Pope was born there, and had lived there until she had married Joe McFarlane, a Methodist lay preacher from Nevis, the neighbouring island and the ever dissenting second third of the trinity, consisting of Anguilla, which fled the trinity, some years before. Great Trinity of Islands the national anthem then went; here there was reversed mathematics: one from three still left three, blood was thicker than water, and none of them had fallen down, although the other had gone its way helped by an attempted coup led by the then opposition leader. He was among the shortest men in the three island state, and was referred to by supporters and non - supporters alike, as Patsy.

There were two entrances to the cemetery of the cathedral: a wrought iron gate at the very front just off the main road which even in those years when they were children was never closed; cars couldn't drive in through there. The other entrance called the West Gate, took you passed the first entrance, right, passed the vestry on the left and sharp right to the doors of the church. Its rolling lawns and tombstones were then accessible by foot. Milton hated cemeteries and had never been to a funeral.

That the cousins wanted to meet there was further proof to him that they were not quite well. The reverend had already pointed out the small tablet of stone to Frank before they arrived and they could see him at the first entrance about twenty metres from the gate. Milton had more interest in the old church and walked in, leaving Idris to join Frank there.

Idris sat down for a rest on the low wall at the side of the door of the church and waved at Frank about three hundred metres away. Frank waved back. It would be one of those walks thought Idris, so he got up, in trepidation. The distance seemed too far in his present state. But he set out any way. He was curious what Frank had found, and liked the well ordered way in which the cemetery was set out, with the headstones and tombstones either side of the pathway lined with dates and royal palms. Two thirds of the way down, he stopped to admire the dates and royal palms, and waved at Frank. Frank waved him to hurry up. He waved back and just as he reached, Pervase came in through the wrought iron gate.

"Where's she?" asked Pervase.

Frank laughed. "Here she is," he said, pointing at a tablet of stone in the ground.

Idris, joining them, said: "Is anything written on it:"

"It looks as if there used to be a cross in the ground," said Frank.

"Well, there is hardly anything there now, isn't it?" said Pervase.

Frank pulled the tablet of concrete up and found the other part of the cross underneath the mould, and read the inscription on it: "Here lies Susan McFarlane nee Pope, Beloved daughter of the reverend Andrew George Pope, born eighteen hundred and seventy nine, died nineteen hundred and thirty five. And may her soul rest in peace."

"I see," said Pervase.

"Ehem," Frank muttered, more to himself than the other two; in fact to one in particular.

Idris was crying.

"Here we go again," said Frank. "Always bawling under crisis; just like when we were growing up, bawling, while he's fighting you and planning how to hurt you next; you unforgiving soul!"

"Leave him alone," said Pervase. "Let him cry."

"Come on man," said Frank. "Pull yourself together; it's just one of those things."

"Its life," said Pervase. "But …."

"But what?" asked Frank.

Pervase smirked and broke into Creole: "So whahappen; dis man conceive ha all on his own; she aint got no mudder?" And he laughed.

"That's why you cryin', don't it Idris?"

Idris stopped crying and gave a nervous laugh. "She belonged to him: like a donkey, a horse, a cow, a dog, a sheep, a goat, a pair of shoes, and a doll." He paused, rubbing his feet into the lawn. "I think he treated his dogs better."

"That's not nice," protested Frank. "You are talking about your great ancestor."

"Listen Frank," said Idris.

"Guys, guys, take it easy!" said Pervase.

"See, just as I say; one minute bawling down the place, the next is violent reaction." And he laughed. So Pervase laughed and Idris gave a resentful chuckle. After a few minutes in silence, they walked out through the wrought iron gates; Idris leaving the car to be brought to the entrance by Milton.

Milton had already looked at the stained glass windows in the cathedral; he liked the idea, but they reminded him too much of death. So after looking at them he had wandered to the vestry, and had a talk with the reverend Roland Bradbury.

"It's good to see your family is taking an interest in the church again," said the reverend. "You ought to have your children, baptised and confirmed here. After all, your great – great grandmother is buried in those grounds and I believe part of this house stands on your land."

"We nat her 'bout de land reverend," he replied.

"I know," replied, the reverend. "But why is it that none of her descendants come to this church; none of the reverend Andrew Pope's black descendants come to his church, it's not good for your family, but I suppose I can't be over stepping my calling here. I know you resent white people."

"No, we doant," said Milton. "Look at you, you're all right - we doant resent you. You're a man of God - not like he, a rapist!"

The reverend was on the verge of laughter, shocked by his frankness. "You're very frank," he said.

Milton took it literally. "I aint Frank," he said. "Frank is the other funny one that went to England and come back mad; I aint mad, mi name is Milton, like in Paradise Lost. You know de book?"

"Yes, one of the best works in English, ever."

"Good," said Milton. He stood in silence looking at the mango tree laden with fruits. "All you who came afta him, always been kind to us; his great - grandson and daughter is back home now, praps they'll come to his church one day." He looked over the mango tree. "Am helping myself to a mango off a dat tree; want one?"

"Yes," said reverend Roland Bradbury. Milton walked to the trunk of the tree and clambered up, picking two ripe mangoes from the top. "Catch," he called out, throwing them at the reverend, who caught them, laughing.

He climbed down. The reverend gave him his mango, which he rubbed clean with his shirt and bit into it.

"It's sweet," he said.

"Good," said the reverend, following suit. He chewed and swallowed. "It's good," he said.

"You more than welcome here on this land. You is a man of de soil. Here's Calvin's card," dipping into his pocket and handing him the business card.

The reverend took it. "Is Calvin the one who is in charge?" he asked.

"Only of certain things: I tink Idris is the wan 'o is really in charge; den I tink it's Pervase; den I tink is Frank; den another time I tink it's even me whu is in charge. I doant knuw whu is really in charge." He paused as if in thought. "Sometimes I swear de old reverend is de wan whu is really in charge, but I can't be sure for no one ever talks about him. You is an Englishman and knuw 'bout dese tings. Whu du tink is really in charge?" He took another bite of his mango.

"I wouldn't be able to comment on these things. It's your family and you must know; so I can't really make informed comment. Nor would I wish to. Thanks, though."

"Well, OK then, I like your mango. Could we have a couple of bucket full every year for about thirty dollars each; it will help de church?"

The reverend laughed. "Mr. McFarlane; you are a very shrewd business person."

"McFarlane - Wiggley, reverend," he said. "Must go now; call Calvin…. please!"

Idris, Pervase and Frank were waiting in the ice cream bar left of the wrought iron gate. They were still unsettled by the lack of a proper gravestone for Susan. As Milton approached Frank was first to speak.

"Milton, we sent our drivers home; we riding wid yiu." Milton liked the change to Creole; it showed that they were really staying home for good.

"Good," he replied.

"And why didn't yiu come to the grave; it's your great-great grandmother as well – why didn't yiu come?"

"I don't like cemeteries," he replied. "But guess wha?"

There was a pause, and they waited in anticipation. Milton said nothing. Then as they showed their impatience he said:

"Why didn't yiu guys come and meet de reverend. He's a nice man; he's giving us mangoes for the restaurant, soon as Calvin or one of you authorises payment. Now, where we going?"

"Sandy Beach," said Frank.

Chapter Forty Seven

It was three o'clock and Mulki looked at her watch. Then she pulled Yasmin towards her and whispered in her ear. Kathryn was off getting ice cream cones for the children with Patrick and Paddy in tow, while two shadowy characters sat in dark sunglasses, observing the children; around the ice cream parlour, there were two equally shadowy characters attending them. They paid for the ice cream, without asking, and helped to take them back to the sandy area where they were all seated, enjoying the sun and the fresh sea air.

"Don't be looking at your watches all the time, please," said Cuffay.

"Yes, please," said Tegramond, "try…. pleasing not to attract attention. You are home now!"

Milton pulled up outside the sandy arena: parked and headed for the leisure spot. Pervase, Idris and Frank followed. He was right, he thought. Sometimes he is really in charge. Before they left the car they had emptied their pockets and given him all the money on their persons. This amounted to two thousand dollars." "This is for the credit union," Frank told him. "At least, what's left of it after the party?" That said: Pervase produced a cheque for the partner hand in his village. "Who can't match that we will pay out," said Idris. "That's right," said Frank.

Milton was glad that they weren't going back. Since they arrived employment had been good for every one; houses were going up every day and there was good produce from the estates. He was proud to be a McFarlane.

"There they are," said Pervase.

"With the hill people again," replied Milton.

"Your friends," said Pervase and laughed.

"Look who is turning up," said Frank, and he laughed: "My, if it isn't my cousin your wife."

"You know how the old saying goes, don't you? Cousin and cousin makes dozens," said Idris.

"Leave it alone," said Milton, and accelerated his walk, and when they reached the others he saw that Nadia and Rosaria had joined the party.

The steel band was competing with the reggae and calypso grandees, and the moko Jumbies were on stage, the drummers, drumming away on the big drums, and the other members of the troupe with maracas, bells, tambourines, and shakers of all kinds. The two flute players were scaling in that eerie way like two Jumbies arguing. Every fourth beat, the big drums resounded and the stilts man pranced around rather than danced.

The bright costumes of red, yellow, green, and here and there sprinkles of purple and blue were eye – catching and mesmerising.

The crowds stopped what they were doing and turned towards the troupes. The man dressed as a bull ran amok, shaking his clattered whip, cracking it and threatening the crowd to a whipping. The man in the mitre, who seemed to be the one in charge, blew his whistle, and his shapely assistants, all girls, dressed in Amerindian costumes blew theirs, and the music stopped. Then the warriors came on cracking their whips at each other and then the crowds.

The master of ceremonies brought them to order. He cracked his whip, which sounded like thunder and the big drums rolled loudly and the shakers rattled and as he began to speak, a solitary drummer interrupted on the repeater drum. He feigned annoyance and walked towards the culprit, cracked his whip, and held his staff above his head; this was his rod of correction.

Idris found his wife and children and stood with them watching in anticipation. Mulki kissed his hands, and put them around her waist. Pervase and Yasmin, Frank, Kathryn, Milton and Nadia stood together, flanked by the four shadowy hill people, with Patrick and Paddy, while an unidentified young man who had taken a liking to Rosaria was shooed away.

Jane arrived with James and the twins and Pervase's children. They were surprised but delighted as Calvin had turned up with three other hill people.

"I am de king o' Egypt," shouted the master of ceremonies. The drums rolled and someone clapped thunder. The crowds clapped and laughed, and someone shouted:

"Come down; cum arf de stage, man!"

The master of ceremonies located the owner of the dissenting voice and cracked his whip in his direction, and stood pointing with his rod of correction.

"Silence dat wan!" he shouted to the bull.

The bull ran towards the culprit and set upon a lean middle aged man. He cracked his whip threateningly until the man broke the circle and ran away, hiding behind his friends. There was uproar. The people clapped and laughed.

There was a burst of music for three minutes and then the master of ceremonies stopped it.

"Play maas, man!" a voice shouted from the crowd. There was a four minutes burst of moko music, until the king of Egypt stopped it.

He cracked his whip three times, and repeated three times: "I am de king o' Egypt; I am de king o' Egypt; I am de king o' Egypt."

"We hear you," shouted a lone voice in the crowd. The king ignored this, and the drum answered with three claps of thunder.

"And I come to crucify," continued the king. This drew laughter and applause from the crowds; those who had whistles blew them, or whistled themselves, and those who did not, shouted approval, made monkey or ape noises and clapped. The king's assistants started to wind.

"Hoi!" "Hoi!" "Hoi!" "Hoi!" The crowd shouted in approval. The steel band started up, and the reggae and calypso grandees joined in; the flute players took over and the king stopped the music.

The warriors lifted three crosses to which three men were tied, and the music started up. Then it stopped.

"I am de king o' Egypt, I come here to crucify."

"We hear dat aready," cried a voice. "Nuw get arne widit!" The crowds clapped and the repeater drums rattled, and ended with a clap of thunder.

"Nuw dis is Barabbas and dis is Barnabas, and dis is Christ, de light o' de worrrld," said the king of Egypt, tripling his "r." "Which one should I crucify?"

"Crucify Jesas," someone shouted from the crowd. Since he is de light of de worrrld, we need light."

"No! No! No!" shouted another. "Crucify Barabbas, he's a bad man!"

"Noo!" chanted another. "Crucify Barnabas, he too fast in de crucifixion business, he shouldna be there."

The crowd erupted with laughter. The flute players began to play, the dancers to wind, and the king of Egypt to dance and sing:

"Ah will crucify dem, mek wi crucify dem, cum and crucify dem, de robba and de tief an de light a de worrrld."

This drew whistles from the crowds, with whooping and cat – calls, others made barking noises and cries of approval, as he slid from one side of the stage to the other:

"Cruci ... cruci crucify dem."

"Yes," shouted the crowd. "Crucify dem, yes. Crucufy dem all."

And they took up the chant, mimicking the dancing girls, and the king of Egypt:

"Cruci ... cruci crucify dem." "Mek wi crucify dem, cum and crucify dem, de robba and de tief an de light a de worrrld."

The warriors begun to dance twirling their sticks and the dancing girls to sway, and the bands took up the tune, and the people began to sway and dance to the music. Then a few of the warriors distributed bowls of tomatoes to the crowd, and encouraged them to throw them at the victims on the crosses, and the music floated on the air, from the beach to the mountains and out to sea.

And Barabbas and Barnabas and Jesus were brought down from their crosses to tumultuous applause from the crowd and untied, they took up the chant:

"Cruci … cruci crucify wi.

Luuk huw dem crucify wi. Cruci … cruci crucify wi. Lawd luuk huw dey crucify wi."

Then they began the dance of Dancing on the Bones of the Dead and Stepping on Ants.

"Yes," shouted the crowd. "Crucify dem, yes. Crucify dem."

Then the warriors joined in:

"Captain Morgan crucify dem

John Hawkins crucify dem. De robba and de tief and de light up de worrrld."

Chapter Forty Eight

In August two men arrived on the island asking for the estates of the McFarlanes. At first they were given the run around, until local police officers ascertained that they had come from England with a warrant to arrest Idris for abducting his own children. The mothers had not consented to their staying in the islands longer than a month. They had already been gone more than half of the following year. The Privy Council in England had assigned a prosecution against Ralph Regan Jamieson McFarlane, also known as Idris McFarlane – Suleiman.

And Pervase knew that if they got through to Idris that he soon will be next. Perhaps, even now Abby was planning her next copy cat move. But like Idris, he too was a McFarlane and ready to die. "Who was it the slave had to kill? The slave had to kill the master to be set free!" He, too, knew who to kill. And like Idris his reasoning was clear. The children had quite forgotten England; for this was their once in a life time, to be the most important children in the world; a world in which they played second fiddle to no one. As descendants of the black Kalinago, chieftains of the Leeward Island Caribs, they were as Aunt Rosa had insisted, already royal. Their grand parents Jamie, called Norris, and Blanche, daughter of Anna, had left them a river with its own legend. Their images of themselves had changed as did their lineage and they could never fit into the mould of English life, in which their future was cast. There were no more advertisements of dark children in rags, beady eyed, rattling tin cans for their last supper. They were landowners; they owned a river. They were the descendants of a Nevisian by the name of Joe McFarlane, and Susan Pope, with her roots in the Tegrania. They weren't immigrants; they held proper passports, they rode horses and bicycles on their grand fathers' and grand mothers' land and ate oranges and mangoes picked off trees planted by their grand parents' and great - grand parents' hands. They were hybrids of a certain pedigree: Anna their maternal great - grand mother had been god mother and great - aunt to the third Jamie McFarlane. It mattered to a closed society no matter how modern it pretended to be. They were home, and when they went into town, they were no longer little "blackies," neither privately in the quiet of suburban or aristocratic homes, or uttered more overtly under hot breaths in Essex or Kent, neither did they hear their parents being called any names, but were treated with respect. They were citizens, not ethnic minorities.

On their land there were date trees, palm trees; they picked avocadoes when they refused to have them picked for them, they ate fresh strawberries off their land. They could aspire to be anything they dreamt they wanted to be, and read their own dreams.

The present development was an effrontery to Idris. The slavers needed his offspring and his little cousins to play second fiddle to theirs all the days of their lives. They wanted him dangling like a stuffed puppet on their strings, remotely controlled; and in England they had watched him dangle while they had put on that Cheshire cat smile of theirs and sneered every time they'd asked some stupid question at an interview, ad lib questions, which they did not ask anybody else. Then rubbing salt into the wound by demanding what equal opportunities meant to him, and then pontificate what it meant to them. As if such words on paper ever meant anything. And not only had he been dangled, opportunities were dangled to his face like stale carrots that rabbits of other warrens had already chewed on. That he had seen the results of relative deprivation, the trauma of mind that constant poverty and harassment had brought upon the Caribbeans, who seemed to be especially targeted by the system to enforce a childish conservatism, as if racks and thumbscrews were no longer needed to enforce conformity. There was always the self inflicted inferiority of white violence backed up by white power, legitimised by the legal system and the imperialist past. He wanted to kill, even if it meant his own death. They were Andrew George Pope's people and he had had enough of them. He was ready to die. He knew who to kill. He thought of his hero Cyril Briggs and those molten, red-hot summer nights in America, when it was either kill or be killed, when lynched black bodies burned to cinder on charcoals of fire, and prepared to die.

So when Calvin brought the family to St Pauls Capisterre and the crew set sail for Sabad, he thought it an unnecessary precaution; as if he was attempting to thwart fate. But Calvin had other thoughts in mind. The cars weren't going to pass the spot that night. Perhaps another night, but Calvin had made it his duty to study the world. He had, like his cousins, amassed the complete library left by the "old bastard," and he admired Genghis Khan, who while being

Mongol had sired an entire race of people who were different to himself. That is the way of the true conquerors; their souls belonged to themselves, but their hearts to the world, and they were owned spiritually by a new people that they had created.

More than all the black descendants of Andrew Pope he admired Andrew Pope; even loved him. He had seen his photograph at the vestry with his daughter. He bore no resentment. For Calvin England had made the others soft, he was glad that he'd never been there. They were off to Sabad to see if they could find his grave in Windward Village, and he was certain that they would, because the reverend at the cathedral had good contacts there; they always ran there, to the island of the Makambos after they had broken oath with their God who seemed to like them more, because he was their God and they were his people; he looked like them and suffered the same weaknesses. They were created in his own image: Physically frail, effeminate, emotionally weak, but intellectually evil.

He was sure of another thing: in any society in the world there were dark forces, to which access was determined by pedigree, and to optimise such access was predetermined by possession of the fuel that oiled the wheels of capitalism, that was money and it generated power. St Kitts was a microcosm of the world, and he had power; they had power. You fought your own turf and did not budge an inch. He was sure Andrew wouldn't have budged either.

In the hills beyond the ridge, where Anna had taken Idris to see heaven and where he had seen the edge of the world, the Tegrania, the remnant of her mother's people had hidden among the caves under Mt Liamuiga, after the massacre at Bloody Point. And she had taken him there to be healed because his soul was sick after he had witnessed a terrible sign, a sin of sight. Cuffay and Tegramond were painting their faces; they believed in the old ways that they could become invisible at night, and they were right because camouflage is an exact science. They moved like shadows in the caves above Nicola Town, where spring is more like springtime than anywhere else on earth. And at nine o'clock had made their way to the lodge, near the site at Bloody River, on which New Yellow Crescent Estates stood. They had fought a major battle there before but had died, but tonight they had outwitted the other army; they were the ones with expert reconnaissance this time.

At first when they arrived Chief Inspector Allan Bonham and Roger Pack were the epitome of etiquette and forbearance. Three weeks into their investigation in which the locals had thrown stones at their cars and lobbied the local police, who could no longer cooperate with them for fear of reprisals, they had become frustrated. After all this was a former colony and England still figured, the queen was the head of state; the Privy Council could encourage an invasion. There was something called International Law; their law as they saw it and as the locals saw it. The difference being that this was not a street in England where you targeted black driven vehicles: people who held no status. You had to be sensitive; you had to approach the situation as you would any landowner or powerful man in England, or anywhere else for that matter. The rules were the same; respect of power and property. That was the rule of law wherever you happened to be.

The two men sat in the car at the beginning of the private road that led to New Yellow Crescent Estates. They didn't know why they were lured there. The chief of police on the island Jackson Butt, had suggested some oddity about drugs and Colombians and perhaps, reconnaissance would help his local police, but they were there, anyhow. They were waiting for a Shogun jeep with three children, perhaps, another car with two twins, perhaps, another couple of cars with family members, they couldn't be certain about the others, but they were sure of the first car.

When it started to rain heavily in the August night, and the temperature dropped so low in the dusk that they felt chilly at that hour in the tropics, they ought to have known that unpredictability spelt trouble, and then when the galling bird was seen leaving its nest in the trees where the river met the old town, with its cumbersome wings in comical night flight that they needed no further omens. But they were strangers and weren't to know that the spirit of Tegramond was roaming the rainforests crying for his three lost daughters whose skulls were broken against the rocks, murdered at Bloody Point when the French and the English, divided up his beloved Liamuiga and changed its name forever; that it was the night of the rolling calf and Jack o' Lantern when a light could be seen on the mountains that followed the voice of Tegrania, the wife of Tegramond, wailing, as they searched for their lost children.

The river was gushing, there was an overflowing in the mountains and cloud bursts in the sky and the source of the river had filled to overflowing with the recent night rains, and it sped down through the valley noisily. The ghaut began to run as two shadowy figures arrived at the lodge and waited. Calvin had given the watch full instructions that on no account should any members of his family are stopped at the entrance to their property.

He had taken precautions in light of recent developments. And they knew the shadowy figures were the hill people. They didn't know them by any other names except, sekunya or the hill people. So when they turned all the lights off and there was only the clap of thunder and a new burst of rain in the August night, they heard nothing when they struck, having crept up to the car with its engine turned off, waiting to intercept the Shogun Jeep - then they wrapped them in crocus bags and carried them in the green darkness along the coast, going south to the narrows where they waited for the launch to rendezvous that would take them like caught fish to Guadeloupe, then onto America as cadavers. It really didn't matter that they were white. They had done it to their own before, so why not strangers, who were their enemies? They would have done it to anyone who would deny them the right to choose between liberty and death, to act decisively so that they no longer remained dangling men.

Nearing the islands of the Makambos as the schooner tacked for Windward Village. At his desk below deck, Idris smoothed out the paper on which he had written a poem; he had done it in his own handwriting, just as they had taught him in that school in the village that saw itself as a town, even as a city, before he went to England, as Mas Luke had insisted all those years ago, that good handwriting reflected the writer's state of mind. Mulki sat impatient with excitement, rubbing her round belly; she was six months pregnant. He cleared his throat, took a sip of her banana cordial and read:

The African Queen

When amber lit, your eyes call me hunter;
You are an altar of fire on a mountain aflame with sacrifices,
And when the sheets of our bed from perfection ruffled,
Assume the scents and textures of low savannah grasslands,
We consummate our love with melanite fervour;
With black light we embrace on morning glory – embellished grass,

Meeting at a place of brooks, we are a perfect fit,
And have come full centuries to embrace this harmony and love,
Your love cries bring angels down from heaven,
Drawn to witness the commingling of spiritual bliss and fire,
You ingest music from the spheres and make body and soul one.
This sparks the new embers of black fire and lights,

The emperor's humble shields, we are ancestors ridden,
They clap their hands at your nakedness,
For you are the loves at the shrine,

And we are ridden by the loas of the habitat of our natures:
We are elephants in the long grass in the land of dreamtime:
In honour of the old bull Olorun, conqueror of the heart of Olokun,
When impassioned at the Pentecost of creation,
She lost all her wiles and her wits to him, and gave him her soul,
I now take your heart this blood – red dawn,

You are Erzulie, the Dahomy enchantress,
Wholesome and feminine mother of no comparisons:

You are manifested as Nyankoton, the rainbow wife of Onyankopong,
And as Olokun in metamorphosis,

And Mulki, you ascend the horizon and I am burnt
By the sparks that fly from the tips of your wings,
And when you descend we are beaten by troop of the colours,
And you are a covenant of fire on a mountain of miracles.

Calvin appeared in the doorway of the cabin and walked in, "Coz we're in the Makambos," he said. Idris handed the sheet of paper to Mulki, then rose and as he extended his hand to be shaken, Calvin put his arm around his shoulder and kissed him on the neck. They both laughed, because they knew that this was the beginning of the coming of age for their little small island, that sought now no longer to be a victim, voiceless and being spoken for, but a challenge to be men and women, who were much the same as other men and women elsewhere in the world. They were the living, subject to life as to death, like people everywhere, subject to the joys of life before that inevitable decay in old age sets in, if they lived that long, and then whatever became of their fight only one thing would ever matter. They would die like men and women everywhere to pay the price of their freedom, as one renaissance poet had exhorted the neighbourhood militias in America, in nineteen hundred and nineteen: "face the murderous cowardly pack, pressed to the wall, dying, but fighting back!" Simple it was - a fact of life - as in the way an apple falls.